PRAISE FOR DOUGLAS CORLEONE

Falls to Pieces

"*Falls to Pieces* twists and turns at breakneck speed in its exploration of parental devotion, the secrets kept by those we love, and the lengths some people go to in order to escape the past."

—Riley Sager, *New York Times* bestselling author of *Middle of the Night*

"[A] psychological thriller that's very much in the vein of Gillian Flynn or Lisa Jewell . . . Fans of the genre should be urged to pick this one up, and fans of the author can safely be told that this book is just as good as his previous ones."

—*Booklist*

"A twisty, fast-paced thriller from a gifted storyteller. Corleone masterfully combines great characters, a setting in Hawaii that is lush and forbidding, and a tense, dark plot."

—William Landay, *New York Times* bestselling author of *Defending Jacob*

The Rough Cut

"A sharply plotted legal drama with a double-barreled climax."

—*Kirkus Reviews*

"Another winner from this accomplished mystery writer."

—*Booklist*

"Clever, witty . . . Corleone offers a thoughtful look at how easily the legal system and the media can be manipulated."

—*Publishers Weekly*

Robert Ludlum's The Janson Equation

"[Corleone] is a perfect choice to pen the latest in the Janson series . . . [he's] a first-class storyteller, and he brings a jolt of energy to this series and a step up to the Ludlum brand."

—*Booklist*

"Corleone keeps the story bouncing along in true Ludlum style, surprising and confounding at every turn, and steering confidently to a satisfying ending."

—*BN Reads*, June's Top Picks in Thrillers

Good as Gone

"[A] heart-wrenching, adrenaline-producing adventure that . . . leaves the reader gasping for breath at the end."

—*Huffington Post*

"Once the story kicks into high gear, which is pretty much at the top of page 2, it doesn't let up, period."

—*Booklist* (starred review)

"A torrid chase . . . *Good as Gone* leaves you with the deep, uncomplicated pleasure of watching a skilled professional kick major ass."

—*Kirkus Reviews*

"An adrenaline rush."

—*Publishers Weekly*

"*Good as Gone* is everything I want in a thriller—an ingenious plot, breathless pace, and one of the coolest new heroes to come along in years. My only question is, when can I read the next Simon Fisk thriller?"

—David Ellis, *New York Times* bestselling author of *Look Closer*

"*Good as Gone* delivers a lightning-fast pace, surprising and heartfelt twists, and action aplenty."

—Jeff Abbott, *New York Times* bestselling author of *An Ambush of Widows*

"*Good as Gone* is as good as it gets. Simon Fisk is a fascinating character, and Douglas Corleone has crafted one hell of a thriller. It is a pleasure to recommend this nonstop novel to my readers."

—Michael Palmer, *New York Times* bestselling author of *A Heartbeat Away*

"A terrific international thriller. I expected to be entertained when I picked up a novel by Douglas Corleone and was rewarded handsomely. Highly recommended."

—James Grippando, *New York Times* bestselling author of *Goodbye Girl*

"*Good as Gone* goes from zero to sixty in under six seconds and never lets off the gas! If you like your thrillers filled with nonstop action in a race against time through Europe's underbelly, hop in and take a ride."

—Andrew Gross, *New York Times* bestselling author of *15 Seconds*

"*Good as Gone* is the can't-put-it-down thriller of the year that propels Douglas Corleone into Lee Child territory. Yeah, it's that good."

—Jason Starr, international bestselling author of *The Next Time I Die*

Payoff

"A lean, mean pedal-to-the-metal thriller. The novel accelerates to high speed almost immediately and doesn't slow down until the book is finished. Another winner."

—*Booklist*

"If James Bond were in the business of rescuing kidnapped children, he might easily be mistaken for Simon Fisk . . . a character worth rooting for."

—*Publishers Weekly*

Gone Cold

"A heart-pounding third installment . . . In this unstoppable page-turner with its wicked humor, detailed settings, and action-packed scenes, Corleone keeps you on the edge of your seat."

—*Honolulu Star-Advertiser*

"Corleone's prose is lean, his plotting tight, and his characters vividly drawn. [Simon] Fisk is one of the more interesting series leads in the contemporary thriller genre."

—*Booklist*

Beyond Gone

"[A] blend of action and suspense fueled by well-placed surprises."

—*Kirkus Reviews*

One Man's Paradise

"Fans of John Grisham, Lisa Scottoline, and other legal thriller authors will enjoy this for the sheer pleasure of seeing a master defense attorney at work in the courtroom."

—*Library Journal*

"This novel won the Minotaur Books / Mystery Writers of America First Crime Novel Award, and it's no wonder. Former defense lawyer Corleone has created a crafty and memorable character and placed him in a suspenseful and layered story . . . A sequel to this fine debut would seem almost mandatory."

—*Booklist*

Praise for *Night on Fire*

"Douglas Corleone . . . follows his auspicious debut (*One Man's Paradise*) with an equally enjoyable successor."

—*San Diego Union-Tribune*

"Douglas Corleone's second look at the seedy side of life, lawyering, and untimely death on Oahu in the twenty-first century . . . is a page-turner in the best sense of the word."

—*Honolulu Star-Advertiser*

"Kevin [Corvelli] tries a mean case and tells a fine story."

—*Kirkus Reviews*

"The John Grisham–style twists and turns and cinematic courtroom scenes keep the pages turning."

—*Library Journal*

Last Lawyer Standing

"Corvelli is a likable, pill-popping lawyer, and the secondary characters are Elmore Leonard quirky."

—*Booklist*

"More plot twists than you can shake a stick at."

—*Kirkus Reviews*

LIVE THROUGH THIS

OTHER TITLES BY DOUGLAS CORLEONE

Falls to Pieces

The Rough Cut

Beyond Gone

Robert Ludlum's The Janson Equation

Gone Cold

Payoff

Good as Gone

Last Lawyer Standing

Night on Fire

One Man's Paradise

LIVE THROUGH THIS

DOUGLAS CORLEONE

This is a work of fiction. Names, characters, organizations, places, events, and incidents are either products of the author's imagination or are used fictitiously. Otherwise, any resemblance to actual persons, living or dead, is purely coincidental.

Published by Thomas & Mercer, Seattle

www.apub.com

EU product safety contact:
Amazon Media EU S. à r.l.
38, avenue John F. Kennedy, L-1855 Luxembourg
amazonpublishing-gpsr@amazon.com

ISBN-13: 9781662532610 (paperback)
ISBN-13: 9781662532603 (digital)

Cover design by Ploy Siripant
Cover image: © Patricia Turner / ArcAngel Images; © ASDF, © Ljupco Smokovski, © hary_cz / Adobe Stock; © foxie / Shutterstock

Printed in the United States of America

For Ray McManamon,
whose friendship got me through

Man is sometimes extraordinarily, passionately, in love with suffering.

—Fyodor Dostoevsky, *Notes from Underground* (1864)

PART I

Day One | We Were Merely Freshmen

1
Homecoming, November 1993

The Morning Of

The morning after the dance, I woke to one of those hangovers that felt personal. I shut my eyes tight against the pink daylight bleeding through my lids. Then I cracked one and stared up at a ceiling of twinkling stars.

Not my room.

Images from the night before spun through my skull like the betting wheels on the Wildwood Boardwalk: pregame at Cormac Hall, a party ball of cheap beer at the Heights, dancing in the dark auditorium, spotting Jess flirting with Kip Ulrich by the bleachers—her smile too familiar—then seething and staggering back to the dorms. Buzzed. Drunk. On the brink of a blackout.

Alone.

So whose dorm was this?

I caught a whiff of vanilla and lavender beneath the dank scent of whiskey and sweat. Not Fenton's room, which invariably reeked of weeks-old socks. No, this wasn't even the right building. This was

D'Amelio Hall, the freshman girls' dorm, where boys were forbidden past midnight under penalty of expulsion and a lifetime of Hail Marys.

Panic jolted me upright. A mess of blond hair spilled across the pillow beside me, a bare shoulder rising with each breath. Past it, a digital clock glowed 6:12 a.m.

Damn.

RAs patrolled the halls between six and seven to confirm the building remained devoid of guys overnight. One of the unfavorable hallmarks of a Roman Catholic college.

I sat there, heart pounding, hungover, suddenly hyperaware of how far I'd fallen in a few short months. I used to think I was one of the nice guys. Smarter, better, above all this. The kind of guy Jess believed in. But lately, I'd been chasing oblivion like it owed me.

I stole a glance outside the window, grateful to be on the first floor. An earlier adventure at D'Amelio cost me a severely sprained wrist and the quarterback position on our intramural flag-football team. I had no intention of risking intramural basketball for the muddled memory of a one-night stand.

I looked at the girl again. Still asleep, still anonymous.

Something about the way her hand curled under the pillow made me want to disappear.

Guilt crept up my throat.

Jess—*my* Jess or my *ex* Jess—the Jess I'd fallen for during Freshman Orientation, lived just one floor up, a few doors down. Maybe she'd seen me enter D'Amelio Hall last night. Maybe she'd catch me sneaking out of someone else's bed like a third-string extra on *Melrose Place.*

I swiftly threw on the jeans and flannel I found crumpled on the floor. Pulled on my muddied Timberland boots without tying them.

A rustle in the hallway hurried me even more.

I moved quickly, unlocking the window, hoping the bristling late-November breeze wouldn't wake the girl whose face I still hadn't seen.

As I climbed onto her desk, I spotted an English lit paper. *By Stacy Rennick.* The sweet, quiet French Canadian from my creative writing class, who wore a black leather jacket and always found a seat next to me.

Shame heated my cheeks. My self-loathing stung sharper than the headache.

Quietly, I hung my legs out the window and steeled myself for the short drop.

What if someone sees me?

What if it's Jess? Or one of her friends?

Voices from the hall propelled me out the window prematurely.

After landing awkwardly on the dewy lawn, I quickly took inventory. No broken bones, no sprains or strains, no bleeding. Just grass-stained jeans, mud-splattered boots, and a soul in need of cleansing.

As I made my way toward Cormac Hall, the freshman boys' dorm, I passed Professor Garland, my adviser and professor in criminal law and sociology.

Garland was former FBI, with a face made of stone. The kind of guy who took pride in catching rule-breakers and didn't miss much.

"Morning, Professor," I mumbled, speech still slurred from the previous evening's debauchery. I probably stank of booze too. Could practically *feel* the dark hard liquors seeping through my pores, blending with my nervous sweat.

"Mr. Dryer," he said with the slightest dip of his chin, his gaze falling on my loose bootlaces.

I kept moving, grateful for the lack of follow-up. But Garland probably filed moments like this one away for lectures on the correlation between binge drinking and bad decisions.

Fishing for my keys outside Cormac, I glimpsed the sky and felt like I was staring into a boundless gray abyss. I used to love mornings like this. When the sky looked like a clean slate capable of becoming anything.

When my fingers finally found metal, I was relieved. The new-key fees were already eating into my considerable term-paper profits.

As I opened the door to Cormac, I heard the scream.

Shrill, raw, human.

Unlike anything outside of slasher films.

I spun back toward the girls' dorm and reasoned it was still autumn. Some cheesy Halloween paraphernalia was bound to be hanging around.

But before I crossed the threshold, a second shriek echoed through the valley, this one even louder and sharper.

"Oh God! Jess!"

Each word reverberated in my stomach. Especially the last one.

My legs moved before my brain did. Because if something had happened to her—if something was *happening*—I didn't care who saw me, what rules I broke, or how much I stank of whiskey and shame.

Suddenly sober and alert, I peered through the thickening fog, which had transformed the campus's three hundred acres of rolling green hills into a scene resembling Victorian London.

I wanted to run, *should* have run, but my bootlaces were loose, and I imagined twisting an ankle and spending the day at urgent care.

I started back toward D'Amelio slowly, then accelerated, gathering steam as I went.

After all, another bottle of pain pills *would* make for one hell of a homecoming weekend.

Especially after last night. Especially after what happened.

Especially after what I'd done.

2
Homecoming, November 2023

Mornings arrive faster these days. No hangovers—not one in twenty-five years. But with no real schedule or routine, the days bleed into one another, no single rotation on the earth's axis standing out from the others.

Except today.

Today there's a mark on my calendar, because it's the morning of Homecoming 2023 at Center Valley University, and I'm as bursting with nervous excitement as I was freshman year. My literary agent Creighton's right. I need to rebrand, write something more powerful, maybe even brave enough to borrow from my own life.

Which has never come easy.

It's time to end my thirty-year streak of avoiding the site where Jess died.

Time to learn the truth about what happened to her.

The medical examiner's report was inconclusive as to the manner of death. Unless new evidence emerges, the manner will officially remain "undetermined," leaving open all three conceivable possibilities.

Accident.

Suicide.

Homicide.

The *cause* of death is clearer. Gorier.

Anyone who witnessed the aftermath didn't need to read the autopsy report to know that when Jess Karras struck the ground, her head made the initial impact.

Her skull fractured.

Her brain hemorrhaged.

Death was instantaneous.

There were no signs of a struggle atop the roof of D'Amelio Hall, though that doesn't mean a struggle didn't occur.

This trip isn't some rash decision. I'd been mulling it for months. Yet I wasn't *sure* until this morning, which adds a pinch of sunny spontaneity—something in short supply over the course of my adult life.

I'm framing the story, *We Were Merely Freshmen*, as a search for reconnection—not just with our four friends, but with Jess. Who, if I'm honest, is the only girl I've ever really fallen in love with in my forty-seven years.

Given the stakes and how little I remember, this could become a search for redemption.

Which piles some unwelcome weight onto this weekend. Like the final exam you find only in nightmares, where you haven't gone to class all semester and need to wing an oral presentation in your underwear.

Before I can reason my way out of it, I spring from the bed, shower, and dress. I pack a small suitcase and stuff it into my Prius before doubt catches up.

While closing the trunk, I pause and ponder whether this is the right decision—*of course it isn't; the hard way never is*—but I need to go just the same.

So I gas up the hybrid near my home in North Jersey, enter I-287 west, and aim for eastern Pennsylvania, an experience that feels less like a road trip than a temporal shift.

Less like I'm heading to a college reunion than traveling thirty years back in time—to a world that didn't want me and a life I left behind.

I haven't set foot on campus since the mid-nineties, when I was expelled. And I *wouldn't* be now if my last book hadn't sputtered.

After nineteen novels, my series—and by extension, my lead character—is running out of steam.

Or maybe I am.

Hotshot defense attorney Del Danzinger just isn't speaking to me these days.

At least, not like he used to.

The critics dug *Danzinger for the Defense*. But it moved fewer than ten thousand copies. And those numbers don't cut it anymore.

My recent breakup with Alissa didn't help. After our split, I chose not to tour and steered clear of social media. Even though the decision to end the relationship was mine, I felt like I lost something.

Like I dropped something precious on purpose.

As if maybe *Gregg Dryer* didn't break things off at all, but some third party controlling my tongue.

There's a reason I feel that way. Despite decades in therapy, I still can't quite put my finger on it. But it seems to have started when my life did—at Center Valley College in 1993.

If nothing else, something that year altered my timeline. This weekend I intend to find out what it was, who did it—and, most vitally, *why.*

After three decades, it's time someone is held to account.

Even if that someone is me.

Especially if it's me.

3

During the ninety-minute drive, I can't shake the feeling that my attending Homecoming is an admission. Maybe I was wrong to give up back then, to give in, to let them close the books on Jess Karras with her manner of death still undetermined.

Suicide always seemed like the tidy answer. Too easy. Arguably, against the weight of the evidence.

To me, Jess's death *felt* less like a suicide than stranger-to-stranger violence, a cold-blooded theft in the middle of the night. A slap in the face of every future she might've had, with or without me.

At least that's my pitch. That's the *book.*

But the book has rattled something loose inside me. Now I need more than a theory. I need the truth.

If I can't know what *could've* been, I need to learn why it never was. I need to know for certain whether Jess took her own life. Or someone took it from her.

Then again, Jess and I weren't even dating when she died.

For a moment I wonder if I'm just scraping the past, digging for new material. Putting Del Danzinger to bed while Gregg Dryer finally takes the spotlight.

Whether I'm fabricating my own motivations.

But no, there are reasons I never completely believed it.

Good reasons. *Strong* ones.

As I cross the border into Pennsylvania, barbed memories tighten around me like a straitjacket.

I crank up the volume on the Cranberries' "Zombie" to drown them out.

I also ease off the accelerator. I need no reminding of how often the Pennsylvania State Police caught me speeding along this stretch. Five points on my license for doing 96 in a 55. A suspension, then driving while suspended. Thousands in fines, nearly jail time.

But that was when I was young and dumb, full of testosterone and self-righteousness.

Now I'm older. Slower. Behind the wheel of a silent silver Prius instead of a shiny red Mitsubishi Eclipse with vanity plates reading 2BAD4U and a bumper sticker touting NWA's "Fuck tha Police."

What the hell was I thinking?

Still, today's decision feels eerily familiar. Like when I left for Paris without Chloé, the woman I once thought I'd marry.

My impulsiveness has quieted over the years but never disappeared. It's still part of me, buzzing in the back of my head, hiding in the shadows, waiting to seize opportunities.

Just knowing it's still there scares me sometimes. Has since freshman year.

I've always been terrified of losing control.

And yet, I can't help but miss it a bit. The rush, the risk.

Without it, life starts to feel like a stale daytime drama.

Which is to say, it doesn't feel like much.

Maybe this weekend will change that.

Maybe I'll move past Danzinger, past Alissa.

Maybe I'll feel new again.

My phone jingles, jarring me out of a deep highway hypnosis.

I stab the speaker button. "Dryer," I say.

"Gregg-o! How's tricks?"

Creighton. My literary agent.

Young, loud, and maddeningly enthusiastic, he's one of those 30 Under 30 types.

What drew me to him was the hunger in his eyes. In the photo on his agency's website, anyway.

It's a look I had once. A look that fades with time.

By forty, I couldn't even fake it.

Once you've coasted for twenty years, not needing to bite and claw for every scrap, you become complacent. Go into a type of hibernation. It's only once you're poked and prodded that you wake, agitated and in search of your appetite.

That's how I feel today.

I not only *want* something to thrill me.

I want to *want* something to thrill me.

I'm only beginning to now—and it feels good.

Today's conversation with Creighton is mercifully brief. A friend at Trigger Finger Press needs a favor. He wants me to blurb a debut novel by Monday.

I don't know how much weight my name carries anymore, but I'm in no position to say no. After two decades with the Big Five, it might be time to find a new home. To be championed by an editor eager to give my books the push they need to be seen. To be read. To be felt.

Or maybe I just want to roll the dice of life again and see what happens.

With gusto, I tell Creighton to send the manuscript to the usual email, then end the call and lower the window, eager yet a little lonelier than I was with him on the line.

But then I take in a crisp breath of autumn air and turn up "Smells Like Teen Spirit."

Exhilaration surges through my chest.

A familiar sign flashes by:

Welcome to Allentown

In a few more miles, I'll reach Center Valley, Pennsylvania.
The only place that's ever truly felt like home.
Maybe because it was new.
Maybe because it was dangerous.

4

When I finally reach campus, I'm nicked by a thorn of nostalgia. But that's to be expected. What throws me is how *young* this class of freshmen looks. So much closer to my friends' kids' ages than my own.

Still, I can see myself out there, clear as yesterday. Chugging cheap Canadian beer from a red Solo cup, playing volleyball shirtless on the main lawn, all collarbones and cockiness.

If that seventeen-year-old kid looked into the future at me now, would he even recognize himself?

Would he be proud?

Disappointed?

Or would he be too lost in the moment to care?

When I pull into the freshman lot, I don't spin into a space with squealing tires like I did in '93. I don't risk mowing down the mobs of eager teenagers and their fretful parents, who've now been apart for three whole months.

The clinging, the tears (ostensibly of pride), tell the story. For some parents, this is less a celebration than a confirmation of their loss.

And I feel it, too, in a strange way. If Chloé and I had married, our kids might've started college this year.

At my age, it's impossible not to peer down the paths not taken. And easier to kick yourself for wrong turns. Even harder to pat yourself on the back for the right ones.

Chloé was arguably the last woman I ever wildly cared about. The last relationship I let matter. The last person I let inside.

After Chloé, I tucked myself under the warm comforter of a singles existence. Since then, I've avoided stepping out into the cold.

No one can break your heart if you don't let them touch it.

That may sound grim. But it's a damn good way to keep yourself whole.

And that's how I've felt for so long, I can hardly imagine feeling otherwise.

You and me both, Danzinger whispers.

Hearing his voice after all this time jolts me like I just stuck my finger into a light socket.

Meantime, a kid with a blue Solo cup suddenly raps on my window, nearly giving me a heart attack. As I lower the glass, my free hand feels around the glove box for my tranquilizers.

Despite all my progress, social anxiety is something I've never been able to shake. Fortunately, for writers like me, it's practically a prerequisite.

But it also means I stay tight with my benzo buddies—Team Klonopin.

"Can't park here, bro. Students only. Parents and alumni gotta hit the Heights."

His Philly accent reminds me of Fenton, and I wonder again whether he'll make the drive from Doylestown. Deep down, I hope he does. He cracks me up like no one else. Though I'm not sure if he'd make this weekend easier—or messier.

"Is that a beer?" I nod toward the blue Solo cup.

He grins and lifts it forward like a trophy. "*En-er-gy* drink, bro."

He thinks I'm a narc, but I only asked because—for the first time in years—I feel this sudden strange, stupid craving to blaze a path to the nearest keg.

But I have twenty-five years in my pocket.

I'll never go near alcohol again.

Even if this campus *is* where I first fell in love with it.

"All right," I tell him. "I'll move."

I wait until he walks away, then kill the engine and watch the freshmen. It's not just their youth that stuns me; it's their diversity, their sense of purpose, their height.

My friends' kids are tall, but I'd assumed they were outliers. Now I'm thinking they might just be making them bigger these days.

I pull out my phone and open Facebook, realizing I've made no plans to meet anyone. My Messenger inbox is packed.

Three indie authors asking how I "made" it, as if I have. Two suspiciously beautiful women with extravagant bios like *"Fly high"* and *"Nothing is impossible."* Bots. Every stock image with hundreds of likes and comments, all from men my age or older, thirsty for a mirage in the desert.

Finally, I find a message from Toni Cullen, one of my first friends freshman year.

Hey, don't know if your really coming

but do u wanna meet at Black Pepper?

The misspelling of *you're* reminds me Center Valley isn't exactly Ivy League. The single Ivy I wanted to apply to was simply too close to home. Too close to *her*. Mommy dearest.

Toni's already checked in at the Black Pepper Pub, our off-campus hangout those first few months following orientation.

One night, after a wild drive to Veterans Stadium to watch their Phillies pummel my Mets, our clique of six—Toni and Kip, Fenton and Liv, Jess and I—marched down South Street in search of flawless fake IDs.

That was the dream. Not just a thirty-pack in a dorm but an actual bar with a brass rail and five-dollar pitchers. Adulthood without accountability.

After Jess died, those IDs were seized and placed into evidence at the Center Valley Police Department. Another symbol of our overnight loss.

Toni. Her message earlier this year planted the idea to come back. Just staring at her profile pic makes me ache for the version of myself who used to make her laugh.

She was sharp. Loud, fearless.

The one of us most likely to risk sex in public.

Of the three girls in our group, she was the one most like me. Probably why nothing ever happened between us.

Sometimes, opposites attract.

Other times, likeness pushes us apart.

When you don't admire yourself—and I *really* didn't back then (hell, I still don't like that kid *now*)—you're not exactly looking for your twin.

Still, Toni Cullen—Jess's best friend, Liv's roommate, and one of the last people to see Jess alive—is as good a place to start as any.

As is the Black Pepper, where I can finally prove that I can sit in a bar in the Commonwealth of Pennsylvania without a drink in front of me.

I restart the Prius, glance back at the file I just picked up from the Center Valley Police Department. I loathe myself for even *wanting* to drink at such a pivotal moment.

But if I'm honest, maybe the demons I fought on this campus thirty years ago were never truly vanquished.

Some just hid in the shadows. Others changed form.

And some?

Some might still be here in Center Valley.

Waiting to finish me off.

5
Freshman Orientation, August 1993

The Roof, Part 1

"Get off the roof!"

It was Saturday, the second night of Freshman Orientation, and the six of us—Toni and Kip, Liv and Fenton, and Jess and I—were drinking Schlitz and passing a joint on the roof of D'Amelio Hall, laughing our asses off while the Violent Femmes' "Blister in the Sun" blared from a boom box.

We were in clear violation of at least nine provisions of our brand-new *Student Handbook*.

"Get off the roof, dumbasses!"

Someone wanted us off the roof.

"Get off the friggin' *roof!"*

Someone wanted us off the roof *really* bad.

None of the others seemed to notice, so I said nothing. Maybe it was the first-floor crew from Cormac again. We'd nearly come to blows the night before, after Fenton arranged for my twenty-one-year-old Panamanian suitemate to score us a bottle of Uncle Vlad vodka. In exchange for the first floor's soberest driver, we promised them a thirty-pack of Natty Light.

Fenton returned upstairs empty-handed. "He got pulled over."

"For DUI?" I said.

"Failure to signal."

"Then where's the bottle?"

"He got a hundred-dollar ticket. Says the vodka's theirs now."

I was seventeen and had never even tasted vodka, but I wasn't about to lose a bottle to someone else's bad driving.

Fenton and I stormed to the end of the third-floor hallway and started downstairs with the others falling in behind us.

What happened next is a blur. I vaguely recall seeking out a guy I knew *wasn't* a hothead. I figured this could be settled with a firm look and a little bluff.

Next thing I knew, we were in someone's room.

There was shouting.

There was shoving.

A bottle or two went flying over our heads.

Then a pair of baseball players—the thieves' suitemates—stepped in, warning us that if their Coors Light party ball got confiscated, we'd get stomped.

Fenton and I retreated upstairs, each with a looted pint of Southern Comfort stuffed into our back pocket.

Although there were no immediate consequences for the fracas, that night I realized something uncomfortable that I'd soon conveniently and repeatedly forget.

I had my mother's rage trapped somewhere deep inside me.

The fury was caged. But it was hungry.

And alcohol was its key to escape.

Tonight we'd fired down warm shots of SoCo, then strolled to D'Amelio to see what Liv and Toni were up to. We'd met them that morning at a hangover brunch in the cafeteria, still shaking off the blackout that cut Friday night short.

I was instantly infatuated with Liv—olive skin and jet-black hair, a serene, wholesome vibe that made me fantasize about a wife, a Labrador, and a mortgage. Fenton conveniently preferred Toni, figuring her to be low maintenance.

The girls had other ideas.

Toni showed up at my room before we met them that evening and laid it out: Liv thought I was "bad news." Toni, meanwhile, intended to dodge Fenton after spotting his brutal oral herpes flare-up.

We found the girls in a single a few doors down on D'Amelio's second floor. The room belonged to a third girl—Jess—who sat cross-legged in cutoff denim shorts on two single beds pushed together.

She offered us drinks, but her gaze left me speechless, a rarity back then when I had alcohol in me.

Van Morrison was playing "Brown-Eyed Girl." Maybe. Or maybe I've grafted that onto the memory like a soundtrack onto a scene.

Either way, for a good three minutes, I was trapped in Jess's wide brown eyes. And for the first time in my life, I felt like someone could *see* me. Not look at, but actually see me.

As if I was visible, physical.

As if I wasn't a ghost.

Liv faded from my mind.

But it wasn't just Jess's eyes. It was the brushstroke of freckles across her nose. Her old high school boys' soccer tee. The way she radiated this effortless beauty, meant to impress no one.

Jess was the kind of down-to-earth, all-American girl I'd assumed existed only in movies.

Best of all, nothing about her screamed New Jersey.

Gazing at her, I never felt farther from home.

Never farther from my mother.

Later, on the roof, we huddled close for warmth, despite the August heat, and Jess and I paired off like it was written into the script. We kissed between bursts of laughter. Our conversation flowed as if we'd known each other forever.

She loved dolphins.

And R.E.M.

And baseball—though she later admitted that was a lie.

She was Catholic but into karma, maybe even reincarnation. If so, she'd come back as a dolphin off the coast of Maui.

Her favorite movie was *Aladdin*, her favorite show, *Mad About You*. She didn't have a favorite song but kept "Losing My Religion" on repeat.

She rode horses. Once. Because of that Tom Petty song.

She adored her mother. "No, really," she said like she could read the skepticism behind my eyes. "I'm still her baby girl."

The proof was a dorm room packed with plushies: dolphins, sea turtles, tigers, bears, and more monkeys than she could name.

One teddy bear even kept her secrets.

Beneath her luxurious comforter were Wonder Woman sheets, sometimes switched out for Strawberry Shortcake.

She also had a boyfriend, Frank Handly, a high school senior back in Nazareth.

Weird, sure, but when I raised a brow, she shot back, "Would you say the same if I were a *guy* with a girlfriend back home in high school?"

She had me there.

She said it was "all but over." She'd stopped taking his calls.

Said she hoped Frank would take the hint.

I hoped so too.

Of course, I didn't know I'd be in the same position six weeks later.

Jess wasn't a loner, not even close. She lived alone only because her roommate bailed before orientation. But even with Liv and Toni nearby, she felt a little left out not having a roommate of her own.

As the night unfolded, Liv curled up with Fenton, Toni with Kip. Jess and I rolled our eyes and bet on which pair would flame out first.

Not us, though.

We were already making plans for next weekend. Talking about fall break. Thanksgiving. Even New Year's Eve.

Without realizing it—without even knowing what love *was*—I'd fallen. Hard and fully.

Thirty years later, I still haven't completely recovered.

6
Homecoming 2023

As I pull into the Black Pepper lot, a chime alerts me that the manuscript from Trigger Finger Press has arrived. I settle into a space on the near-empty blacktop and open the Kindle app on my phone.

The novel Creighton wants me to read is titled *You Oughta Know* by C. C. Candiotti. I scan the jacket copy.

When bored housewife Kerry Maven receives a text from a past lover, the ensuing affair rekindles a fire but unburies a trauma—the death of a romantic rival under mysterious circumstances.

As she investigates, all evidence points in one disheartening direction: toward the man she once loved and still desires.

Should Kerry expose the truth or just walk away? Should she deliver her lover to justice—or keep bringing a killer to bed?

The description makes my stomach tighten. A cold, familiar electricity coils up through my chest. A jilted ex-lover. A mysterious death. A journey back in time to find the truth.

Themes that are hardly rare. But fiction is never better than when it cuts too close to home. This book fits the bill.

I'm excited to read it.

Only thing is, I'd rather be *writing* about reopening a cold case myself than actually doing it.

Whether *Freshmen* becomes a memoir or semiautobiographical novel, I still don't know. But I've decided to treat the investigation like Del Danzinger. Follow the clues, build a case, and keep it together long enough to find an answer.

It's fitting, really. Law school was never about the law for me. It was a hunger to be the hero of the novels and shows I consumed in my teens. Turow's Rusty Sabich. Grisham's Mitch McDeere. *The Practice*'s Bobby Donnell.

Except practicing law in the real world is nothing like fiction. It's messy, it's drawn out, it's miserable. Sometimes brutal. And in criminal defense, one thing is almost always true: Justice means somebody has to lose.

But as a *novelist*, I'm drawn to an investigation like a fly to a . . .

Awful analogy. No wonder the *Times* snubbed my latest.

To be fair, I did spend law school shadowing defense attorney JaMarcus Cooke around Providence, Rhode Island. Fueled by idealism, I received a rude awakening. Lying clients who missed court dates almost as often as payments. Being dealt loss after loss at trial. Having people ask you over dinner how you can sleep at night. How you can face yourself in the mirror in the morning.

When a client took a swing at JaMarcus in the courthouse hallway, I realized I'd rather gamble on publishing than keep risking my face.

Even then, I never worked a cold case. The term alone conjures images of stacked Bankers Boxes in dimly lit evidence rooms, dust so thick it dulls your thoughts.

These are the forgotten: the forgotten cases, the forgotten victims, the forgotten killers.

Except not this weekend.

This weekend, there's one case and one victim I intend to remember.

And maybe one killer about to learn that some people never forgive.

And some of us never forget.

Before my arrival, I contacted the Center Valley Police Department and got Chief Cheryl Lindsay, who was a rookie when it all happened. After pleading my case, she agreed to bypass the red tape and have Jess's file ready for pickup.

Now that it's sitting in my back seat, I can't bring myself to open it.

And it's more than mere hesitation—it's dread.

I text Toni, who replies that she's taken a drive but will be back at the Black Pepper in ten.

Eventually, I crack open the folder.

Jess stares up at me, frozen in time. As if she's been waiting. For thirty years. In all that time, I never seriously considered returning here. For me, Center Valley vanished from the map in the spring of '94.

I don't know how long I'm staring, blinking away unexpected tears, before an old beige Taurus pulls into the lot.

Toni's behind the wheel.

My chest lifts. My eyes dry. It's silly, sudden, and undeniable.

Back then, Toni was everything I admired. Charismatic, gutsy, unafraid to call bullshit—especially on the people she loved.

Even as I gravitated toward Jess's softness, I always respected Toni's fire. The way she entered a party like a Molotov cocktail. Stirring things up. Making some of us laugh and others cry.

She wasn't out to be liked. She was out to *live*.

When we sat around fantasizing about our futures, Toni didn't talk about husbands or houses. She talked about *movement*. Boston, LA, San Francisco. Maybe Chicago. Maybe a walk-on role as Hooker #2 in an episode of *Law & Order*.

She didn't care if they cut her lines or killed her off by page 2.

She just wanted the experience.

As far as I know, she never left Pennsylvania after graduation. She taught elementary school. Married a guy who struggled to hold a job. Raised a few kids in a house a block from her parents. They vacationed in Hershey, spent their honeymoon in the Poconos.

And maybe that's just what she needed. A life that didn't require adding so much fuel to the fire. A place to rest, to recuperate. A place to *stay.*

The moment she steps out of her Taurus feels unreal.

Fleeting and euphoric and impossibly right.

Like that perfect point in a music festival, when the lights hit just right, and your favorite grunge band takes the stage, and every substance you've ingested crests at once.

It's like 1993 all over again.

And for a second—just one—I let myself feel electrified about being here.

7

Entering the Black Pepper Pub feels less like stepping back in time than slipping into another dimension. One where Jess is alive and happy, burned by the aches and ironies of middle age instead of erased from it.

For a moment, I picture her across the table. Those big brown eyes. That brushstroke of freckles. Auburn hair that always smelled of strawberries.

For an instant, her face replaces Toni's.

Then she's gone.

"It kinda gives me the chills just being here," Toni says.

"Why's that?"

"I haven't been to the Pepper since our IDs were seized. The last time I was here . . ." Her voice catches. "It was with Jess."

Hearing her name out loud knocks the wind out of me. I wasn't ready for it. I figured I'd have to ease into that night, gently nudge Toni toward the past. But maybe she sees Jess as the elephant we need to clear from the room before anything else is said.

I miss my window to respond when Toni interprets my silence as reluctance and pivots.

"So, you're married?" she says.

"Nope. Came close once, though. You?"

Between my college and law school friends, I've lost track of married couples on social media. Few boast about their divorce and even fewer change their status. But spouses tend to vanish into thin air from posted family photos like Mob rats.

"Still holding it together," she says. "Our youngest left for college in August."

"Congratulations."

I should ask where her kid goes. I know how small talk works, I just don't do it well. My brain checks out. Language is replaced by static, then by an L train that drowns out the world.

". . . when we dropped her off," she says.

"That's . . ."

A server arrives before I finish the thought. Toni orders a glass of pinot grigio. I go with a Diet Coke, though every cell in my body suddenly craves a pint of Heineken.

We agree to split a basket of curly fries.

Once the server leaves, Toni asks, "Do you keep in touch with anyone else?"

"Just Fenton. You?"

"Still friends with Liv. She's arriving tonight. Kip too." She hesitates. "You never liked him, did you."

"What makes you say that?"

"Just a vibe I caught back then."

She's not wrong, I suppose. But my feelings about Kip are less about dislike than doubt. Last time I saw Jess alive, she was laughing at his jokes, touching his arm.

Kip had no alibi. Just the word of a holier-than-thou RA named Troy, who swore Kip returned to Cormac Hall alone. Same RA who nudged the cops to look harder at me.

When I pressed my suspicions about Kip to Detective Harbaugh, he said, "No one on campus thinks he has it in him to kill someone."

"Of course he does," I'd said. "We all do."

If a client ever uttered anything so stupid in front of my old boss, JaMarcus would've dropped them on the spot and refunded their money from the wad in his pocket.

As for Toni, I don't need to reread her statement to recall what she told police. She left the dance early with Liv to meet two senior guys at the Heights: J. P. and Rocco. Liv didn't hit it off with J. P., but Toni stayed behind with Rocco. Her alibi was clean.

By then, our precious little clique of six had already splintered.

A few weeks after our first rooftop night, Toni dumped Kip for choosing Parcheesi over sex. Ten days later, Liv gave up on Fenton for the opposite reason. She was a strict Catholic saving herself for marriage. Fenton was a self-proclaimed sexual degenerate.

"Kip's a math teacher now," Toni says. "Married with a litter of kids in Scranton."

Thankfully, our drinks arrive.

As I study Toni over the rim of my glass, a memory surfaces. Her climbing into bed with Fenton while I tried to slip out the door. Her boldness, her laughter. Her refusal to be afraid of anything she could see coming.

She's still beautiful. Different now. Realer. Weathered in a good way. I can't say when she was more striking.

"Where are you staying?" I ask.

Only in this bar, in this town, could a Diet Coke taste like it's missing Bacardi 151.

Instinctively, I glance at her left hand. She's not wearing a wedding ring. Not that that means anything anymore.

Funny how even the *absence* of a ring brings me back to the diamond I'd left behind when I flew to Paris without Chloé. Hoping, absurdly, that she'd be waiting for me at the airport, despite having torn up her ticket and left the pieces on my floor.

The mind sharpens things in strange and terrible ways while you're sipping rumless cola and waiting on curly fries in your old college town.

"I'm staying here at the Pepper," Toni says. "Rented a room upstairs."

The rooms upstairs were revolting thirty years ago. If they aged like the bar, I can't imagine spending a night. I booked a room at the

Allentown Marriott, fifteen minutes from campus. No frills, but no roaches either. At least not according to Yelp.

"I stopped by the freshman dorms earlier," I tell her.

Toni and the others remained at Center Valley through graduation. As sophomores in Wilkes. As juniors in the Heights. Senior year off campus near Lehigh University. They lived the full four-year experience.

"Are you happy to be back in Center Valley?" she asks, then quickly adds, "I mean, aside from what happened freshman year . . ."

"Can you set it aside?" I ask, not unkindly. "Can you separate that semester from the rest?"

She freezes. Caught by the question. Or maybe my tone was sharper than I intended.

"She was your best friend," I say, more gently.

"I know. I mean, I was destroyed when Jess died. But we all moved on, didn't we?" She hesitates. "Would you have left Center Valley if you weren't . . ."

"Expelled?" I offer, grinning. "I don't know."

The truth is more complicated.

Once Jess died, I wanted to leave but had nowhere to go. I was still seventeen and had long ago vowed never to return home. Not while my mother was alive.

By the time the dust settled, it was December. Too late to transfer. Especially with my three incompletes.

So I stayed. Remained in the dorms for winter break. Spent a few days with Fenton's family in Philly, then came back to a campus buried under snow.

We passed the time the only way we knew how: drinking, partying, slowly unraveling.

Fenton and I were both placed on residential probation after he was caught twice having girls in his room and I racked up a half dozen alcohol violations.

I didn't even try to hide it.

After Jess, I refused to live sober.

This was college, after all. Everyone drank. Who could tell the difference between a kid blowing off steam and someone spiraling?

The curly fries arrive.

As I smack the 57 on the ketchup bottle, a different image surfaces. The trail of blood leaking from Jess's mouth into the soil. Exposed bone near her left shoulder blade.

Is it a memory? A flashback?

Or just the visual echo of a photo Detective Harbough showed me again and again, hoping to get a reaction?

I can't tell anymore. What's real. What's reconstructed.

When you can't trust your memories, you lose your grip on everything—identity, truth, time. And that's when you start questioning who you really are. Why you're really here. Why you're doing what you're doing.

When I look up, Toni is watching me, concerned.

"Sorry," I say, struggling to pull myself back. "I was just thinking . . ."

I've spent my adult life navigating systems designed to obscure truth. Academia, the legal system, the publishing world, even society itself as it drifted further into algorithms and curated feeds.

I accepted Jess's suicide because that's what I was told. When Harbaugh closed the case, the possibility she was murdered began to feel like a remote twist. More recently, something to keep in my pocket in case *Freshmen* needed a stronger hook.

But now? Now that I'm back here, back in the town, taking in the air, the smell of the Black Pepper—I'm not so sure anymore.

Now I'm remembering things differently. Or maybe just remembering more clearly.

And I'm not convinced we ever really *knew* what happened.

I stare at Toni and weigh whether now is the right moment. I don't want to scare her off.

After some thought, I decide this weekend there *are* no right moments. Only wrong ones.

So I go for it.

"Toni, do you really believe Jess jumped off the roof of your dorm?"

8
Freshman Orientation 1993
The Roof, Part 2

"We're staying," I told Fenton as he and Liv stood to head back downstairs.

"We're gonna watch the sunrise," Jess added, her smile glowing in the moonlight.

We were lying on our backs on a Winnie the Pooh blanket Jess retrieved from her room. A chill crept in, but I barely felt it. Above us stretched a panorama of stars—more than I'd ever seen from New Jersey. I was pretty sure the sun rose in the east, but couldn't remember which direction was east. It might creep up behind us and make me look ridiculous.

But then, who cared?

I felt more alive—more magnificent, more *present*—than I ever felt in my seventeen years. I heard every cricket, felt every shift in the wind. I was conscious of every breath.

"We should do this every night for the rest of our lives," she said.

I didn't disagree but imagined I'd like a few hours of sleep between drinking and class.

"I saw you over at the Heights last night," she said. "You were really loaded."

"Seriously?"

The first night of orientation—Friday—was already a blur. Shaky and misshapen like a fever dream. Although it was thrilling, I hardly remembered anything. Just spikes of adrenaline, shards of sensations, half-formed impressions, scraps of sensory overload. Everything else was static. White noise.

From what I'd read about binge drinking, those memories didn't just disappear. They never even formed. The events were never recorded. Trying to remember was like rewinding a blank VHS tape and playing it over and over, hoping a movie appears.

Still, I had fragments. Feelings. Glimpses.

The day started with meeting Fenton outside the dining hall. He wore jeans, a tight white tank top, and a red, white, and blue do-rag with a star in the center.

"Who are you supposed to be?" I asked. "Evel Knievel?"

In the caf, still buzzed from the twelve-pack of Miller Genuine Draft and Jell-O shots that christened my college life the night before, I devoured the best Belgian waffles north of Disney World. Three cups of coffee later, I was wired and only slightly hungover.

After breakfast, we hit the main lawn, where at least a dozen volleyball nets had been erected under the August sun.

Fenton squinted. "They got a basketball court 'round here? And maybe some shade?"

That's when I knew I'd found the right friend. Philly and Jersey weren't so different after all.

Most of the other students were from rural Pennsylvania, where the Second Amendment meant at least as much as the rest of them, and probably more. Where crucifixes weren't just wall art and jewelry. Where f-bombs caused folks to take cover.

They eyed us like we were intruders.

Discerning glances scorched my flesh. I'd always felt pale, yet next to them, I was somehow fifty shades darker. More ethnic, more suspect. I looked like I didn't belong.

Fenton either fit in or didn't care.

Next thing I knew, we were shirtless and showboating, setting each other up for spikes and chugging from Solo cups between points.

"They call this a 'dry campus,'" Fenton said later, laughing hard and loud. "What a crock."

From that day forward, for years, I couldn't fathom a world without alcohol. Couldn't picture being all there, all the time, with only a book to disappear into.

Because my mother could pull you out of a book.

She'd done it so many times, I'd lost count.

And, living or dead, she'd find a way to do it for the rest of my life.

"Who was that girl you hooked up with last night?" Jess asked on the blanket on the roof.

It hit me like a sucker punch.

"I didn't hook up with anyone," I said.

"You were upstairs with someone at the Heights. I saw you go."

"I swear, I'd tell you. I blacked out around the same time as the sky. Fenton and I were drinking all day."

"It's okay." She playfully smacked my arm. "We hadn't even met yet."

"I honestly don't remember anything after dinner."

"I met Fenton last night," she said. "He's funny."

That surprised me. He hadn't mentioned it.

"He could barely function," she added.

That explained it.

We lay there in silence. I felt her body shift closer.

"What did she look like?" I asked finally.

Jess shrugged. "I only caught a glimpse. Saw some girl leading you upstairs."

"Upstairs? I didn't think they allowed people upstairs."

"She must know someone in high places."

"Or low," I said, forcing a laugh. "Well, I woke up in my own bed this morning. Alone. With a hangover from hell. So if someone got lucky, it wasn't me."

"Look," she whispered, pointing. "There they are. The first rays."

The sky at the edge of the horizon had turned the color of tangerines and steel.

It looked magical.

But only because of her.

I'd seen sunrises before.

But this was the first I ever *felt*.

"So," I said, "you love dolphins, R.E.M., and sunrises. Anything I'm missing?"

She turned to me and kissed me gently. "Only my mom."

She kissed me again—slower, deeper—holding my gaze long after our lips parted.

"At least for now," she whispered as our tongues brushed.

If true kisses are supposed to mean something—and I think they are—then that kiss qualified as my first.

9

Homecoming 2023

An hour after leaving Toni, I sit in my room at the Allentown Marriott, perusing the file in connection with the investigation into Jess's death.

Triggers exist everywhere. Her birth certificate clipped neatly to her death record. Copies of her Pennsylvania driver's licenses (both real and the fake one procured in Philly) and her Center Valley student ID. In all three photos, she's smiling. Gazing into the lens as though she knows someone will be staring back at her decades later.

I can almost hear her pleas.

But no. That's just grief talking. Or ego.

At best, wishful thinking; at worst, grandiosity.

At first glance, I find nothing I haven't seen before. Detective Harbaugh had already shoved most of the evidence across a steel table at me in Interrogation Room A. First, photos of the bloody clothes Jess died in, then a list of phone calls made and received in the two months leading to her death.

Some of the calls are to me.

Many more are *from* me.

Harbaugh said I was obsessed.

He was wrong.

Of the three couples, yes, Jess and I lasted the longest. Which was still only six weeks. We'd never exchanged promises, never spoken our feelings aloud.

I never called her my girlfriend.

She never called me her boyfriend.

So how did six weeks give rise to a lifetime fixation?

Shrink after shrink has asked me that question. There's no single, straightforward answer. But here's the closest I get.

Those six weeks were the first time I'd escaped not just my mother's house but her gravity, along with the trauma, the rage, the constant need to disappear. Jess wasn't just a girl—she was the moment I stopped running *from* something and started running *toward* something.

Jess was everything my mother wasn't. Kind, generous, affectionate. She laughed. She rooted for me. She read my stories. She made me feel possible.

In a lifetime of memories, those six weeks shine the brightest. Everything else blurs in comparison. Even the highlights. And there were many.

Maybe that's why this preoccupation lasted so long.

Or maybe it's because Jess wasn't the only love I found that fall.

I also fell hard for alcohol.

For the first time, I could slow my thoughts. Soften the noise. Blunt the sharp edges of existence. For a few hours a night (and later, most of the day) I could forget.

Forget her voice.

Forget her face.

Forget my mother ever existed.

Books had always been my first escape. But alcohol let me forget in real time. My mother's voice couldn't pull me out of oblivion no matter how hard she tried. And it let me pretend I belonged. In dorms, at parties, in crowds.

It was the first time I felt a part of the world.

The first time I felt the world might want me in it.

"She already *had* a boyfriend," I remember shouting at Harbaugh one night at the station. "Some high school kid in Nazareth."

"Unlike you," he said, "there's no evidence Frank Handly was on campus that night."

He was right.

My alibi was Stacy Rennick, who'd been warned by both Harbaugh and her family attorney not to speak with me. I didn't know what she told them. Whether she said she fell asleep first. Whether she admitted she couldn't say for sure if I'd left her bed during the night.

Back then, there were no cell phones. No late-night texts or missed calls. Just landlines. And there were no calls between our rooms that night.

If I'd gone upstairs and knocked, wouldn't Jess have just let me in? Why would she have taken me up to the roof?

Unless someone else was there. But then, why did no one come forward?

Unless I invited *her* up there.

Unless I lured her to the roof for a purpose.

If that's the case, a good criminal lawyer would draw only one inference.

It wasn't just a moment of rage, a crime of passion.

It was *premeditated.* Which means life without parole.

Or back then, death by lethal injection.

"What if I told you Stacy Rennick could only account for your whereabouts for forty-five minutes that night?" Harbaugh once asked.

"I'd tell you to blow it out your ass," I snapped.

Whatever that meant. I'd been hooked on the Jerky Boys.

Harbaugh disliked me from the start—"Nice bumper sticker ya got there, kid"—but I did myself no favors. Later, working with JaMarcus, I hated the way I'd behaved. Not because it was rude but dumb. Harbaugh wanted to get into my head, under my skin, and I opened the door and rolled out the red carpet.

I played right into his hands.

In law school, I'd cringe thinking about that version of me. I'd tell JaMarcus's more arrogant clients: "Sometimes, innocence isn't enough. Sometimes, you need to keep your cool. Sometimes, you have to keep your mouth shut and let the process play out."

But then, I've always made things harder on myself. My penchant for self-destruction could be my real motive for reopening this rough-and-tumble murder investigation.

Because little good can come from resolving it.

Other than a book deal. And another year of living with a roof over my head. Having food to eat. Health insurance.

Now, reading Stacy Rennick's statement, I can confirm Harbaugh lied to me. Stacy not only said I spent the entire night but that she was sober. Which solidified my alibi and hers. Not that she ever needed one. Harbaugh had zeroed in on our disbanded clique of six from orientation from the start. Toni, Liv, Kip, Fenton. Me.

As suspects, Liv and Toni made sense. They remained in Jess's orbit. And from what I gleaned the night of her death, Jess hadn't entirely written off Kip.

But Fenton and I were a different story. The girls had moved on from us weeks earlier.

I slap a closed folder down on the nightstand. It's six p.m., and Toni and I are meeting Liv at McCartney Hall for the alumni dinner.

Of the five of us, Liv was the only one without an alibi.

She left the dance early, went with Toni to the Heights, but didn't stay long. She claimed after leaving Toni behind with Rocco, she returned to her room, alone.

She scoffed at the very notion of needing an alibi.

But she'd been drinking.

She knew the roof.

And according to Fenton, she might've even had a motive, however thin. Although I highly doubt it, Fenton suggested soon after their breakup that Liv had a thing for me and was disappointed with how things turned out.

My guess is, only the second part is true.

Standing in front of the mirror, I close my eyes. I look terrible. I'm not used to being with people. Not real ones anyway. Not for a while. I'm shaking, I'm sweating. My nerves feel like razor wire.

After decades of sobriety, I stare at the minifridge as if it's talking to me. The Klonopin isn't working. After years on Prozac and Wellbutrin, they no longer have much of an effect either. But altogether, they create a floor to keep me from spiraling too fast, too far.

I've been avoiding situations like these since Del Danzinger solidified himself as my meal ticket with *Danzinger on Death Row*.

There's no way I can meet them like this. I reach into my pocket and grasp the twenty-five-year chip that seems to have lost some significance since my arrival.

My sponsor died suddenly only weeks after I received it, and I never got around to finding another one. Not that another would've been of any use. No one could possibly fill his shoes.

Meantime, COVID hit, and the meetings went online. The few in-person ones became ghost towns—and I stopped going altogether. Probably not one of my better decisions.

I'd justified it by asking myself: Does five or six years of heavy drinking as a student make you an alcoholic for life? Or had AA been a solution in search of a problem? Was alcoholism simply a scapegoat? Something to blame? An excuse, not just for past behavior but present and future isolation?

Once I was sober, did I keep going to meetings for the wrong reasons?

As a writer working from home, how many people would I've seen if not for AA? Did I keep going only for Del Danzinger's sake? How many of my fellow members' stories sparked my imagination and formed the premise of a book? *Danzinger's Demons*, *Danzinger's Descent*, *Danzinger's Downfall.*

Meantime, I'm prescribed benzos for anxiety, amphetamines for concentration, especially when I'm on deadline. I take muscle relaxers, sometimes even opiates, for chronic neck and back pain. I never became addicted to any of it.

I finally bend on one achy knee and open the minifridge.

I tell myself I'll have only one before I leave.

In the back of my mind, small and quiet, another voice whispers: *Or none at all.*

That voice belongs to my former sponsor.

That voice belongs to JaMarcus.

God rest his soul.

10

None of the redbrick buildings on campus look smaller than they did thirty years ago. Even at night, everything appears elephantine. McCartney Hall—named for the musician Damian, not Paul—is no exception. What was once a cozy cafeteria is now a sleek city-grade eatery.

"Am I the only imbecile who didn't wear a suit to this thing?" I ask Toni as we step inside.

"No," she says, pointing toward a guy face-deep in a burrito. "That imbecile didn't either."

"I've missed that sense of humor."

"My sense of humor missed you too."

We're each carrying a card with our table number.

"Seven, seven, seven," I mutter, my speech otherwise just fine because I abstained.

Thanks again, JaMarcus.

Despite my promise, seven would've been the number of drinks I slammed back at the hotel if I'd gone through with my plan to have one. Because after the first, why not a second? Then a third to dim the brightness. A fourth to dull the surrounding sound. A fifth to blunt the biting glances I feel as I move through a crowd. A sixth for small talk. A seventh to drown out my mother's constant criticisms, even now.

I would've hated myself for it. Not in some cinematic, tortured genius way. In the quiet, exhausted way you hate yourself for breaking a promise you meant to keep.

Twenty-five years of sobriety would've been erased with the first sip. That first sip was the hardest back then and, luckily, it was the hardest tonight.

Because after that first sip, it's all liquid sunshine and rainbows.

Until it isn't.

Still, I'd edged close to the brink. And this time, JaMarcus wouldn't be there to pick up the pieces if I fell.

I want to do better, be better. But want alone doesn't rewrite history. And I fear maybe this is just who I am in Pennsylvania.

Perhaps our so-called *permanent record* is more important than we thought.

"Ah, there we are," Toni says, giving me a nudge.

I'll need to excuse myself soon. Pop an Adderall in the men's room to unpack the heaviness in my head, to stave off the emptiness and boredom always a blink away.

My diagnoses have shifted over the years depending on the psychiatrist du jour. ADHD and CPTSD are the latest. Nine letters. One more and I win a free Italian sub at Jersey Mike's.

Of course, psychiatry's not a perfect science.

Like Dory, the best you can do is just keep swimming.

Already seated at table 7 is Liv Latham, dressed in deep purple, her smooth olive skin and dark eyes somehow unchanged. I did a deep dive online before Homecoming. Saw the photos, the gated home in Haverford, the puffy husband, the two perfect daughters. Her life curated, filtered, complete.

She's a self-styled stay-at-home mom with several side hustles: freelance writer, wellness coach, a Four-Diamond ambassador for the Sculpted Summer pyramid scheme.

Armed with this, I can approach our talk like a cross-examination. Yes or no questions. No superfluous words, no unnecessary explanations.

No blather.

As she tells me about her newest product—specialized deodorants, "they're not just for pits anymore"—my eyes lock on the crucifix hanging from the thin gold chain around her neck. The cross still makes me flinch like a vampire in an old movie.

As a kid, I believed that proved I was Satan's spawn. Not knowing who my father was—and my mother working like a Cold War spy to keep it that way—didn't help allay my fears.

When Toni wanders off to flirt near the bar, I see my opening.

"This is my first time back in thirty years," I say, setting aside my water glass.

"I was surprised you came," Liv replies.

"Why?"

We'd corresponded earlier this year. Her last message largely convinced me to come.

She rolls her eyes. "Really?"

Just like that, I see the eighteen-year-old Liv again. Pretty, playful, pointed. Razor-sharp.

"If I knew you'd be here," she adds, "I would've brought your books to be autographed."

It catches me off guard, not the idea of signing them, but the fact that she reads them. If she didn't like me, I doubted she'd like Del Danzinger. Even Creighton the Great thinks we're the same cat. As if I had so little imagination.

Del Danzinger isn't me.

He's better than me.

More JaMarcus Cooke than Gregg Dryer.

"I'm thinking of setting the next one here," I say.

"In Center Valley?"

"At the college. A fictional version of our first semester."

Liv presses her lips together. "What do you mean '*our*'?"

"The five of us," I say, watching closely. "And Jess."

Her reaction is immediate, a jolt of indignant energy. "You want to *profit* from Jess's suicide?"

"Profit?" I laugh dryly. "Clearly, you're unfamiliar with the publishing industry. No. Not profit from it. Explore. Investigate. Try to understand what happened."

I glance toward the bar. Toni's still talking to a man I think I half remember. They both have chilled martinis in their hands, hers with onions, his with olives. Both drinks look outlandishly delicious.

"Were you in love with her?" Liv asks, bluntly.

I pause, wanting to rebuke her; the witness isn't allowed to ask counsel questions. "I had feelings, sure. We were close those first six weeks. But when it ended, it ended."

"Did it, though?"

Before I can reply, she asks, "Who did you punch at the Saint Patrick's Day party? The one that got you expelled?"

I wasn't expecting that. "You know who."

She sips her wine like she's proven her point. "You were still pining for her. Still calling her before Homecoming."

"I was seventeen." I force a laugh. "I was drunk-dialing, not sending her sonnets."

Suddenly, I feel like I'm being owned by a hostile witness.

So I flip the script. "Besides, Fenton said you never particularly cared for Jess."

"What does that have to do with anything?"

She doesn't deny it, which unsettles me. It's so unexpected.

"You're the only one without an alibi," I remind her.

She doesn't flinch. "I left Toni behind with Rocco at the Heights and went straight to my room."

"Did you see Jess?"

We all know the timeline. We lived it. We recited it for investigators dozens of times. But timelines are tools. They can be rewritten. On paper *and* in our minds.

"Is this why you came back?" she asks coldly. "To interrogate your friends?"

"*Are* we friends?"

"On Facebook."

Her response guts me. This *is* what constitutes friendship these days. Algorithmic proximity. Why bother calling someone when you constantly see their updates? Why visit when they appear first thing on your smartphone every day? Why ask how they're feeling when they're obviously fine, snapping happy pictures at picnics and barbecues, smiling for family photos at theme parks and restaurants. All is hunky-dory in Faceland and, let's face it, that's the only version we care to see.

"And back then?" I ask. "Were we friends?"

"I thought so. If you need to ask . . ."

When she trails off, I remain silent. Hurt and guilty, but mostly disarmed.

Finally, I circle back. "*Did* you see Jess later that night?"

"She was still at the dance when I got back to my room."

"You didn't answer my question."

"You're being ridiculous."

"Because I have questions about Jess?"

She narrows her eyes. "Because you have questions about *me*."

The words are like a head-on collision. I scan for Toni but can't find her. Suddenly, every stranger in this dining hall is a juror eyeing me like a defendant sporting their orange jumpsuit to trial.

I lean in. Quiet, careful. "Jess could've stopped by, maybe looking for Toni. Maybe you went up to the roof. Something could've happened." I reach for her hand, which is warmer than expected. It's something I did with ease when I had drinks in me. Which is partly why I miss drinking more than I admit. The electricity of a casual human touch is undeniable. "I don't need justice, Liv. I just need the truth."

"You mean, you need an ending to your book."

"No, my book ends however I want it to. Real life doesn't."

She locks eyes with me. "You're still obsessed with her."

I pull back. My jaw tightens. I feel the vein twitch above my right eye. "That was Harbaugh's theory. He wanted you and the others to turn on me. That's what cops do. They divide and conquer."

She says nothing.

I lean in again. Softer now. "Look, I read your statement. You didn't tell Harbaugh everything. You didn't get back to the room, pop *Ghost* in the VCR, fall asleep, and wake to the scream, did you?"

"I woke before the scream," she says flatly. "Not because of it."

My breath catches.

She just admitted to lying in her statement.

Legally, the case will go nowhere. Not thirty years later, without hard evidence. After all, there was no skin found under Jess's nails, no defensive wounds, no sexual assault. Nothing that might yield conclusive DNA evidence pointing to the killer. But emotionally, it changes everything.

"I woke around six," Liv says, unprompted. "The night before, I finished *Ghost* and fell asleep, just like I said. When I got up, I started worrying about Toni. Her bed hadn't been slept in. I threw on some sweats and was about to jog over to the Heights."

She looks at me like she's challenging me to keep up.

"First, I wanted to leave Toni a note on our whiteboard in case we missed each other. But I had to erase something," she says cryptically.

"Erase what?"

"Four words. Meant for someone else. Left on the wrong door by someone drunk."

Her voice is icy, final.

"What did they say?" I ask.

She doesn't blink or speak for what feels like forever.

Then she says, "The note read, '*One last sunrise, Jess?*'"

11
September 1993
Labor Day Weekend

Roughly one week after Freshman Orientation, we got a badly needed three-day weekend, courtesy of the American labor force.

Fenton and I had already decided that academics at Center Valley College were a joke. He was majoring in psychology, I in criminal justice, but our first-year schedules were nearly identical: intro-level liberal arts classes that felt like high school with higher tuition.

"Don't do it, dude," Fenton said in aisle 3 of Pop's Pharmacy. "Don't buy condoms."

"What? Why not?"

"It's bad luck."

"Says the guy with raging herpes."

Given the simplicity of our syllabi, I'd decided to use my grandmother's blank check at the college bookstore . . . *creatively.* With Fenton at my side, I searched the shelves for the priciest textbooks in the store. Although I was an English and history guy, the real money was in advanced math and science.

"Big money, big money, big money," Fenton chanted as I lifted each heavier volume. "No whammies, stop!"

I held up a massive brick called *Top Topics in Topography*. Even thicker than the abstract algebra books.

"Wait," Fenton said, "that's a graduate-level course."

"So? This is *Bookstore Bingo*. There are very few rules."

I had no intention of keeping any of the texts. If I didn't slit the plastic or mark the pages, the bookstore had a "no questions asked" return policy, which I'd already tested by sneaking extra books into my roommate's pile. We returned them the next day for a full cash refund. My roommate was so enamored with my ingenuity, he called his folks and told them he needed a second check to buy additional books for his classes.

"Aren't you going to buy anything for your actual courses?" Fenton asked.

I handed him the topography textbook. "How about I cut you in and borrow yours?"

But Center Valley's Catholic bookstore didn't sell condoms. Hence our venture to Pop's Pharmacy, a few miles away, near Lehigh.

There, I examined the selection like a wine snob.

Fenton groaned. "I'm telling you, Gregg, it's bad luck."

"Bad luck is an STD, man. Bad luck is a positive pregnancy test."

"Without fail," Fenton argued, "every guy who buys condoms for a specific girl ends up tossing them. If you need one, you'll find one."

"You're *that* superstitious?"

"I'm Catholic."

In those days I didn't put much stock in Fenton's blanket statements. Hours earlier, after hearing the new Guns N' Roses album, he'd declared, "Axl Rose should cover *every* song *ever*." He retracted the statement in a group text twenty years later.

"I'm sure they'll serve their purpose at some point," I told him.

"Your funeral, dude."

"If it makes you feel better, you can pay at the register."

"Are you nuts? I'm not going anywhere *near* those things until I seal the deal. Dude, you can't trick the condoms. They'll screw you every time."

I continued studying the prophylactics. "Are you getting anywhere with Liv?" I asked.

"I have a wide lead off first, looking to steal second." He frowned. "But it's not as if there's a cornucopia waiting for me."

Liv may not have been the obvious bombshell—bookish, small-chested, demure—but if it weren't for Jess, I'd have been envious. All right, I *was* envious. There was something about Liv that clung to me. Maybe because she didn't give anything away easily—not approval, not attention. You had to earn it.

"She thinks I'm bad news," I said.

Fenton shrugged. "She thinks *everyone's* bad news. She even says Jess is bad news for being too free-spirited."

"No freer than Toni." Toni had been the most open with us, happily sharing that she and her ex humped like jackrabbits.

I finally grabbed a three-pack, just in case there was something to Fenton's ridiculous superstition.

"I don't know," he said. "Toni at least broke up with her boyfriend before coming here."

"Jess is never seeing that high school kid again."

"I don't doubt that," Fenton said as we approached the register. "But yesterday, Liv told me, Jess couldn't take her eyes off Macmillan's six-pack between quarters of the flag football game."

Mike Macmillan played varsity baseball, which made him Center Valley royalty. The kind of guy they let slide into the back row of every lecture hall with his hoodie up and his hat pulled low.

Meanwhile, I refused to engage in any extracurricular that didn't let you drink Miller High Life on the sidelines. Not out of any joy, not to bond with my team or celebrate the score, but to escape reality. To numb myself. To climb out of my head for as long as I could, as often as I could.

As I grabbed the paper bag, Fenton hit me with what had become the most crucial question in our daily lives. "What are we drinking tonight?"

I grinned, recalling the prior weekend and our brush with the first floor. "I kind of dig that Southern Comfort stuff."

Back in the dorm that night, after the laughter faded and the buzz wore off, I lay on the top bunk staring at the ceiling tiles, Jess's name echoing in my head like the end of a prayer I didn't know I'd been reciting.

All the talk, all the posturing, the scheming and jokes—it was armor, wasn't it?

And underneath it, the truth:

Jess already took up too much of my headspace.

Not for what we were.

But for what we might still become.

12
Homecoming 2023

When an Uber drops me back at the Allentown Marriott at eleven, I head straight to my room and open the minifridge.

Stare at its contents.

“Alcoholism is an allergy,” JaMarcus once told me, smoking a menthol in the faculty parking lot.

At the time, he was Professor Cooke of my undergrad criminal procedure course at Bristol University, where he worked as an adjunct in the Criminal Justice and Black Studies Departments.

“When you have an allergy,” he added, “let’s say of nuts, you stay away from them because your throat might close.”

He paused for effect, as if posturing for a jury. “If you’re allergic to alcohol, you damn well better keep clear of it or you’ll break out in handcuffs. And that’s if you’re lucky. If you’re behind the wheel . . .”

He trailed off as he took a puff, but I already knew. His son Russell died in a motorcycle crash around my age just a few years earlier. Killed by a guy who’d been barely over the legal limit.

To the very end, JaMarcus refused to take DUI cases.

Checking my watch, I consider calling Fenton, finding out where he is and whether he’s coming at all, but decide against it because I’m stuck in one of those rare but memorable moments where everything seems hopeless.

Liv just turned my entire investigation upside down, and I don't like what shook out—mostly because I'm not sure it doesn't implicate me. Not in the way Liv thinks, maybe, but in the ways it matters.

She didn't accuse me outright. But the inference was clear. She thinks I wrote that note on her whiteboard. *One last sunrise, Jess?* She thinks I mistook her door for Jess's. And by erasing it and staying silent, she believes she protected me.

Which means Liv believes I killed Jess.

Or was at least *there* when she went over the edge.

"You were blacked out that night, weren't you?" she asked at dinner.

I'd already admitted that to Harbaugh. There were gaps—long ones I couldn't account for. But that didn't make me a murderer then. And it sure as hell doesn't make me one now.

Even if I didn't have an alibi in Stacy Rennick, Liv couldn't possibly have known if the handwriting was mine. I'd scribbled plenty of dumb crap on their whiteboard those first few weeks. Mostly obscene sketches Fenton and I found hilarious. The girls, not so much.

Besides, I wasn't the only guy who went to the roof. It wasn't a sacred space.

Who knows if Jess took Mike Macmillan at some point after our split in October. They were only together briefly. A week or so that felt like months. She dumped him after learning he had a girlfriend about to visit campus.

By Homecoming weekend, the girlfriend had come and gone, and Macmillan was a free agent again. And while he moved on, sometimes plans fell through. Some nights even baseball players got shot down.

Maybe he went to D'Amelio searching for Jess.

Maybe he found her.

There were no phone calls between them, but Macmillan knew D'Amelio. Knew the halls. Could've knocked on doors, written on whiteboards, and waited. Maybe long enough for her to return and find *him.*

Then there's Kip Ulrich, the last person I saw with Jess. They were flirting at the dance, touching, laughing. Maybe they continued things afterward. Maybe an argument broke out and escalated.

The Cormac RA claimed to have seen Kip enter the dorm, but there's no proof he stayed there. His roommate was in Philly. The security guy barely watched the doors. The girl behind the reception desk at D'Amelio was even more indifferent.

And why didn't Kip show tonight? He was supposed to meet Toni. Maybe he backed out because she told him she'd be with me.

Maybe he's afraid. Or maybe he thinks *I* did it.

Maybe Fenton does too.

Fenton knew me better than anyone. I told him everything those first few months. I knew I'd never see my friends from home again, not while my mother was alive, and I was desperate for companionship. Especially after Jess.

I remember how I felt in the days before Homecoming. Not the specifics, but the ache. That rattling feeling of unfinished business. That desperate need for closure.

Because Jess and I didn't break up. We just . . . stopped.

One day we were together. The next we weren't.

Without a word. Without a *why*.

We'd never defined the relationship, but maybe a posthumous label would've helped me let go. If I knew what we were to each other, I'd have understood what we weren't.

I'd have understood what I lost.

And what I never had to begin with.

Now, alone in my hotel room with nothing but the hum of the fridge and faint traffic outside, her name still hangs there—*Jess*—like a ghost with something left unsaid, a story untold.

Not Jess, the girl, not even her soul. Not her truth or tragedy. Just her name. Four soft letters that once lit me up and now lie in my gut like lead.

I try to tell myself she was a chapter. Not the whole book.

A lapse, not the loss.

But even after all this time, after all that bluster, all the blaming and rationalizing, I still can't shake the feeling that some part of me never left that rooftop.

And that some part of her is still waiting for me there, so we could lie on our backs—holding hands and gazing up at the stars—patiently awaiting the first rays of the day.

13

Tossing the open file onto the bed, I check the time. Too early to sleep, even if I hadn't taken sixty milligrams of Adderall to survive the alumni dinner.

I scroll through my phone, thumbing through old texts and Facebook messages. Nothing from Toni. I consider calling her but can't recall how we left things at dinner. Was she staying behind? Bringing someone back to her room above the Black Pepper?

A crazy thought: *Should I call Alissa?*

Her kids will still be awake.

She'll be asleep. Or she'll pretend to be. I can't blame her. She seemed really hurt by the breakup. I'm not sure I gave her any real reason for it.

I'm not sure I had any real reason to give.

I again consider calling Fenton but decide to wait until morning.

But that leaves tonight.

And the long, cold, dark hours that lie ahead, like a silent, empty stretch of highway heading nowhere good.

Minutes later, I stare at the screen and debate calling an old law school buddy who's been divorced a few years. But he's probably out on a date. Or home with one.

"I'm telling you, bro," he said recently. "You don't even have to leave your house anymore. Women just show up."

I sigh with resignation. Open the App Store.

Between my contentedness with being alone and living in a fairly urban area, I haven't needed to resort to apps. But here I'm in unfamiliar territory. Rural Pennsylvania.

And I find myself not only alone but lonely.

The kind of lonely that creeps under your skin, disguises itself as curiosity, and whispers: *Just see who's out there.*

That voice is Fenton's.

With blurred vision and a dull ache above my left eye, I type *dating apps*. I expect Tinder to pop up first, but it's buried beneath sponsored ads. The list below is a mile long. There's an app for every race, religion, age group, kink, and zodiac sign.

Nothing appeals.

Eventually, I scroll back up and click "Get" on the Editor's Choice.

I enter the required information. Upload the first decent photo I find.

Before long, I'm swiping left and right like a pro.

Well, mostly left.

That's when I see her.

A photo I've not only seen before but studied.

It's Liv.

Only here, she goes by *Lily*.

It's one of her Facebook photos—same angle, same lighting—but with her husband skillfully cropped out.

My thumb hovers over the screen.

If I can see her, she can probably see me.

I check the profile. It doesn't feel abandoned. Her location is listed as ten miles from campus. This isn't some dusty leftover account. This is live.

I should swipe left. That's the safe move. No notification. No fallout.

No possibility of waking up in the middle of a potential murder investigation *and* a thorny custody battle.

But then . . .

What if this is the way in?

What if she knows more about Jess than she's letting on? What if this is my chance to get closer—not to Liv, but to the truth?

Even I'm not sure I believe what I'm telling myself. But maybe choosing intel over sex is exactly the choice I need to make.

Maybe this isn't a temptation.

Maybe it's a tactic.

Or maybe I'm lying to myself because I miss feeling seen.

I stare down at Liv's photo.

Then close my eyes.

And swipe right.

A fresh current of nervous electricity courses through me. Shame. Excitement. Strategy. Hunger. All tangled together like a live wire.

I wait.

And I wonder. Teetering between:

What will she do? And:

What the hell have I just done?

14

An hour later, Liv and I sit across from each other at the Coop, the nickname bestowed on the Coopersburg Diner long before our first three a.m. visit freshman year. How many times Fenton and I ate here after a night of heavy drinking, I don't know. Lucky for us, the Coop was used to drunk college kids acting like idiots.

"I guess I should explain," she says.

"No explanations necessary."

"Les is a good guy. I just get the shivers whenever he touches me."

I don't know how to respond to that. "So," I tease, "your profile mentioned you were looking for a wild night. Didn't expect you to pick the Coop."

She smiles. Even in the diner's unforgiving light, Liv looks years younger than her age. From her Facebook page, I gathered her husband makes some serious money. If the rich are prettier because they can afford to be, she's the rule and he's the exception.

"Your profile hardly mentions *anything*," she says. "I wasn't sure what kind of night you had in mind. Especially if it ended up being with me."

The frost I always sensed from her thaws with every word. Maybe it was never frost. Just shyness with a pinch of insecurity. Now, across the table, she's warm, goofy even.

While we eat—Cobb salad for her, hot open-faced roast beef sandwich with brown gravy for me—she laughs loud and long, at one point rubbing her spoon on her sweater and affixing it to her nose, drawing stares from nearby tables.

"You caught me off guard with the whole whiteboard thing," I say, twisting my water glass, wishing it was the amber lager that just passed by. "But I didn't write the message. I wasn't on the second floor of D'Amelio that night."

"Right, you were on the first floor. With Stacy Rennick." She takes a sip of water, as if the name leaves a bad taste. "I didn't see her at the alumni dinner."

"I think she still lives in Canada," I offer, mostly guessing. "I doubt she'll show this weekend."

"Then we may never see her again."

"Why not?"

"I don't plan on coming back here next year, do you?" Her smile flickers. "Or has tonight turned you into a hardcore Homecoming junkie?"

"We still have a few milestones left, don't we?"

She arches her brows. "You really want to see what these people look like in their fifties? It's hard enough now. Soon it'll just be . . . sad."

I shrug. "I thought everyone looked pretty good, considering."

"Considering what?"

I lean in, lower my voice as if it's a secret. "You and I—we're the same age as Archie and Edith Bunker on *All in the Family*."

She chuckles as the busboy clears our table.

"You believe me, don't you?" I say once he's gone.

"That we're the Bunkers' age on—"

"That I didn't write that message on your whiteboard thirty years ago," I say firmly.

Her sad smile flattens. "Harbaugh played the voicemails, Gregg."

My cheeks flush hot. "That means nothing. I never threatened her. Never even attempted to win her back. Before murder, don't you think I would've tried flowers?"

"But you invited her back to the roof in those voicemails."

"Because that's where we went. *All* of us. Not just me." My chest tightens. "Did she go up there with anyone else after breaking things off with me? Maybe Kip or Macmillan?"

The server pours our coffee. Liv shrugs. "I never returned to the roof after breaking things off with Fenton."

"Do you know if he's coming this weekend?"

She lifts a shoulder. She doesn't know, doesn't care.

"Gregg, you admitted you blacked out that night. How do you know you didn't come upstairs and scribble on our whiteboard?"

The truth is, I don't.

Blackouts were the monster beneath my bed for years, beginning with the first night of Freshman Orientation. They didn't let go until I stopped drinking completely.

Until JaMarcus Cooke started strong-arming me into going to meetings.

Until he offered me a deal I couldn't turn down.

"I was with Stacy all night," I say, sidestepping. "But that note on your whiteboard *is* a key piece of evidence the cops never had. We can't just dismiss it."

"A piece of evidence in what? The police aren't reopening a thirty-year-old case."

I'm Caesar at the Rubicon. "No. But that doesn't mean *we* can't finally know for sure what happened to Jess."

Her face sharpens. "We? This is all about your book deal, isn't it."

"No, we established that back at McCartney Hall."

"Then what is it? Why this obsession?"

I set my palm against the table harder than intended.

Plates and glasses rattle.

Diners glance our way.

The vein above my eye—Alissa's favorite barometer of my frustration—is probably twitching as if I just got tased.

I smile to reassure everyone I'm not dangerous.

They don't look reassured.

"I'm *not* obsessed, Liv." I lower my voice. "Jess's death affected everything that came after it. Don't you *feel* that?"

She looks at me like I'm speaking in tongues. "You think if Jess hadn't died, you'd still be with her?"

I shrug as if it's irrelevant, as though I'd never given it a second thought.

Still, I can't help but make the argument. "I don't know. Anything's possible, right? Fenton married Amy. Kip married his college sweetheart too."

It sounds ridiculous. But on some bizarre level, I know it's possible. Possible that, in an infinite multiverse, countless Greggs and Jesses made it to this Homecoming together.

If Jess hadn't died, we might've worked it out. At least in the short term. Maybe forever. Or as close as forever comes in a world in which everything survives moment to moment.

Just a week before she died, we'd almost gotten back together in her dorm.

The Night of a Thousand Plushies.

I hate thinking about that night, about the possibilities. Every time I do, it singes something inside me.

"I've never felt stronger for anyone," I say.

"That's because we feel *everything* stronger when we're teenagers."

"No, Liv. It's still there," I say, surprising myself with the vehemence in my voice. "It's in my bones."

She doesn't flinch. "That's nostalgia. Maybe not for Center Valley. Maybe not even for Jess. Maybe it's for your youth."

I drop my face into my hands, rub my burning eyes. "I was still young when I left Pennsylvania."

"But you didn't leave. You'd been expelled. Banished. Don't you think that's why you feel so differently than me and Toni?"

She's not wrong.

My expulsion haunted me for years.

The nightmare started on a cold March night at a party at the Heights.

I still hear my fist connecting with Macmillan's temple.

After he dropped, I'd turned and faced Fenton.

"What the hell did you do?" he shouted at me.

I looked down at the unmoving body at my feet.

"Get the hell out of here," Fenton yelled, shoving me toward the door. "They called campus police."

I ran.

As Pearl Jam's "Jeremy" replaced Nirvana's "Lithium" on the stereo at Heights number 9, I dashed through the night to Cormac Hall, where I hid among the second-floor science majors.

"I got my life back on track," I tell Liv. "I finished college. Law school. Passed the bar. Even got my Rhode Island law license." I shift gears. "But that's not the point. It doesn't matter if Jess and I would've made it. What matters is she lost her life. And I need to know why. Even if I never saw her again between that night and this, I need to know why she's not sitting with us here at this table tonight."

She goes quiet. "I understand."

I study her. "Do you *really* believe Jess committed suicide?"

It's a question I admit I still can't answer. As close as we were, I knew Jess had secrets she'd never share. At times, she became sad and withdrew. Some nights she cried without knowing (or admitting) why.

Between the alcohol and whatever went through her mind when she drifted into space like she did, it's certainly possible she jumped. Yet it's just as possible she didn't.

Liv glances at her watch, then reaches across the table and takes my hands as I took hers earlier. Her touch is warm saline coursing up my veins.

She looks into my eyes and says, like she's offering a slice of cake, "Wanna skip a second cup of coffee and finish this conversation back at your hotel room?"

It's almost as if she knew I intended to ask the waitress to bring my next cup of coffee with some Baileys and a shot of Jameson.

15

Minutes later, an UberX driven by a guy named Max pulls in front of the Coop, and off we go to Allentown, my heart pounding against my chest.

What the hell am I doing?

That message on Liv's door is now the best lead I have. I should be chasing it, calling Toni, asking if she remembers ghostly traces of the note, or whether Liv ever mentioned it. Failing that, I should be hunting down whoever wrote it. Because that person—man or woman—is likely the one who killed Jess.

When Max drops us at the Marriott, I need to study the exterior to remember which room is mine. I spot the back of my Prius and use it like the needle on a compass.

Outside my door, I fish through my pockets for the key card, but Liv's already pushing it open with her finger.

"Pretty sure I closed that when I left," I say. "Wait here. Let me go in first."

"Afraid there's gonna be a hooker waiting for—"

Her joke dies on her lips. My eyes register the chaos.

The flat-screen is shattered. Lamps smashed. Chairs overturned. Shampoo, conditioner, toothpaste, and shaving cream are smeared across the king-size bed like frosting. The mirror over the dresser has spiderwebbed. Broken bottles and crushed cans litter the battlefield like fallen soldiers. The minifridge has been cleared out.

I bolt toward the nightstand and pull open the drawer. My pills are gone.

I scan the room. So is the police file on Jess.

This was no random burglary.

I rush to the window and rip back the drape.

A message is scrawled across the window in alternating streams of ketchup and mustard.

Go home

"Oh my God," Liv gasps.

That's not *remotely* how I'd imagined her shouting those words tonight.

Although Allentown PD responds, it's the Center Valley chief of police who has questions for me.

Chief Cheryl Lindsay was fresh out of the academy back in 1993 when she was dispatched to the scene of a possible suicide on the CVC campus. Back then, she was ten years older than us. Now she looks twenty. The job wears on you, I suppose.

She doesn't give off the vibe of someone who phones it in—or someone who gives it her all. If anything, she's fashionably disinterested.

I ask, "Is Liv all—"

"*Mrs. Todeski* is fine," Lindsay cuts in from the bed opposite mine in the vacant room next door. "My patrolman drove her back to the Bethlehem Ritz."

Of course. The rich gossip like anyone else. Liv's husband might even have connections there. Which makes me wonder how she slipped out to begin with—and how she'll explain a police escort to the overnight bellhop.

Probably with a crisp fifty.

"It's been a long time," Lindsay says.

I don't respond. She may not be Harbaugh, but she's still CVPD. And, as much faith as I've lost in the law, I'm still technically a lawyer.

"Okay," she says, exhaling. "So you're going to be as cooperative as you were thirty years ago." She motions with her chin toward the wreckage next door. "You told first responders you think this is connected to Jess Karras."

I remind myself that Lindsay's no ally. Though she had the file ready for me as promised, she knew she couldn't prevent me from getting a copy. All she could do was throw paperwork at me. Eventually, I'd have gotten through it. Pennsylvania has its own Freedom of Information Act called the Right-to-Know Law.

"Not just connected," I say. "It's a warning. Someone's trying to scare me off."

"Because?"

"Because I'm looking into what really happened to her."

"You don't think she killed herself? What evidence are you basing that on?"

"Nothing admissible," I concede. "But I'm not trying to prosecute anyone. I just want answers."

"To ease your conscience?"

I don't take the bait.

"Back then," she says, "you also insisted it wasn't suicide. Even though it wasn't in your interest. You were the prime suspect."

Thirty years and a law degree later, CVPD's file is clear. "Harbaugh botched the investigation. He was fixated on me."

"He was a fine detective," she says, "but prone to tunnel vision. He trusted his gut more than I liked. But his gut was usually right."

I sigh, long and loud. I'm done discussing Harbaugh. "Are they lifting prints?"

"Yes, but it's a hotel room. We don't expect much."

"They stole the case file I picked up yesterday."

"No, we recovered it in the dumpster on Clive Street. A few other things were with it. Signed copies of your new book."

I ignore the jab. "So you're saying I wasn't targeted?"

"As a tourist at a budget motel? Sure, you were targeted. But not in any meaningful way. This is more common than you might think."

"What about the message on the window? '*Go home*?'"

"Sounds like something a burglar might write to a guest they just robbed, doesn't it?"

I can't believe what I'm hearing. This is why I didn't want to loop in the cops. I learned this lesson working for JaMarcus, when he took a case hours away in rural Massachusetts. The gap in quality—between their law enforcement and Providence PD, not to mention the prosecutors—was staggering. Part of him loved it. JaMarcus got to play the small-town hero for a week. He even considered staying and racking up the W's. But another part of him knew he'd miss the challenge of city prosecutors.

"Gregg," Lindsay says. "I'll be honest. You should heed that inartful message and go home. Listen to the condiments. If you came to see old friends, invite them to Jersey. If you're here to solve a case, you're thirty years too late."

"There's no statute of limitations on murder. Why not reopen it? My room is a second crime scene. New evidence means new grounds."

"You know," she says, "even back then, I knew you had the makings of a storyteller. I felt it in my gut."

I blink. "Felt what?"

"Let's just say, I believed you were clever enough to argue Jess didn't commit suicide just to throw us off."

"And now? Three decades later?"

"You have to admit, it sounds like the perfect premise for one of your books. But you'd have to clear your name, leave no doubt. My wife, who's a crime-fic buff, tells me antiheroes aren't in vogue these days."

I scoff but otherwise keep my mouth shut. Like I should've done with Harbaugh.

She says, "The front desk tells me you're booked through the weekend. Why don't you skip the ball game, the concert, and Sunday brunch and go home." She points outside. "If someone wanted to scare you off, they'd have hit your car too. Clearly, whoever did this doesn't even know what you drive."

I'm unconvinced.

If anything, I'm more certain than ever that I'm staying.

"This isn't the Wild West, Chief. You can't run me out of town just because I'm asking the wrong questions."

"I don't care what you do," she says, standing. "But Dean Anson over at the college? She's a different story. Part of your expulsion included a lifetime ban from campus. She's not pressing charges over the alumni dinner. But if you show up at the game, the concert, or brunch, CVPD will be notified. You'll be arrested and forcibly removed."

She starts toward the door.

Her tone strongly implies running me off is exactly what she intends to do. I'm going to find out why.

In a way, I've been running from this my entire life.

I'm through running.

"I'll ask the front desk for a new room," I say as Lindsay opens the door, letting in a gust of cool air. "I'll need it at least through Sunday." I shrug. "Maybe even longer than that."

Because the upside of being an agoraphobic writer with no attachments?

Chances are, you've got nowhere else on earth you need to be.

PART II

Day Two | The Downward Spiral

16
Homecoming 2023

Century Stadium, home of the Center Valley Centaurs, looks nothing like the patchy diamond of dirt and half-moon of faded grass the team played on thirty years ago.

"Beer here!" a vendor shouts.

Are you *kidding* me? Now, *this* is progress.

Fenton whistles, lifts his arm, and the vendor hobbles over with two cold ones. When I decline, Fenton buys one for his left fist and one for his right.

Freshman year we sat on dead grass on a hill above the field, passing a flask and sipping tall cans of Busch hidden in brown paper bags.

I wonder briefly if the university has a writer-in-residence program. Then again, my expulsion and lifetime ban from campus might hinder my application—and, for a writer, I have a crippling fear of rejection. For now, I'm just grateful the young officer at the gate didn't ask me for ID when I pulled into the lot, where I met up with Fenton.

I lift a can of ginger ale to my lips. I don't tell him outright about my sobriety, but to most people the signs are obvious. Especially this weekend, when I'm hanging by a thread. Craving Heineken at the Black Pepper, searching for a keg in the freshman parking lot, staring daggers at the hotel minifridge, drooling at the Coop as a server passes by with someone else's lager. Never mind how I wanted to pounce on Toni's martini glass at dinner last night.

Fenton probably bought two beers counting on my frail willpower.

But that's the old Gregg. This one's new and improved.

Now with a fresh, lemony scent.

"Did I miss anything earthmoving yesterday?" Fenton asks.

Between sips of Canada Dry, I offer the highlights. The freshman lot, a message from Toni, our meetup at the Black Pepper, and the alumni dinner at McCartney Hall, where we ran into Liv.

I glance at the modern scoreboard. Tied 0–0 in the bottom of the third with a kid named Zack Macmillan at the plate.

I point. "Is that . . ."

"Mike's kid, yeah. He's a freshman. Not only made varsity but hits leadoff and plays center."

I survey the stands for Macmillan, which is tricky given my disguise: hood-up hoodie, hat pulled low, sunglasses—basically, a dollar-store Unabomber.

I haven't yet told Fenton the part about Liv, how I found her on some wannabe Tinder app, how we met at the Coop. How she invited herself to my hotel. Or what we walked into at the Allentown Marriott.

I keep it to myself for the time being.

Instead, I ask him about his family. Fenton and Amy live in Doylestown, where he practices clinical psychology with a group of therapists. Amy's been swept away in the gig economy, juggling side hustles and raising what Fenton affectionately calls their "Irish quintuplets." Boy, girl, boy, girl, boy, each born eighteen months apart because they lost track of time and started late.

I tell him briefly about my breakup with Alissa, but my mind's elsewhere. It's on Fenton's beer. It's searching the stands for Macmillan. It's back at the Marriott, saying no to the minifridge while wondering who trashed my room.

Fenton offers the usual post-breakup platitudes: plenty of fish; the right one's right around the corner; you'll find her the moment you stop looking. It reminds me of my magical thinking as a kid, when every penny in the fountain, every broken wishbone, every whispered prayer asked for the same thing.

A father.

("You're the reason he left me. He wanted nothing to do with you.")

Never got one. But then, I never had the sense to stop looking.

"How's Toni?" Fenton asks as the third inning ends.

"Good. Still teaching. Still married. He drives for UPS now, I think. They're adapting to the empty nest."

"And Liv?"

"I probably learned more about her last night than I did freshman year." I hesitate. Thirty years ago, Liv's privacy wouldn't have crossed my mind. Now it gives me pause. But withholding from Fenton also feels like a violation of the Bro Code. "She was sweet," I say. "She seems . . . content."

Our right fielder makes a leaping catch deep in foul territory. Fenton pops up, sloshing beer on my jacket, and howls like he's got thousands riding on the game.

I glance down at the brown leather and want to lick my sleeve.

"Sorry," he says, sheepishly. "This is my one weekend a year, you know? No Amy, no kids. Just fresh air and freedom."

For a second, I feel sorry for Fenton. But then, I remember how happy he looks in those Facebook photos, surrounded by Amy and her ginormous extended family.

"They drive me frigging crazy," he says, laughing like a stoned Seth Rogen, when I bring them up in the fourth. "Her parents, her backwards siblings, and dozens of cousins. It's like *Everybody Loves Raymond* meets *The Beverly Hillbillies* without the laughs."

"But Doylestown seems like a nice—"

"Doylestown is great. But we're not having that herd over to our house. So every weekend we gotta drive two hours out to their farm. The kids love it. They play with the animals. Pet 'em, milk 'em, ride 'em, whatever the hell they do. Meantime, I want to walk out to the shed with my father-in-law's shotgun."

"You fib in your status updates," I say.

He laughs, that same great, hearty laugh I still hear when I'm sitting at my computer in Jersey.

For a moment, Pennsylvania feels like home again.

But it won't last.

Without my meds, especially Team Klonopin, I'm in for a rough ride this weekend. I called Dr. Shaw first thing this morning but got her answering service. I'm still waiting on a callback that might not come until Monday.

"So what finally brought you out this year?" Fenton asks.

Many alums attend *all* of Center Valley's annual homecomings. Most of them live no more than fifty miles away.

But then, everyone else also graduated from here, whereas my time was cut short by the disciplinary committee.

"The thirtieth anniversary," I say.

He frowns. "Gregg, we just had our *twenty-fifth* reunion last year. You're, like, four years early."

I shake my head, thinking about the twenty-five-year chip sitting in my pocket. Ten years ago, I'd be gripping it until it left a welt.

"Thirtieth anniversary of our freshman year," I say, my tone heavier than intended. "The year Jess died."

"Oh, right." He blinks. "Sorry, I completely spaced on that. During Homecoming, too, wasn't it?"

His casual tone jars me. Am I the only one who still cares that our friend died here a few decades ago? Am I the only one who still thinks about her? Who wonders if we know the whole truth?

My Hoboken shrink suggested I perceive time differently. For me, 1993 is yesterday. But pressed on whether I left the tristate area last year, I'd need my phone, calendar, maybe a few alibis.

CPTSD distorts time—profoundly. Not just psychologically or emotionally, but neurologically. Survivors lose the narrative thread.

Life becomes an archive of isolated scenes: sharp, disjointed, often misplaced.

Sometimes, I "lose" hours or days, only to figure it out when I open my manuscript and realize Del Danzinger's been dishing out justice while I was staring into space.

I don't track years so much as eras—*Seinfeld* and *Friends*, then Y2K and 9/11. Iraq and Afghanistan. Cops with machine guns in subway stations. The blight of reality TV. Lindsay, Britney, Paris, Anna Nicole—tragedies rebranded as entertainment.

During those years, I escaped into books, movies.

After Chloé, I flew solo to Europe chasing something I couldn't name. A soulmate like Jess, I suppose. But every evening ended the same. Waking up in a stranger's room, writing a thoughtful, kind, yet plainly conclusive note, then gone by sunrise. Back to my hotel to sleep until noon, only to do it all again.

Meanwhile, having returned to Jersey with a Rhode Island law license, I leaned on the skill that kept me in beer freshman year at Center Valley. Except this time, I wasn't ghostwriting term papers for ballplayers like I was back then—now I was 100 percent legit.

I started writing for magazines and trade journals, any publication that would take me. About everything from Russia's unprotected nukes to Mama Celeste's meatless spaghetti sauce.

The web was killing print, but big businesses and internet startups were starving for super-cheap content. *Lots* of it, about literally *anything*—from the nutritional benefits of eating red ants to the top ten outside-the-box uses for kitty litter.

I wrote as Jack Oceano. Let him take the heat for teaching readers how to rewire their own doorbells.

Still, whether reviewing heavy-duty oven mitts or unscented candles or Paris Hilton's sex tape, Jack gave it his all. Never took any shortcuts.

And while Jack cranked out rankings for the top twenty celebrity nip-slips, I was working on my debut novel, *Another Man's Hell*, introducing hotshot young lawyer Del Danzinger.

Those few hours writing Del were different. As dark and dangerous as Del's world was, I felt safe between those pages, where he won case after case, fought the system and succeeded, and gave his domineering father what he had coming.

Law school, in hindsight, was a three-year wrong turn into madness. A quarter-million-dollar mistake. Instead of pursuing what I was born to do, I detoured through American jurisprudence. It was an error, a glitch in my nervous system, a ghost signal from the past.

Then again, thanks to JaMarcus, it's also how I got clean and sober.

And it's where I finally received permission to write for a living without burying myself beneath a mountain of guilt.

At the plate, Zack Macmillan works a full count, then lines one into center.

"Watch this kid on first," Fenton says. "He'll steal second within three pitches."

Sure enough, the kid breaks on the lift of the pitcher's leg and slides into second while the ball's still in flight.

"Safe!" Fenton shouts.

I pump a fist and play along. But I continue searching for Mike Macmillan.

Back in '93, his teammates swore he was with them at a party the night Jess died. But no one outside the team—or sleeping with them—could vouch for him.

"There's a good reason for that," Harbaugh told me. "The players were holed up with a group of girls. Beer, wine, weed, pizza. There was even a bathroom up there. No reason for them to go downstairs. Plenty of reasons not to."

I rubbed my temples. "You're not listening," I said. "They're lying for him."

"Look," Harbaugh said, "Macmillan filled me in on the Condom Incident. It was a dick move, and you were humiliated. He may be an asshole. But he's not the killer."

I leaned back, feigning exasperation. I knew I was the prime suspect, no matter what they called me. But I believed in my innocence—and, back then, I still believed in the system. I kept talking, hoping they'd solve it.

But deep down?

I never believed Mike Macmillan killed Jess.

Given what we knew, there was only one conclusion I could draw if Jess didn't die by suicide.

The trouble is, it's a conclusion I've never been able to live with.

17
September 1993
Veterans Stadium

We reached the ballpark in record time, thanks to me doing 110 along the shoulder of the Pennsylvania Turnpike. The weather was perfect, and it was my first time seeing the Mets play outside Shea Stadium. In my head, I was flying.

We'd packed my Eclipse beyond capacity, with Toni and Liv squeezed onto Kip and Fenton's laps in the back. Jess rode shotgun, visibly thrilled by the speed, her hand gripping the armrest with exhilaration and fear. The tiny red sports car darted in and out of traffic like a pinball, its radar detector chirping every few miles.

At Veterans Stadium, we sat along the first base line, closer to the field than I'd ever been. It was a Tuesday night, the lowly Mets were in town, and the forecast had called for rain. The stadium was practically empty.

Jess and I sat a few rows above our friends.

Talking. Eating hot dogs, drinking Coke. Laughing. Kissing.

Paying zero attention to the game.

The Mets lost in a rout, though I don't remember the score. I *do* remember rooting for ex-Met Lenny Dykstra, long before his spectacular self-destruction: bankruptcy fraud, drug busts, grand theft auto, indecent exposure. A stint in federal prison.

In 1986, he, Darryl Strawberry, and Doc Gooden were my heroes.

Later I'd wonder: Had I known somehow? Been drawn to fallen angels even then?

Or was I just a Mets fan because I lived within driving distance of Queens?

But then, why did I despise the Yankees, the pretty boys in pinstripes, always clean-shaven and perfectly coiffed under George Steinbrenner's tyranny?

I mean, let Don Mattingly wear his damn sideburns.

He's a Gold Glove first baseman hitting over .300.

Later that night, we hit the South Street Headhouse District in search of bulletproof fake IDs. The cost cleaned me out, but I was already ghostwriting papers for upperclassmen, mostly athletes allergic to academics. Low expectations led to high grades, and soon I held a client list from CVC, Lehigh, Moravian, even Temple.

Business was good.

Life was better.

I had a best friend in Fenton. A de facto girlfriend in Jess. A clique of six when I'd never truly belonged anywhere before. Center Valley College, soon to rebrand as a university, felt like the home I never had. And those five friends, even Kip Ulrich, felt like family.

Back on campus, I pulled the Eclipse into the dark freshman lot. The four others piled out to stretch their legs (and probably thank God for surviving my driving), but Jess stayed behind. She placed her hand over mine and whispered, "Wait."

Once we were alone, she pulled me toward her and kissed me, deeply, hungrily.

Moments later, we were in the back seat, Jess straddling me, the fogged-up glass sealing us off from the world. We could hear voices outside, but the windows of the Eclipse had turned to brick.

I'd left the condoms in the room.

Never even thought to keep one in the car.

We made out and dry-humped for what might've been hours—my greatest regret, jeans instead of sweats (because *ouch*). My greatest triumph? Remaining entirely sober and remembering every delicious moment.

We kept pausing to look at each other. Tilting our heads back, gazing like we were whispering secrets without saying a word.

Afterward, I tried to act casual. Like the night was no big deal.

But the truth?

I was already in love with her.

This was just the first time I admitted to myself how much that meant.

18
Homecoming 2023

Following the Centaurs' 3 to 2 win, the droves head out of the stadium. Fenton and I hang back so I won't be recognized in the lot. When he suddenly slips two fingers between his lips and shrills directly into my ear, I'm sure I've gone deaf.

He's spotted Kip Ulrich and is waving him over.

Kip's gone completely bald.

Yet he wouldn't shave his head with us for Spring Fling.

Thankfully, we're all holding drinks, so no one reaches out for a post-COVID fist bump.

"Hey," Kip says, acknowledging me for the first time in thirty years.

We dispense with the small talk. Kip doesn't want to be around me, and I don't blame him—even if he didn't have anything to do with Jess's death. In hindsight, I was pretty horrible to him back then.

"Are you guys going to the concert tonight?" he asks Fenton.

"Hell yeah," Fenton says. "How often do you get to see Hootie and the Blowfish live?"

"Guess who's opening for them?" Kip grins like it's an inside joke. "Waiting for Rain."

They high-five. Waiting for Rain was a local favorite of the Lehigh County pub circuit in the early nineties. I'd always thought we followed them around ironically.

I consider how to approach Kip about Jess without scaring him off. Better to do it tonight at the concert, once he's a few beers deep. Loosen the threads, then tug.

According to the case file, which Chief Lindsay finally returned to me (somewhat worse for wear and missing some documents), Kip's statement was short and clean. He left Jess at the dance shortly before it ended, went straight back to his dorm, and fell asleep early. His RA, Troy, corroborated it. Kip even volunteered for a polygraph.

Harbaugh considered that sufficient to rule him out.

But a polygraph can be beaten.

And in my years shadowing JaMarcus Cooke around Providence, I learned bluffing can be just as effective as taking one.

JaMarcus even bluffed a time or two himself.

We reach the lot and spend several minutes searching for my Prius. When I finally spot it, my heart sinks into my stomach.

All four tires: slashed.

Every window: shattered.

Across the driver's side in thick red paint: another two-word message.

Fock off

"Oh, come on," I say, palming my face. "Those are my wheels."

Fenton scratches his head. "That's the first typo I've seen in paint."

We scan the lot, but whoever did this is long gone. They must've hit the car during the game, while the blacktop was packed with taller, wider vehicles.

I debate whether to call campus police or CVPD.

Then realize I can't call either.

Technically, I'm trespassing. And I don't doubt Chief Lindsay would haul me in. Dean Anson might press charges just for spite. Either way, it'd end my investigation.

An investigation few people know about, which essentially narrows the list of suspects down to law enforcement, Jess's other love interests, and my friends.

My neck and shoulder muscles tense, sharp and sudden, like a piano wire pulled too tight. A harbinger of what's to come.

Pain.

The kind of pain that sends you on a Swiss Exit if it's constant as opposed to chronic.

I know what it wants: heat wraps, ice packs, muscle relaxers, and enough NSAIDs to kill a town.

But I don't have that kind of time to spare.

Jess deserves better.

Something shifted in me after last night's break-in.

This is no longer just about the book.

Not even about redemption.

I *need* to know what happened to her. *Really* know. Because some part of me still believes she could've been saved. And that I'm the one who should've saved her.

"You want a ride?" Fenton asks when we reach his SUV.

"Do you remember how to get to Nazareth?"

He looks at me, puzzled. "Um, I've got GPS—that's proven effective at getting me places the last twenty years. But what's in Nazareth?"

I open the passenger door and slide in. "I'll fill you in on the way."

19

Nazareth is a thirty-minute drive from Center Valley along PA 378 heading north. As we ride, Fenton punches up a playlist that could've been a mixtape in the center console of my '93 Eclipse. "Hey Jealousy," "Hard to Handle," "Creep." Each song more familiar than the last, each mile pulling us deeper into Jess's universe, closer to her hometown.

Named for the biblical village where Jesus spent his wonder years, Nazareth is small, less than two square miles of solid land, no water in sight. Ironic, given her love of dolphins. But then, Jess was always a contradiction. Someone who could love you fiercely one day and feel like a stranger the next.

Or maybe that's just what I've told myself ever since the night I found her on Macmillan's lap.

The night of the Lap Glance.

"I didn't see Macmillan at the stadium," I say, turning down "Suck My Kiss."

"How could you miss him?" Fenton says. "He weighs, like, three fifty now. He and his wife were behind home plate."

A twinge of satisfaction makes me want to slap myself. "Guess MLB never came calling?"

"Calling? He never took another at-bat after spring '94."

"Injured?"

"Are you serious?"

"I was tossed in April," I remind him. "I didn't know—or care—what happened to the Centaurs after that."

Before he can reply, I point out our exit, which then spits us out behind a jam-packed school bus.

"Mind telling me where we're going?" he asks.

"To visit a middle-aged cable installer who plays with model trains."

Fenton cracks a smile. "What the hell's going on?"

It's time. "I had an ulterior motive for coming to Homecoming," I admit. "I want to put to rest what happened to Jess. For real this time."

Fenton's smile fades. "Dude, you *know* what happened. She jumped."

That was everyone's fallback. The easiest answer. Clean. Convenient. If it was suicide, there was no killer. No campus threat. No PR crisis. No drop in enrollment or incoming applications. Case closed.

The more I think about it, the more convinced I am there was a cover-up.

"The medical examiner's report was inconclusive," I say.

"Gregg, she had problems. You know that better than anyone."

"Not the kind of problems you solve with a swan dive from three stories."

Jess had her shadows, sure, but she loved life. You could see it in her eyes, hear it in her voice. Whatever darkness was there wasn't powerful enough to snuff out her radiance.

After the damage to my room and car, it seems almost obvious.

Someone helped her off that roof.

Fenton slows behind the school bus, which is carrying a football team. "Didn't they find a ton of booze in her system?"

She was drunk, yeah. And baked. Also had Ritalin in her system. But no SSRIs. That surprised me. She'd told me she was on Prozac. We used to joke about being pharmaceutically compatible.

"She didn't leave a note," I say. "Jess would've left a note."

Not because most jumpers do but because *Jess* would have. She listened to lyrics. Kept notes I wrote to her on cocktail napkins. Movie stubs. She needed things to *mean* something. If she'd chosen to go, she'd have left words behind, not a mystery.

Because even when she *did* drink or smoke weed, as she did that night, she was present. The *real* her never vanished like it did in others. If anything, she became *more* Jess. And Jess wasn't impulsive. She was thoughtful. She liked to sleep on things.

And she never would've allowed her mother to suffer like she has, never knowing what happened to her daughter. If she *had* to do it, she'd have made things easier on her mom, not harder.

A pale ass presses against the rear glass of the school bus.

Charming.

Fenton laughs. "Look. Above the door it says 'Emergency Exit,' with an arrow pointed downward, right at that kid's—"

"Did you sleep with her?" I ask suddenly.

One night, I saw Jess and Fenton leave a party together. When I returned to Cormac, Fenton wasn't there. I walked to D'Amelio and knocked on Jess's door. No answer.

"What? No, man. I never banged Jess. Just Toni. And Traci. Barb, Donna, Shannon and her roommate, what's-her-face." He scrunches his brows. "That last one, she was on the rag. Got the tampon string stuck in my teeth. *So* gross."

"Remind me why we were friends."

Fenton slept his way through freshman year. Given his laissez-faire attitude toward sex, I wouldn't be shocked if he didn't even see sleeping with Jess as a betrayal.

"What would it matter if I did?" he asks. "I mean, you were with her, what, six weeks? She moved on. To Macmillan, maybe others."

It's consistent with what he told Harbaugh. He never mentioned the others to me, maybe to spare my feelings.

Or maybe because he was one of them.

Or maybe he only told Harbaugh there were others to deflect suspicion from himself.

"Where were you that night?" I ask, evenly.

"I was at Colleen's. You remember her, right? Sophomore. Wilkes Hall."

"You stayed all night?"

"Didn't want to get written up by the RA. Wilkes was always locked down tight."

"You knew Colleen from high school?"

"Since middle school. We'd been close."

That, I remember. After Jess died, Colleen and Fenton behaved more like squabbling siblings. They'd never slept together before, and never again. But she adored him. She would've vouched for him no matter what.

Even if he asked her to lie.

The GPS tells us to take the next right. He flicks on his blinker. A dull, rhythmic *tap, tap, tap* starts in my head, and suddenly I'm a kid again, riding shotgun in my mother's mud-brown Oldsmobile.

Tap, tap, tap. *Her left blinker.*

It's 1983. Mommy pulls into the gas station near school. I wait to hear the ding ding *as our tires cross the black tube.*

Ding ding.

I open Paul Zindel's The Pigman *on my lap. I only get car sick when the car is moving. So I can read when we stop and it won't make me puke all over the car, which makes Mommy wish I died in her belly.*

("Throw up again and I swear I'll leave you here with the trash.")

Using my finger, I find where I left off at the light. As I read, I track each word as if I'm singing along to a sing-along song.

The words make me feel better.

They calm my tummy, clear my head.

I don't know why.

Only that I want to be in the world with the Pigman more than I want to be in the car with Mommy.

"So, this cable installer," Fenton says as he makes the turn and the tapping stops. "Is this the dude Jess dated from high school?"

"Frank Handly, yeah. I saw him at her funeral. As far as he knew, they were still together when she died. Or at least that's what he told Harbaugh."

"You think he lied?"

"He had no alibi. He could've been on campus that night."

"Except no one saw him."

"No one was *looking* for him. No one even knew what he looked like."

There were problems with Frank as a suspect. A spotless record. No calls between them in the final weeks. But sometimes silence says everything. Weeks of no contact would've sent me to campus looking for her.

Fenton pulls to the curb. The property's in Frank's name. Transferred after his mother died in a car crash outside town. Toddler toys are scattered across the browning lawn. Leaves in every stage of decay blanket the yard. The house leans to the left.

Still, something about it says someone tries.

To me, that means something.

Second thoughts vanish the moment Fenton opens his door.

We walk up the cracked path and climb two crumbling steps. I jab at the bell.

Inside: chaos.

A kid screams.

A dog unleashes a frenzied barking spree.

A woman yells at the kid to shut up. Or maybe at the dog. Either way, yelling like that makes my gut tighten. Makes me seven again, bracing for impact.

("Don't blame me for what you are! Garbage in, garbage out. You should thank me for lugging it around for nine months.")

Some people inherit money and property. I got her words buzzing around inside my head like a jar of flies.

The door swings open. A woman dressed in a lavender sweatshirt depicting two obese cats nuzzling one another stares at us like we're selling vacuum cleaners door-to-door.

She's mid- to late fifties, which doesn't explain the toddler.

"Mrs. Handly?"

I take her silence as confirmation.

"Is your husband Frank home?"

"What do you want with Frank?" Her voice drills into me like Roseanne's.

"We're in town for our college homecoming," I say. "We knew him. Thought we'd say hi while we're here."

"Frank didn't *go* to college," she snaps, slamming the door in our faces.

Thwack!

The sound lights me up like a fire alarm. Growing up, no door in my house closed without maximum force, maximum noise, maximum fear. Like a handgun going off near your ear.

Fenton and I stand there, gobsmacked.

"Can I help you, gentlemen?"

The voice behind us is male. Middle-aged. He's dressed in a Comcast uniform, has dirty-blond hair and a starter mustache he needs to ditch, fast.

Damn that new Top Gun *movie.*

"Frank Handly?" His name is sewn into a patch on his shirt.

"That's right," he says gently.

"Sorry to trouble you," I say. "We're in town for a reunion. We had a mutual friend." I hesitate. "Jess Karras?"

His eyes widen. "Jess? She died. Long time ago. You went to that college with her?"

His face sours on the word *college.* Like maybe higher education was to blame.

The front door opens again. Barking, screaming, mayhem.

"Sorry," I say to them both. "Didn't realize there was a toddler in the house."

"What do you think all that crap on our lawn is for?" his wife yells. "To lure strays?"

Frank sighs. "Go back inside. I'll be there in a minute."

I catch a glimpse of the kid—spinning in circles, arms raised like a cracked-out superhero.

"Cute son," I offer.

"He's not our son, *Einstein*," she barks. "For God's sake, I haven't had my period since Obama."

"He's our grandson," Frank says, apologetically.

When his wife slams the door shut a second time—*thwack*—my insides jump. Pain begins to radiate from my neck into my shoulders.

"We . . . started young," Frank says. "And our daughter started even younger. But Todd's the best thing in the world."

"He's a frigging *delight*!" his wife shouts from inside.

Frank gestures up the block. "Maybe we better finish this at the dog park, where it's quieter."

20

The dog park down the street from Frank Handly's house smells like dog crap. I sit beside him on a green bench, careful to avoid the white splatters of pigeon droppings. Fenton's a few yards off, jawing with some heavyset guy walking a black-and-rust rottweiler.

"So, you and Jess were friends?" Frank asks, tentative.

He's nervous, though I can't say why. Then again, I've known since I was young that I can intimidate without meaning to. "Something in the eyes," said a friend back at Bishop Connolly High. "Makes me glad you didn't juice with the rest of us."

"Freshman year, yeah," I say. "You were still with her at the time?"

He shrugs. "Honestly, I got the sense she moved on. We hadn't talked for weeks before she . . . died."

"You think she killed herself?"

"Well, that's what they told me. That she jumped from her dorm roof."

"Who told you?"

"Some detective. I don't remember his name. Kinda reminded me of Dirty Harry."

"Dirty Harbaugh," I say, though the guy looked more like Ron Swanson from *Parks and Recreation*. "How long were you two together?"

"All of my junior year. Then that summer. But once she left for college, things faded fast. First week, we talked every day. Then the calls got shorter. Less frequent. Then nothing. She never invited me to campus. After a while, I could pretty much tell it was over."

"Do you know why she ended it?"

He lifts his shoulders. "She was never in her room when I called. Or she wasn't answering. I assumed there was someone else."

I remember the ringing. Her phone constantly going off. Enough that I'd asked her to unplug it. I might've done more than ask.

"You ever visit campus?"

"A few times. I tried her dorm. No one knew where she was. Or they weren't saying. One time, some girl down the hall called campus security, so I left. After that, I just looped around campus, hoping to spot her."

"Were you hurt?"

He arches his brows. "Sure, I'd been dumped."

It's honest. More honest than I'd be with a stranger.

"What was she like while you dated?"

He shakes his head. "She ran hot and cold, ya know? One week she was all over me, the next she'd pull back. I figured I just didn't get her. That maybe I wasn't supposed to." He pauses. "That summer, all she could talk about was college. Even when we were lying on the couch or messing around on the mattress in my mom's attic."

My stomach registers that last bit with a quiet protest.

"Was she on any meds?"

"Her doctor gave her something for sadness. It lifted her for a while, but after her prom . . ."

"Something happen at prom?"

"Nah, that's just around the time she started pulling away. I don't know if she stayed on the meds. She didn't like talking about that stuff. Her sadness, I mean. I had a hard time reading her, but I think she was ashamed."

"Was any of it situational?"

He shrugs. "Her dad split when she was, like, ten. She said it didn't bother her. He'd never been Dad of the Year. But I think she cared more about how it affected her mom."

"Is her mom still around?"

"Yeah. Same house as back then. Just a few blocks over."

Anxiety curls in my chest. "Did Jess ever talk about hurting herself?"

"Jokingly. Once we even talked about how we'd do it. I said a nice, clean gunshot to the head." He pantomimes it for me—finger to his temple, head jerking sideways. "Jess said pills. That way her mom could have an open casket."

Briefly, I'm back in that little church in Nazareth. Closed casket. A short, stocky priest reciting from the book of John. Jess's mom sobbing in the front pew. Once crying out like her soul had just burst.

It didn't surprise me. I'd seen such fervent grief working funerals as an altar boy.

Not that suicide is a selfish act. But as someone who's been around it, I know those at risk tend to think of others ahead of themselves. And I can't imagine Jess putting her mom through the grief of losing a daughter, let alone forcing a closed casket.

Still, college suicides are more prevalent than you'd think. Half of all students report feeling depressed. And most mental illnesses emerge around that age.

I started Prozac during my senior year of high school.

In my case, there was an obvious cause. She went by Diana Dryer.

Jess, by contrast, had what most would call a decent childhood. Her dad fled, yes, and he'd been in some trouble with the law. A Drunk & Disorderly, a DUI, but never anything violent. After he left, she wasn't bounced between homes. No rumors of abuse. No signs of bullying or trauma. Money was tight but never catastrophic. There was food on the table. A roof over their heads.

Neither Frank nor I ever heard anything darker.

Neither did Harbaugh, according to his notes.

Freshmen have their own style of stressors. First time away from home. Pressure to fit in. The fear of being alone. Will they find love? Make friends? Figure out who they are?

I didn't get homesick. Not for a second.

But others did. I even saw it in Jess at times. I mistook it for her missing Frank. I didn't react to it well.

The SSRIs . . .

Did I discourage her from taking them?

Did I take her sadness as heartache? Did I frame her depression as something small and temporary and easy to dismiss? Something I'd need to compete with?

The notion is too terrible to think but too possible to ignore. Because as much as I remember from those months, there's so much I don't. So much I can't access. Not just because of the drinking. Some memories just don't stick.

The ones tied to guilt . . . I avoided. But, aside from the night of the Phillies game, I also don't recall a moment of being sober. Yet I must've been at some point.

As we pull away from the curb in front of the Handlys' house, I reflect on my own lifelong search for identity.

When you grow up without a father (or even a template), it's difficult to picture the man you're meant to become. So you search for him in other people. In books, in movies, in shopping malls. You try on the faces of strangers, asking yourself, *Is this who I'm supposed to be?*

At least I did.

But for those first six weeks of freshman year, Jess made me feel like I'd already found him. And he was someone better than my mother.

Someone honest and warm.

Someone real.

Someone who could love—and be loved—without flinching.

Not only someone smart but someone good.

21
September 1993
The Library Bench

"Jess," I called out, chasing her to her junker in the freshman lot. "You can't drive."

She spun around. "My *God*, Gregg. *You're* gonna lecture me about driving drunk? Do you think I don't know you and Fenton go to the Coop or Pepper every night after I go to bed?"

"Exactly," I said. "Never with you in the car."

"What?"

I'd expected her to know what I meant. "I didn't even drink the night we drove to Philly."

Jess blinked. "What diff does it make if I'm in the car?"

"It makes a big *diff*," I said, trying but failing to keep a straight face.

"Why?" she asked. "For reals."

Come with, what diff, for reals. I loved the way she spoke. Like she was generating jargon, coining phrases, as she went along. Conjuring neologisms in the best way, like Stephen King. Maybe the slang was real and regional, but to me at seventeen, it felt inventive and exotic.

Right now, she looked at me like she'd just seen the deadlights.

"I wouldn't risk your life," I said, thinking that'd be the end of it.

"What about yours?"

("What I gave you, I can take. And no one would ever give a shit.")

I wasn't prepared for the follow-up. To me, it seemed obvious. Something that didn't need explaining. *Of course* I placed more value on her life than mine. It was an objective assessment.

("No one else gives a damn whether you're alive or dead. Not a soul except for me.")

Jess stepped toward me. Placed a hand on my cheek.

"What the hell did she do to you?" she said.

Even with my mother's voice rattling around in my head, I wasn't entirely sure what she meant. Because I had no idea how much I'd told her. Or when.

Twenty minutes later, we sat on a bench in view of the Francis Magee Memorial Library.

She said, "I'm worried, that's all. My mom hasn't answered the phone all day. It's not like her."

"Maybe she got back late and went to bed."

"She'd wake up with the phone."

"Maybe she had a few drinks." I was only half joking.

"She doesn't drink," she said as if I should've known it. "She *can't*. Doesn't mix well with her meds."

It didn't escape my notice that, even though I was sober-*ish*, she hadn't asked me to drive. She might not have gone if I just insisted on "coming with." She cared about my life more than hers.

"Look," I said, checking my watch. It was too late to go back to the dorms together. "Let's make a few calls from the pay phone. We'll call around Nazareth. Friends, neighbors. Hospitals, police stations. If we can't find her, we'll ask the police to do a wellness check."

I'd done one once for my grandmother after a hurricane killed the power and downed her telephone lines in Port St. Lucie. Because my mother didn't give a damn. To her it wasn't worth the cost of a long-distance call.

"They'll do that?"

"If not, we'll call a cab and get a ride out there."

Jess shook her head, tears forming in the corners of her eyes. "It'd cost a fortune."

"Professor Garland assigned his senior prelaw class a major paper due at the end of the semester. I take half the cash up front. I'm flush. We can catch a cab to Vegas if we need to."

She smiled. I hoped it was too dark to see my cheeks burning neon pink as I pictured us entering a chapel on the Strip.

She held my face between her hands, clearly feeling the heat in my cheeks after all.

"How could anybody hurt you?" she asked.

She appraised me like a mechanic, nodding as if to say I wasn't totaled. With some work, I could be fixed. Spared. Maybe even made cherry.

But then, that's what she did. I'd seen it every day. She made people feel comfortable. Whether they were shy and awkward, angry or cynical, she let them know she understood.

She made outsiders feel like they were inside. And if she couldn't do that, she let them know she was outside *with* them. No matter how cold.

Not just classmates but caf workers and professors, maintenance workers, even campus security. Even the young heavyset one, Nash, who creeped her out. She had a way about her. She wasn't just smart, she was emotionally fluent.

She could read people in a way I never could. She made me think of how far I'd need to go to become a lawyer like Al Pacino in *. . . And Justice for All*. She knew how to ask the question behind the question. For me there were only blank spaces and more punctuation.

In the weeks we were together, I didn't need to tell her when I was falling off a cliff.

She was already at the bottom, waiting with a net.

I so badly wanted to be that person for her.

But what if she learned it from her mother?

What if, like any language, emotions became harder to master the older you grew?

22
Homecoming 2023

Minutes after leaving Frank at the dog park, we arrive at a small pale-yellow home that could be a twin to the one we just left. A decades-old slate-gray Dodge Aries rests in the driveway.

"I think I'm going to sit this one out," Fenton says as he pulls to the curb.

"You ever meet her mom?"

"At the funeral, yeah."

I think back. Recall the flask in my coat pocket. The sunglasses I wore, even inside the church. I didn't want to see or *be* seen. I wanted to disappear. Slip back into invisibility, the way I was before Jess noticed me. Back when I believed if I stayed still long enough, the world would forget I was there.

For all the attention I drew, I might as well have been invisible. Still, I wondered if people were intentionally avoiding me or giving me space the way teammates give their pitcher the silent treatment in the late innings of a no-hitter.

Had I even introduced myself to Jess's mom that day?

Or was I too afraid?

Fenton doesn't remember. After Jess's death, he and I drifted apart for a while. We didn't sit together at the service. I don't remember much either. But I remember her—Mrs. Karras—blurry through whatever spirit I'd packed in that flask. Something respectable, I'm sure. A single malt scotch, maybe. Not Jäger or Wild Turkey like some amateur.

I happened to have plenty of cash. Professor Bannon-O'Donnell had assigned her students a ten-page paper on irony in Joseph Heller's *Catch-22*. Every baseball player came knocking on my door.

Each had read the novel, of course. Each understood the assignment and could do it on their own. But each needed to practice nonstop for their exhibition game against King's College.

If they didn't hand in their paper, they'd be ineligible to play.

Not one of them recognized that the situation itself constituted a catch-22.

The money was so good, I almost dropped my own courses to write full-time.

But that would've interfered with my drinking schedule.

Now Fenton stares at a house across the street.

I choose my angle. "I'll be back when I'm back."

I step out of the car, dizzy, fill my lungs, and shut his door.

Then start up the path to Jess's childhood home.

"Name's Bruce Cutler," I say.

John Gotti's former attorney is always the first fake name to pop into my head. I met him once at a national criminal defense dinner at Tavern on the Green while working with JaMarcus. After entertaining us with hours of Mafia stories, he pulled me aside and, in his grizzled voice, said: "Remember, though, kid. There's no such thing as the Mafia." Then he tousled my hair like I was some baby Mob lawyer in training.

Fortunately, Mrs. Evelyn Karras has either never heard of Bruce Cutler or doesn't care.

"I'm an activist," I tell her, "working on a campaign to strengthen legislation to prevent suicide on college campuses."

She doesn't react.

Gently, I ask if I can come inside.

She studies me, trying to place me on the spectrum between threat, nuisance, and long-lost company.

Then she steps aside and invites me in.

The moment I enter her living room, I wish I'd braced myself.

The mantel over the fireplace is packed—end to end—with framed photos of Jess. Ages five through eighteen. A life that ended just months after orientation at Center Valley. By her own will. Or by someone else's.

Maybe by mine.

She offers me something to drink as I sit on the sofa. I'm tempted to ask for scotch on the rocks.

Instead, I politely decline. "I won't take up much of your time."

She looks around the empty room, then back at me as if I'm a jackass.

No surprise there.

She eases into the chair across from me. "What can I do for you, Mr. Cutter?"

I don't correct her. *Cutter* would've been a smarter choice.

"I understand you lost a daughter on a college campus in the early nineties. First, let me say how sorry I am for your loss."

She bows her head. I hope my words don't ring hollow. Somehow, I doubt they could sound anything but sincere.

"I also understand the manner of death—suicide, homicide, or accident—was never officially determined."

"Officially, no."

I can't help but scan the mantel again.

Jess on a boardwalk, holding both parents' hands. Jess in second grade, with ponytails and missing front teeth. Jess at her twelfth birthday party, candles waiting to be blown out. Jess in her eighth-grade graduation photo, wearing big silver braces. Jess with Frank Handly at her senior prom. Jess in the CVC parking lot, smiling wide, carrying a box labeled STUFFIES.

Move-in day.

Then nothing.

"Can I get you a tissue, Mr. Cutter?" she says.

I wipe my eyes. "Sorry, I just . . ."

I just, what?

"Your daughter looks lovely."

Centered among the frames is a worn teddy bear, a bit of stuffing breaking free from its neck like chest hair from Fenton's flannel.

"Have you lost someone?" she asks.

I lost your daughter.

I lost Jess.

"To campus suicide?" I say. "No. But my uncle did. He was a schoolteacher. Passed away a few years ago."

I take a breath. This part is true. And never gets easier.

"My uncle lost a former student. A female freshman at UPenn. Afterward he helped to pass legislation in New Jersey to prevent campus suicides. Before he passed on, his hope was to expand that effort nationwide. Starting here in Pennsylvania, where she died."

"How noble," she says. Then, sharper: "But my Jess didn't die by suicide. Or accident." Her eyes harden. "She was murdered."

Her words knock the air from my lungs. I sway slightly.

If she notices, she says nothing.

"Is that what the police believed?" I manage.

"It's what I *know*."

A chill climbs up my spine. When it reaches the point where the pain is already unbearable, it heightens it. I stretch my neck, wondering if my being here is a tremendous mistake.

"May I ask how you're so sure?" I say.

"She told me."

"Sorry?"

"She visits me," Evelyn says. "She has since the day she died."

I seal my lips, which parted on their own.

"At first, she came by occasionally, when I needed cheering up. She could always tell when I was blue, even while she was alive. But lately, she visits more often. She asks how I want things arranged when I get there."

"When you get there," I echo, nodding.

She smiles wistfully. "She promised to take care of everything. But that's Jess. Always generous. Always helping."

I hesitate. "When you get to . . . ?"

She chuckles. "Well, I certainly hope I have a one-way ticket upstairs, not down!"

I glance at the crucifix on the wall, suddenly hyperaware of its presence.

"Heaven," I say.

"Jess calls it by another name. She was always a *stubborn* little Christian. She'd had it in her head she'd be reincarnated . . ."

As a dolphin, I nearly finish. *In the waters off Maui.*

I wonder if Evelyn Karras was always this religious, or if her faith deepened after Jess died. Or maybe only recently, once the visits became regular. When Jess started providing less comfort and more conversation.

I need to get out of here.

But I can't help myself. "Did Jess happen to tell you . . . the name of her killer?"

"Of *course* she did. I'm her *mother*." She hisses the words as if I'd insulted her.

I blink. "Did you tell the police?"

"I told them," she says, leaning back, her expression tightening. "They never wanted to hear anything. Not from me *or* my private investigator."

I swallow hard. "Would you . . . share that name with me?"

"No," she says without hesitation, her tone leaving no room for negotiation. "Jess was upset with me for even telling the detectives."

I let a moment pass in silence.

"Did she say why?"

Evelyn exhales. "Why do you think, Mr. Cutter?" She leans forward, her voice low and trembling. "She *loves* him."

Her eyes gleam with fury and frustration and something else I can't quite describe.

"She wants to *protect* him. But he doesn't know what love *is*. He never did. Without her, he's incapable of it. She was his only chance." She wipes away angry tears. "And he *killed* her."

What follows is a length of silence so deep, I can hear the mantel clock ticking.

"Wherever he is now," she says, "I hope it's some *nasty*, lonely, living hellscape of his own sick, twisted creation."

23

"You cool?" Fenton asks when I slide back into the car. "You look like you've seen a ghost."

"Not me," I say.

"Did you learn anything?"

I pull out my phone, unlock the screen, and google a name. "No, but we've got another stop to make."

"Dude, let's just go back to campus—"

"One more stop," I say. "It's not far. A couple blocks south of the Moravian Historical Society."

"Another house?"

"An office."

"Whose?"

There was only one name Evelyn Karras *would* give up before I left. "Raymo Moray's."

He pinches his brows. "What, did his parents run out of letters?"

"He added two of his own," I say. "*PI*—and I think Evelyn Karras told him who she believes killed Jess."

"Really?"

"Really."

I leave out that she got the name during a private supernatural one-on-one with her dead daughter.

"You weren't kidding," Fenton says as we stare up at the building directory. "Ray-*mo Mo*-ray. Poor bastard never stood a chance."

"You relate in some way?"

"Not me, but I do regret naming our third kid Alan."

I play with the letters in my head like some sleep-deprived Beautiful Mind. "Ah, Fenton-Al."

He shakes his head, solemn. "I made my child a deadly synthetic opioid responsible for half the accidental deaths in rural Pennsylvania."

I grab his arm and guide him toward the elevator. "He can always use his initials."

"A. F.?" he says, wincing. "Are you *kidding*?"

"Sorry, I didn't think that one through."

At Raymo's office door, Fenton tries to beg off again like he did at Evelyn's.

This time, I hold firm. "You're coming in with me."

The office is roughly the size of a broom closet and just as drafty and cluttered. It stinks of cigarettes and microwave brussels sprouts.

"Jesus," Fenton whispers. "I can *taste* this room."

I shush him, tempted to remind him his dorm once reeked like a sock drawer of Limburger.

"How can I help you gentlemen?" the older man behind the desk asks. He's small, maybe five three, and skinny as a wire. Steve Buscemi-ish, with every tooth striking out on its own.

"Thirty years ago, you worked a case," I say. "An on-campus death at Center Valley College. She was eighteen. A freshman."

"Jess Karras," he says instantly. "And you gentlemen are . . . ?"

This time I give it to him straight. Our true names, just in case he remembers.

Then I tell him I'm writing a true crime story in the tradition of *In Cold Blood*. And Fenton's interested in adapting it for Netflix.

"How well do you guys remember the case?" he asks.

"Well enough," I say, easing into one of two folding chairs opposite his desk. "We reviewed the police file as part of our research."

"I'm afraid everything I could tell you has already been made public."

"Not everything," I tell him.

"How's that?"

"Jess's mom, Evelyn, gave you a name. The name of the person she believes killed Jess."

He chuckles awkwardly. "If her mom solved it, she wouldn't have needed me."

"At some point after she hired you, she told you she received a visit."

"From Detective Harbaugh?" Raymo guesses.

I shake my head. With a single expression, I try to convey sympathy for Jess's mom, an assurance I'm not delusional, and enough confidence that I have good reason for asking.

Evidently, I nail it.

"From *Jess*?" he says, carefully.

"Look," I say. "I know Jess isn't visiting her mom from the spirit world. But I do believe Evelyn's convinced. And I suspect the name is based on something real. Something Evelyn learned or already knew. Maybe something Jess told her before she died."

"Why would you suspect that?"

"Because I saw Evelyn's face when she said it. She believes it with every cell in her body."

Raymo leans back. "She had problems, her mom. Even back then. I'm sure they're worse now. So did Jess. That stuff runs in families."

"That *stuff*?" I repeat, unable to disguise my distaste.

He backpedals. "Sorry, Mr. Dryer, I just don't see the relevance. Our conversations were confidential. I'm duty bound as an investigator . . ."

"Not legally. Pennsylvania offers no privilege for PI-client communications."

"Still, I'm contractually obligated. She could sue me."

"For what damages? And what's the cause of action? Sharing a dream she had thirty years ago?" I lean forward. "Come on, Raymo."

He hesitates. "Maybe if you can get her to sign a release . . ."

"Impossible," I say. "She thinks Jess told her not to tattle."

"Well, there you go. Obviously, she doesn't want me spouting off . . ."

I cross my arms. "Do you really want me to subpoena you over this?"

He smirks, but there's a twitch in it. "Good luck with that. No judge in this state is signing a subpoena for some out-of-state lawyer-slash-former prime suspect who wants to write a self-serving book about a cold case."

He stands, which means the meeting's over.

"I can tell you this," he adds. "I looked at Evelyn's ghost guy. *Hard.* Couldn't find enough to get probable cause, let alone reasonable doubt. Now, if you'll both excuse me . . ."

Fenton and I rise. But something stops me. Something Evelyn said is clawing its way through my gut.

Jess loved her mom more than anyone. Evelyn knew enough about this guy that Jess must've spoken about him. As a lead, it's thin, but it's something.

"Was it someone Jess dated?"

"Oh, because that really narrows the field," he scoffs.

He studies me and softens. "Sorry . . ."

I step forward. Instinctive. Like I would have in college.

I'm not proud of it. But I can be intimidating when I need to be.

And right now, I'll take any help I can get.

"Walk me through the guys she was seeing," I say, firmly, leaning on my Jersey accent.

"Gregg . . ." Fenton warns. "Come on, you can't . . ."

I shake him off. "The guys, Raymo."

"I can't be part of this," Fenton says. "I've got a professional license. This guy's gonna call the cops."

He walks out and shuts the door behind him.

I turn back to the investigator. "The guys."

Raymo Moray swallows like he's dying of thirst. When he finally speaks, he stutters. "W-well, there was the high school kid, obviously." He bows in my direction. "And you."

I nod.

"I don't know if Jess was seeing him or not, but I also took a gander at the guy she was with at the dance—Richter, was it?"

"Ulrich."

"Yeah, him. That guy couldn't kill a room at a comedy club."

"Go on."

"Then there was the ballplayer."

"Mike Macmillan."

"Right. Except he was a rock star at that school. Could get any girl he wanted." He pauses, retreats behind his chair. "At least . . . up until that spring."

"Who else did you look at?"

"Everyone the cops looked at." His eyes flick toward the door. "Including your friend."

"Fenton?"

"The night Jess died, he was with this girl he went to high school with. I was dubious at first, you know? Because, in all the years he'd known her, he hooked up with her just that *one night.*"

"So?"

"So, I questioned her. Took me a year to get to her. She dodged me, told her parents. Their lawyer served me with a cease-and-desist letter. They even threatened a restraining order."

"And?"

"Well, this girl loved that guy, from what I heard. *Loved* him. Gives her incentive to lie for him, right? Or at least keep quiet." He leans forward. "But Evelyn insisted I keep at it. Turns out, she was right to push me. A year later, this girl *hated* him."

"Why?"

He shrugs. "When she finally sits down with me, she admits the scenario was strange. After years of throwing herself at him, he finally gave in and threw her a mercy lay." He holds up his hands. "*Her* words. Not mine."

"She knew that at the time?"

"Nah, that's just it. He poured it on thick, even the next morning. *Too* thick. Told her he loved her. Suddenly, he wants to marry her. Move to Pittsburgh. Help take care of her diabetic fox terrier."

"And afterward?"

"A few days after the death, he cooled. Acted like the whole thing never happened. First, he said the timing wasn't right, with his friend dead and all. Except he and Jess weren't that close, as far as anyone could tell. Eventually, I guess you'd say he ghosted her."

"Your point?"

"This girl Colleen nearly cracked. I thought she was about to recant. You know, retract her alibi. But she didn't." He tilts his head. "Not exactly."

"What does that mean?"

"She told police she was with him at Wilkes Hall. But she told *me* they were together at Cormac."

My stomach tightens. "Which is a hell of a lot closer to D'Amelio," I murmur.

And nowhere near as difficult to sneak in and out of.

"Did she say why she lied?" I ask.

"Yeah, and it makes sense, to an extent. Your buddy asked her to. He didn't want to be too involved in the investigation. He didn't want the hassle. It was November, and finals were coming up."

"But she confirmed she was with him all night, right?"

"She *thinks* so. But she admitted something else. Something she never told police."

"What?"

"She was loaded. They tried to hook up that night. But she got sick to her stomach, then passed out."

"And?"

"Next morning she woke up with her clothes off."

24

When I step into the car, I don't say a word.

Fenton starts the engine, glancing over as if expecting me to announce the next stop on our Nazareth true-crime mystery tour.

"I want to visit Jess," I say.

There's a prolonged silence before he responds.

"She's at Holy Family." His voice is quieter than I've ever heard it. "It's not far from here."

I nod. He pulls away from the curb.

I flick on the radio.

Bush's "Machinehead."

The song blares and I let it.

Then I breathe in, breathe out, as we head toward the cemetery.

I never willingly visited a grave before today. Given my mother's lack of sentiment for humankind, I sort of doubt she ever dragged me to one either.

Unless she used it to scare me.

Used it to terrify me like she did everything else.

("Keep crying like that in public. They'll lock you up in the nuthouse.")

But I never feared graveyards. Just grass and soil with the empty husks of once-living people planted in wooden boxes. Even when I was young, I figured their souls were long gone. Upstairs or down, it didn't matter. They couldn't hurt me.

I didn't think they could hear me either.

So, I never stood staring down at one, thinking of things to say, as I am now.

Fenton shakes his head at the thirty-year-old headstone that's been misused as a bird commode.

"I want to be cremated," he says, surveying the white streaks on the marble.

"Aren't you still Catholic?"

"The church is letting a lot of stuff slide these days."

I already have my phone out. A quick Google search confirms it. Cremation's been cool with Catholics since the sixties.

"Put your phone away," Fenton says.

I look around the mammoth cemetery.

Not a soul in sight.

"Why?"

"It's disrespectful."

"To who?"

"The people . . ." He gestures with his chin toward the ground. "The people below us."

I pocket my phone. Out of habit more than reverence.

I kneel. Brush a few dead leaves from the base of the stone. One sticks to my palm like it doesn't want to be left behind.

I sit back on my heels, unsure what to say. I didn't come with a speech prepared. And this feels too important to wing it.

But then, now that I'm here, I don't even know who I'm talking to.

Jess, the girl I knew for a few months in 1993?

Or the idea of her? The girl I've been carrying around for thirty years like a phantom limb?

I stare at her name etched into the stone. The finality hits me harder than expected.

I should let go.

Six weeks. That's all we had.

So why does it feel like I lost something?

It wasn't just sexual hunger or the drama of college or even the thrill of being young. It was her belief in me. Even now, I remember the way she looked at me, especially after reading my stories.

Like I wasn't some screwup.

Like I wasn't someone with no business being on earth.

Like I wasn't a mistake.

Like maybe I could be something more than the sum of my messed-up upbringing.

Back then, I was barely holding it together. Drinking too much. Lying too easily. Half in love with disaster. Half in love with suffering.

But with Jess, I almost believed I could be human. Like she'd seen something under the wreckage worth saving.

And what did I see in her?

Everything.

The way she thought. The way she challenged me. The way she got quiet sometimes when the conversation turned inward. Like she had this vast inner world she didn't quite know how to explain.

Or maybe she didn't want to.

Maybe she didn't have the time or patience to turn her byzantine feelings into words.

Either way, there was such depth there; I saw it in her eyes. Real, honest-to-God depth.

And I'd never seen that in someone my age before.

Or, if I'm honest with myself, ever since.

I feel Fenton looming above me like a storm cloud over the Himalayas.

I don't want to suspect him.

But something's off.

Why lie about the dorm?

If he and that girl Colleen were really in Cormac, why change the story? He wasn't stupid. He had to know that if the truth came out, all hell would come down on him, even if he was innocent.

Unless he had something to cover up, why take such a tremendous chance?

I try to dismiss it. Try to believe it's nothing. A mix-up. A memory warped by time. Or maybe even something sinister on her part.

After all, Colleen only revealed the lie when she became furious with Fenton for rejecting her.

Even after telling Raymo, she refused to tell the police. Harbaugh wouldn't listen to Raymo or Evelyn because the first time she told him she knew the killer's identity, she also told him how she found out. Harbaugh wasn't the kind of guy to believe in ghost stories.

But then, maybe a year later, when Colleen got mad at Fenton, she spoke to a lawyer. Any criminal attorney worth their salt would've told her she'd be opening herself up to criminal liability for being an accessory after the fact. Not to mention the potential of it becoming a rape investigation. One that would never go anywhere but change both their lives irreparably.

I keep coming back to the lie.

The lie that placed Fenton much farther from D'Amelio Hall.

A half mile down the path, at least.

And in virtual lockdown.

Colleen admitted she passed out.

My stomach tightens. My neck and shoulder pain deepen like they're syncing into something ancient and rageful inside me. My reptilian brain at work.

"Part of me didn't think she'd be here this long," Fenton says suddenly. "I mean, her name. On a stone. Those flowers there can't be more than a few weeks old."

"What are you saying?"

"I don't know. It's just kind of . . . heavy."

I don't respond, still staring at the stone, my head finally flooded with questions for Jess.

I want to ask if she loved me. If she even liked me.

Whether she told her mom about me.

If it was *me* she meant to protect.

I want to ask her what she saw the night she died.

I want to ask her what she saw in me—and whether it's still there.

And, selfishly, I want to ask her why she left me. Why she never told me we were over.

Of course, the stone isn't going to answer.

So I rise off my knees.

Make the sign of the cross for the first time in decades.

Then Fenton and I return to the car and leave Jess behind.

This time, probably forever.

25

October 1993

The Lap Glance

I was already a six-pack and two shots deep as we crossed the freshman lot from Cormac to D'Amelio. I held my flask out behind me and urged Fenton to catch up.

"I'm walking as fast as I can, man."

"Not walking," I said. "Catch up drinking."

"Dude, the amount you've been putting back . . ." He caught up and took the flask. "You're gonna put yourself in the hospital."

"We're in college," I reminded him. "We bought the ticket. Might as well take the ride."

"Except they don't hand out new livers when you graduate."

I stopped and snatched the flask from his hand. "If you want, you're welcome to stay back at Cormac, playing crazy 8s with Kip and what's-his-face."

"It's not that. I'm all for getting sloppy. But when you stagger into Theology at eight a.m. on a Tuesday reeking of Jim Beam, you draw attention. Not just to yourself either."

"Look who's talking, Mr. Let's Get Smashed and Go to the Chapel."

"You know what I mean, man. Since Jess stopped calling, you've turned the volume up to eleven."

"My drinking's got nothing to do with Jess," I lied. "It's just that, now I have more free time. What the hell else are we supposed to do out here in the sticks? Go cow tipping?"

"We can take a night off sometimes. Watch a movie, play some Sega."

"We did that last night."

"Yeah," he said, "while shooting back a half gallon of tequila."

I upended the flask, stuffed it back into my pocket, and continued toward D'Amelio.

Jess and I were over. There'd been no clean break to cast over and wait to heal. Just a slow, torturous week of silence and rumors that she'd been spotted at Wilkes, hanging out with the baseball players in general, and one in particular.

That week, I searched the scant record of our relationship for a reason I could live with. Something that wouldn't destroy me. Some fault that could be fixed. Something I did wrong and could keep myself from doing again. I had plenty of flaws but by then, they were baked in. If it was my drinking, I'd quit. If I'd been flirting with someone, I'd stop. But the timing, the replacement, the silence, all pointed to one thing. I kept returning to: *You're not as good as him.* Those had to be the words she couldn't say.

So, I tried rationalizing. Telling myself it was bound to happen anyway.

Toni left Kip.

Liv left Fenton.

It was just a matter of time.

I told myself I'd just pictured the end differently.

A nail gun to the head. Not dropped into some pot of water about to boil.

Even while we were together, I wasn't entirely dense. I knew it might not last. Fenton mentioning Macmillan at Pop's Pharmacy was the first of several clues. Nothing serious, though. Nothing that made me think she'd vanish. I assumed, at the very least, I'd get the decency of a sit-down. A definitive end. Maybe a rebuttal window.

I didn't even get a phone call.

Was it ever real? Were we just friends with benefits?

Were we ever friends at all?

Was the night we steamed up my Eclipse after the Phillies game just teenage lust?

Were our talks about fall break, about Thanksgiving and New Year's Eve, all just drivel?

Were the hours in bed, singing along to R.E.M. and cracking jokes, just illusions?

If so, how would I ever know the real thing if it came along?

"Listen," Fenton said hours earlier when I floated the friends-with-benefits theory, "neither of us were really friends with those girls. It just felt like we were. It was a vacation, a retreat, nothing more. Besides, their benefits package was lousy."

Fenton never got past first base with Liv.

I'd been taking things slow, rounding second, watching the third-base coach, when Jess—in today's parlance—simply *ghosted* me.

Except you can't really ghost someone on a three-hundred-acre college campus with only a few scattered redbrick buildings. But somehow, she did. In every way that matters.

Silent.

Total.

Final.

Fenton, it turns out, was dead right about the condoms. But I saved them in my desk drawer anyway.

Later, I'd come to regret it.

There had already been a few Jess sightings that week. On campus. In passing. Even in class.

But tonight, as we made our way to Toni and Liv's to pregame before a kegger at the Patio in the woods, I wasn't expecting a run-in. Toni had assured me Jess was headed to Wilkes and forgoing the party at the Patio.

But as we passed Jess's door, it was open just a crack.

I instinctively glanced in.

And froze.

Jess at her desk. On Macmillan's lap. Their lips locked together, tongues touching.

Something swelled in my windpipe. Another something in my stomach.

Fenton noticed that I'd stopped dead in the hall and cleared his throat.

Jess looked over.

We locked eyes.

Then she closed the door.

And turned the lock.

Clunk.

I can still hear that sound. The finality of it.

After years of screamings, beratings, starvation, and being locked in basements—nothing ever hurt like that.

My heart tore in half.

And, to this day, feels only Scotch-taped together.

I wonder sometimes, if I hadn't seen that—what I'd later think of as "the Lap Glance"—would it have been easier? Would any of this have been?

I rarely ran into Macmillan, who was older and lived in Wilkes Hall. He didn't visit Cormac without a purpose. I observed him at parties, gaming on girls, but never with Jess. Their "relationship" was theoretical—something I imagined only in my most gut-ripping moments. Something I drank to forget.

Until I saw them together.

Until I saw her on his lap.

Until her warmth turned ice cold.

Until the dumb jock—and *dumb* he was, we later learned—got the girl. Again.

Only this time, the girl had been mine.

And until that very moment, I think—I always assumed she'd be mine again.

26
Homecoming 2023

It comes on fast. Even faster than usual.

By the time we've made it from Nazareth back to Allentown, I feel like an entirely different person, which is to say, not a person at all.

Trauma leaves imprints. On the body, on the brain.

It hijacks the part responsible for feeling alive.

When you grow up the way I did, you don't outlive the trauma. You live *with* it.

And you're happy just to have gotten out alive.

But the past is always present.

It has teeth. And it bites.

Hard enough to draw blood.

By the time Fenton drops me off at the Marriott, the adrenaline from the past twenty-four hours is gone, baby, gone, and I feel like I'm free-falling through a hole in the earth. A slow, black descent into something weightless and bottomless.

I'm not plummeting so much as coming apart.

There's no crash landing. Just a gradual erasure of the self.

I imagine the darkness becoming mass. Slipping into my mouth. Sinking into my nostrils. Sealing off my breath. And down I go.

The thought isn't exactly unwelcome, but warm, familiar. Like a resolute ex who knows where you live and kept a key.

Back in my room, I realize I'm just standing there. Frozen. TV remote in hand. My own fuzzy reflection staring back at me from the black screen.

Sometimes I don't recognize myself. Even in the clearest of mirrors.

Absently, I tap the remote. The TV comes to life. Sports highlights. A game show. Some loud reality series. No comfort food like an old sitcom you can mouth along to.

I shut it off and sit on the edge of the bed. Try to remember how long I'd been standing there.

I dissociated. Again.

My thoughts and feelings detach themselves from the world, from my body.

Exactly what triggered it—the headstone, the mantel, some buried flashback—I don't know. Only that I now feel hollow. Drained. Like I've just had drinks with a vampire.

"Now that you know what it is," my Hoboken shrink once said, "you'll be able to manage it better."

Not true. Knowing doesn't fix anything. It just gives your symptoms labels to cudgel yourself with.

Worse, it makes you question everything.

What's real?

What's memory?

What's been distorted—or conveniently rearranged?

It's terrifying, not knowing whether you're crazy.

Or how far gone you really are.

The last thing I want to do right now is call someone.

Which means, I probably should.

I pick up my phone. Breathe in, breathe out. Unlock the screen. I thumb open my contacts and—*damn it!*—inadvertently double-tap:

Calling . . . CREIGHTON

My literary agent. *Awesome*. I'll need to pretend I'm making progress. Considering how to craft my blurb for maximum impact.

I silently pray he won't answer.

"Hey," he says, "if it ain't my brotha from anotha motha!"

Anything's possible, I suppose.

But I know enough about Creighton to know we didn't grow up the same. He came from money and a two-parent home. Got into Princeton as a legacy, thanks to his stepfather.

I gave up a full ride at Drew, the far better school, to take out ginormous student loans so I wouldn't be too close to home.

"So, ya start that book yet?" There's a slur in his words. It's not the first time I've heard it. Not just late-night either. During the day too. Sometimes morning.

"It's brilliant," I say. "Can't wait to send you my quote."

"Coolio," he replies, sniffing. One of those long, wet snuffles I know too well from college and law school in Rhode Island. When drinking was no longer enough.

The coke explains his constant exuberance. His energy, his stumbles.

"Trigger Finger is gonna be over the moon!" he says.

I hesitate. I like him, but I'm in no shape to get involved. For all I know, my intervention could backfire. In an hour, I could be on my way to Manhattan, ready to roll a crisp hundred and do a few rails at his side. That's how close I am to the edge.

"You all right, man?" I ask.

It's the first time that I related to him deeper than sea level.

"Yeah, I'm cool." His voice changes. Straightens. Like mine did when I sat, high and hammered, in front of Center Valley's motley disciplinary committee, which included Professor Garland and the Centaurs' first baseman.

"Saw your major deal in *Publishers Marketplace*," I tell him. "Congrats."

He laughs. Genuinely, this time. If he keeps talking, he's likely alone on the Upper East Side, ripping lines off his coffee table.

"My mom suggested agenting," he says. "Said it'd be a good way to earn and learn. I spotted some greats in the slush and shot up from reader to assistant to agent in no time."

He's got a hell of an eye. And he signed *me.*

That's not nothing.

"'Creighton the Great,'" I say.

"When I saw that on the cover of *PW*, I finally embraced the name, ya know? My last name—Pierce—is from my first stepdad. He was kind of a dick, so . . ."

"So you relate to Danzinger," I say.

"In more ways than one." He pauses. "Probably shouldn't tell ya this, being your agent, but between Princeton and joining the agency, I did almost a year in recovery."

Sounds like rehab worked wonders for him. "Alcohol or . . . ?"

"Well, mostly snow. That one became the big *problemo.* The one that dwarfed all the others, right?"

Yeah, I know.

For him, it's powder.

For me, it was rock.

I also know how I got off it. I just never wrote a book on it and don't plan to.

I debate whether to share my full true story. Not just the addictions but my recovery.

Maybe I can be for him what JaMarcus was for me.

But something holds me back.

My own story's dark. Darker than Del Danzinger's.

Maybe too dark even for Creighton.

And, really, how well do I know him anyway?

Besides, one thing's for sure.

All cokeheads talk.

Minutes later, my phone trills.

UNKNOWN CALLER

Normally, I'd ignore it. But since arriving on campus, I've been handing out my number like candy. It could be Liv. Toni. Kip. Fenton. Maybe even Dr. Shaw, who always blocks her number.

I answer, "Dryer."

Silence.

The screen confirms the call's connected. I hit speaker.

Still nothing.

I mute the mic. Set the phone on the desk.

And wait.

The silence thickens, even as it stretches.

My stomach curdles. I can *feel* something coming. A black wave just offshore.

Finally, a voice, a whisper.

"Come tonight and die."

The phone clicks.

The call ends.

My lips part.

But I've got nothing to say.

And no one in the world to say it to.

The irony is, I was probably going to bail on the concert. Curl up. Drift off. Maybe Uber to the Coop in the middle of the night and quietly slip out when the place filled with familiar faces I'd be too sober to speak to.

Maybe I'd have left Center Valley for good.

Left Pennsylvania.

But those four whispered words . . .

They change everything.

Whoever this is thinks I've something left to lose.

They're wrong.

The call doesn't scare me off any more than Chief Lindsay's threats of arrest.

Instead, it snaps me out of it.

Once in middle school, I overheard a teacher whisper, "The only way to get Gregg to do anything is to tell him he can't."

I feel it now. The adrenaline returning.

With it, clarity.

The emptiness and boredom born of trauma vanish when I'm under duress. When there's danger.

Scared animals always return home.

Fear becomes its own comfort zone. The brink. The fight-or-flight fix.

The jab in the vein.

If someone wants me gone, I must be getting close.

I was going to stay in, maybe even return to Jersey.

Now, thanks to four whispered words from an anonymous voice—there's no doubt I'm returning to Center Valley's Century Stadium to see some Hootie and the fucking B-fish this evening.

PART III

Cracked Rear View

27

Back on campus before the concert, we meet up with a large group who'd matriculated in the three years after I left. Fenton and Kip waste no time diving into a debate about whether baseball's juicers deserve a spot in Cooperstown.

Fortunately, Toni hangs back with me.

Some hipster hands us full Solo cups, then drifts off to join the others. I grudgingly dump mine on the grass, trash the cup, and grab a Sprite. We instinctively clink and mutter a wary "cheers" before diving in like we've just crossed the Mojave.

I pretend mine is spiked with Grey Goose. Hell, tonight I'd settle for Uncle Vlad.

"So," she says, "you gonna get lucky tonight?"

"Depends on your definition of lucky, I guess. If I remember right, yours was you, Kip, and six games of Parcheesi?"

She chokes on her beer, spraying half of it through her nose. In the midst of her laughter, she wheezes. "How do you even remember that?"

"I remember everything about those first few months."

Almost everything.

In truth, almost nothing.

What I don't remember, I've filled in. With feelings, fragments. Things I've maybe dreamed or rewritten or invented altogether. To forgive or torture myself, depending on the mood.

I've reworked that year so many times, there isn't a word I haven't revised.

The blackout that first Friday night of orientation wasn't just a gap but a blank check. A permission slip. The kind Jekyll used to continue becoming Hyde.

Because temptation's a hell of a thing.

And guilt dissolves in 80 proof.

Lose yourself deep enough and you come out the other side scrubbed clean. No memories, no consequences.

No real need for remorse.

Like baptism by firewater.

Confession without penance.

The guilt soaked up during my Catholic boyhood slid off me like I was ceramic.

I don't remember that first night or many others. But I remember how they felt. The adrenaline. The power. The relief.

Only by losing control did I feel like I finally had any.

Toni, in particular, was the antithesis of my rigid, joyless micro-family. She dressed modestly but flirted shamelessly—with everyone from varsity stars to uggos. Even after Jess's death, she never apologized for wanting things.

Never apologized for wanting to *live.*

Every time she left a party with someone else, I felt a pinch of jealousy, even with Jess on my arm. Because while I loved Jess, I never gave her *all* of me. I was scared. Afraid to upset the balance, tip the scale in the wrong direction. Terrified the real me wasn't good enough.

When your mother resents your very existence, you expect rejection.

("You're not my son. You're my sentence.")

Worse, you believe you deserve it.

You anticipate withdrawal.

Abandonment becomes the default.

("If I left you on the side of the road, do you really think anyone would come looking?")

But with Toni, I never pretended.

Never felt like an impostor.

Even with Fenton, I was always performing. Always *on*. In character. Always watching myself from the outside. Afraid the real me might slip out and be found lacking.

Not knowing my true self made me want to hide even more.

"You remember everything, huh?" Toni teases, snapping me back. "How about that snowy night you hit the deer?"

Vaguely. The *thump* is what stuck with me. Or maybe I invented that too, as a kind of punishment.

"I remember picking deer fur out of my hood for weeks," I say, gut-punched by the memory of finding blood the next morning.

"The front was smashed," she says, following an adorable hiccup. "It took you forever to get that fixed."

"Because *I'd* been smashed," I say softly, with remorse and self-loathing. "The insurance company had too many questions. If they talked to anyone on campus and found out I was drunk . . ."

"We were so stupid back then."

"Some of us stupider than others."

There's a moment of silence. Maybe for the deer. Though it survived. Caved in my hood, fractured my windshield, then bolted for the hills like it had an appointment.

"I saw it first," Toni says. "It froze in the road. You were flying. There was no stopping in time. If you swerved, we'd have hit a tree. We were lucky."

"Lucky," I echo, dryly. "Didn't feel that way at the time."

"No. But looking back . . ."

She doesn't need to finish. Everything looms larger in the rear view, as cracked as it might be. The Phillies game. The deer. Saint Patrick's Day.

My disciplinary hearing. The expulsion.

Even Jess's death.

That entire year feels larger than life.

Like it's the only one that ever mattered.

"Toni, you were her best friend. What was really going on with Jess before she died?"

Her face stiffens. "I don't know. She didn't tell me."

"But you two were so close."

"Sure, but . . ." She hesitates. "Aside from when you were hooking up, how often were you ever really *alone* with anyone?"

I blink. I wasn't.

Every conversation with Fenton happened with someone else around. Kip. Our roommates. Later, guys like Marc, Johnny, Loggs, and Little Joe. Even our "private talks" were held in the caf, at loud parties, or in a booth at the Coop.

"You're talking about Liv," I say, finally grasping it.

Toni peeks over her shoulder, but Liv's not here yet. "She was like a shadow back then. And not Peter Pan's. Not the kind trying to get *away*."

"Seriously?" This is news to me. "Was she jealous of your friendship with Jess?"

"You know how catty girls can be." She winces. "Shoot. Did I say that out loud?"

She burps (less adorably) and tips her Solo cup. Already empty.

I toss the rest of my Sprite.

"Liv was jealous of Jess," I repeat, slowly, ruminating on this new information. "And she's the only one who never had an alibi."

Toni laughs hard enough to draw glances. "You think *Liv* could kill someone? Have you *seen* her Facebook? The dances? The goofy reels? She's a *superdork*."

She's right. But . . .

"What if it's all an act?" I say.

But Toni's already off with her Solo cup, angling for a refill.

I stand stock-still.

Because now I can't stop thinking . . .

What if everything we believed about that year is a lie?

And what if the person behind Jess's death is someone we never really looked at twice?

28
November 1993
The Night of a Thousand Plushies

By the time Hootie's debut album hit stores in July 1994, I was already expelled from Center Valley. But the wounds were fresh, the nerves exposed.

That summer, crashing on friends' couches and in the back seat of my Eclipse, Hootie's lyrics resounded retroactively.

Songs like "Hold My Hand" and "Let Her Cry" dragged me back, sometimes kicking and screaming, to those first six weeks in Center Valley.

And to Jess.

I spent hours trying to figure out how I lost her.

Eventually, I decided I never stood a chance. Mike Macmillan was simply the better man. Better looking, more athletic, more popular. Dumb as dirt, but Jess didn't care about that. At least, not then. When she finally dumped him—over a girl back home—I should've reached out.

But I didn't.

Pride kept me frozen. Or maybe fear.

Either way, I've hated myself for it ever since.

There was one night, not long before she died, when I ended up alone with her in her room. I don't remember how I got there. The CVPD case file confirms there were no calls between us that night.

Maybe I ran into her outside. Maybe I knocked, cool and defiant, emboldened by too much SoCo. Maybe she let me in without hesitation. Maybe she heard me in the hall and invited me inside.

I don't know. I only know that it happened.

It felt like a second chance. A chance to forgive her without demanding an apology. Because she clearly wasn't going to offer one.

Maybe what we had didn't warrant a label—or an apology. Maybe I mistook our closeness for exclusivity. Maybe she didn't want any attachments.

But then, why did she dump Macmillan over someone else? Why not resume their relationship when his girlfriend returned home?

And why not call me? Ever. Why not give me a reason? It *had* to be a reason that would collapse me: Because he's *better*. Because you're *not enough*. Those had to be the words she couldn't say. The words I couldn't hear.

Why else would her time with him end *our* friendship?

Not wanting to date me and not wanting to have anything to do with me were two different things.

That night—the Night of a Thousand Plushies—she sat on my lap like she had Macmillan's. A girl I didn't recognize snored in a sleeping bag in the corner, some sophomore too drunk to make it back to Wilkes from the Heights.

Jess flirted. Gently. She whispered that she'd missed me. Thought about me. Or maybe I imagined all that. She didn't say she regretted anything. But she looked at me like maybe she did.

She flattered me, saying I looked like a young Andy Garcia, the hot-headed bastard son of Sonny Corleone in *Godfather III*. Or maybe that wasn't the compliment I took it for.

It was nearly midnight. D'Amelio was about to lock down. No dudes allowed.

"I should go," I said.

"You can stay," she said.

We still hadn't kissed, though her lips were there, inches from mine.

Behind my affection was a dull but persistent ache of betrayal. I loved her. That I still *wanted* her—*not* for the night but for a chance at something deeper—erased any doubts about that.

"I think I've woken up on the ground enough this week," I said.

She climbed off my lap and moved toward the bed. "I'm tired." She yawned as if to prove it. Then: "Are you staying?"

I was already following her.

Under the covers, I curled up behind her. Held her. Waited for her to turn back to me. To kiss me, to say something. To stretch the night until sunrise like we used to.

But she didn't turn back.

She fell asleep.

I stayed awake, holding her. Breathing in her hair, which still smelled of strawberries. Wondering if *we* could be something again. Something real. Less fragile, less fleeting. Maybe even forever. Whatever that meant to me at the time.

There was no chance I could sleep.

Eventually, I slid out of bed and pulled on my boots.

Something brushed against my foot. A plushie. I picked it up, squeezed it. In the darkness, I couldn't tell what it was. Bear, cat, lion, dolphin—could've been anything.

I placed it beside her so she wouldn't wake up alone.

Then I noticed a bin under her bed. Dozens packed together like stowaways.

When my eyes adjusted to the moonlight, they became easier to identify. Tiger, puppy, fox, zebra. A sea turtle.

I pulled them out, one by one, and lined them up along her back, in the space I'd just vacated. Giraffe, hippo, whale, dolphin, dolphin, dolphin.

One teddy bear with its head cocked sideways. As if it had survived a hanging like Bela Lugosi's Ygor in the old *Frankenstein* films.

One teddy bear even kept her secrets.

I wondered if *he* was the teddy she confided in. The one with a heart large enough to hold her thoughts. The one she told me about on the roof back in August.

I placed another by her head, one at her feet. Tucked one into the crook of her arm, which she instinctively clutched to her chest.

The rest looked too forlorn to be left belowdecks, so I kept going. Filling every open space on her bed.

When I finished, I saw beauty in it. A strange tableau of innocence. I took a mental snapshot I still carry today.

I don't know why I did it. Maybe I was trying to be cute. Maybe I thought it would make her smile. Make her think of me in the morning, even when she was sober.

Maybe it was my strange way of saying I loved her.

Because I never told her out loud.

And I didn't know if I ever would.

Somehow I made it out of D'Amelio without injury or detection.

Back at Cormac, I drank myself to sleep.

The next day, I looked forward to history class, the only one we shared.

I sat in the rear, staring at the door, waiting.

She walked in wearing denim overalls with brass buttons and a thin brown tank top. It was cold outside, but she flashed me a smile that warmed me to my core, then headed straight for the seat beside me.

"Hey," I said, my heart thumping.

"Hi."

It was the last time she ever spoke to me.

Forty-five minutes later, she stood, said "See ya" in my general direction, and walked out without another word.

No mention of the night before.

Nothing about the plushies.

No acknowledgment at all.

I sat there a long time afterward, trying to understand.

Eventually, I told myself it was just her way.

She just didn't talk about things.

But thirty years later, I still wonder . . .

Was it *her* way?

Or was it mine?

Was that night *my* last chance, and I missed it?

If I'd kissed her, would things have been different?

Or had she already decided that morning that I'd been a mistake?

That inviting me to her bed was a drunken blunder she'd never make again for as long as she lived.

29
Homecoming 2023

At Century Stadium, Waiting for Rain finishes their set, and a roar surges from the throngs. Over the PA, we hear that the Blowfish are in the building. Sound guys scurry across the stage, checking mics and cables.

Beside me, Fenton cheers with the rest.

On his other side, Kip leans over. "Gonna hit the restroom."

"I'll go with you," I tell him.

Kip looks surprised. But this might be my only chance to get him alone.

As he steps into the aisle, I catch a glimpse of a bloated version of the jock I once knew. I do a double take to be sure, but yeah, it's Mike Macmillan. Judging by his size, he hasn't seen anything below his waist in years.

We reach the upper level, where the crowd noise fades beneath us. There's a line for the men's room, so we wait.

Onstage, Darius Rucker performs a mic check.

"Good timing with the concert, huh?" Kip asks.

Hootie and the Blowfish had just returned from a decade hiatus, while Darius Rucker went country pursuing a solo career.

"They recently did a solid cover of 'Losing My Religion,'" Kip offers.

"Jess's favorite," I say.

He shifts slightly. Whether it's the subject or his bladder, I don't know.

"Did you ever hook up with Jess?" I ask in a soft voice.

Kip's eyes widen. "No, never."

"What about the night she died?"

"We *talked* at the dance," he says. "That's it."

"What did you talk about?"

He hesitates. "You sure you want to do this?"

"It's been thirty years. I can handle it."

He sighs in surrender. "She asked about you."

That stops me cold. "Me?"

"She said she'd hung with you recently. That you acted weird. You left her room in the middle of the night. She figured you were mad at her."

"Mad?"

"She said she fell asleep on you."

Puzzled, I'm about to ask him what he means when it hits me like a wrecking ball. I picture her surrounded by the plushies, only now they look less like an act of affection than an accusation.

How did it never occur to me?

That she might've taken the plushies the wrong way.

That she might've thought I was angry because she fell asleep and we didn't hook up.

That she might've assumed I lined the plushies up in her bed to be a jerk.

Had I ever asked where she got them? Were they gifts from Frank Handly? Had they once thrown me into a jealous tailspin during a blackout?

The memory flickers in my mind. Her voice, her touch, the warmth of her back pressed against my chest. Then, the stuffed animals surrounding her like Lilliputians to her Gulliver.

The silence as I left.

The kiss I didn't try.

The chance I didn't take.

As we inch forward in line, the stench of urine wafts out of the men's room. I already know I'm not going in. Which leaves me with little time.

"What did you tell her?" I ask.

"I told her the truth. That we weren't really hanging out anymore."

He doesn't say it, but I know he means because I cut him out.

Fenton and I were always drunk, Kip always clear-eyed. He went home on weekends. Mass on Sundays. Talked about his parents, about the future.

And I hated him for it.

Not because he flaunted it.

But because I didn't have any of it.

Because he was everything I wasn't.

Everything I couldn't be.

The guilt twists my insides.

"I'm sorry," I say when he reaches the front of the line.

"For what?" he asks.

"For everything. I know we didn't get along back then."

He shrugs. "It was thirty years ago, Gregg. I think we've all moved on."

His tone gives me pause. "Moved on from what, exactly?"

"I mean, with the drinking violations. The overnight stays. The stuff that got you and Fenton put on residential probation. I know you thought I ratted you out, but I never did, not once. I swear."

"I never thought that," I say.

If I *had*, I might've broken him in half.

He studies me a moment, befuddled. "Then why didn't you like me?"

I could give him something simple. Something forgettable.

But the truth?

I didn't like Kip not because *he* thought he was superior to me but because *I* thought he was superior. Superior to me like Mike

Macmillan, but not just superficially. Superior to me in all the ways that really mattered.

He was kind.

Disciplined.

Responsible.

Loved.

I hated him because I envied him.

Not just what he had—but who he was.

And who he'd one day become.

30

On the way back from the restroom, someone calls my name.

I turn. Liv smiles, scanning the crowd, worried someone else saw her call out.

"Wait up," she says, jogging toward me with a grace no one our age should possess.

"Why should I?" I tease. "You're late."

I remind myself there are at least two Livs. The goofy superdork from freshman year and Facebook, and the warm, perhaps dangerously hot version who invited herself back to my hotel room last night.

Now, thanks to Toni, there's a third Liv in play: the jealous roommate.

Not jealous over *me*, as Fenton suggested after their breakup, but over Toni's closeness with Jess.

And Liv remains the only one of the five of us without an alibi.

"Where are you sitting?" she asks, flashing a ticket.

"Actually, I was just heading out to the lot. Want to come with?"

Just like that, Jess's phrase sticks to my ribs.

"I might as well," Liv says, peering at the stands. "I'm just gonna get lost out there anyway, and the music's *so* loud."

"Amped for the over-fifty crowd. The ones too vain for hearing aids."

Her smile widens, tugging something in my chest. That look's an invitation. Not for anything specific. Just more. More talk. More laughs. More *us*.

"There's beer in the lot," I say. "Let's grab you one and find someplace quiet to sit."

She nods without hesitation.

And just like that, the guilt sets in.

Because, as usual, I have an ulterior motive.

I wish I didn't. There's a version of Liv I'm starting to like. Maybe even want. *This* Liv. Not Grumpy. Not Goofy. Not the cold, judgmental shadow from freshman year. This third version. The passionate one without a name.

I've seen the other two on Facebook the past two decades.

Is this one real? As present as the others?

I don't know.

Not yet.

But if I can answer that tonight, I might get closer to learning the truth about Jess.

Because where there's passion—like it or not—there are *crimes* of passion.

Twenty minutes later, we're on a bench outside the Francis Magee Memorial Library. From here, "Only Wanna Be with You" echoes faintly from the stadium. The perfect volume.

"This is nice," Liv says once we're settled.

Though the bench sits three, she presses flush against me, her arm leaning into mine.

My pulse quickens.

This *is* nice. The stars—the ones I never see in Jersey. The smell of fresh-cut grass. Crickets chirping in the bushes. A cool breeze on my face. All of it wrapping around me like the childhood I never had.

This valley has always felt more like home than anywhere else.

I'd initially been drawn to its aesthetics in a brochure. The campus could've been painted by Bob Ross. Happy little redbrick buildings peppering rolling green hills. Expansive fields groomed like golf courses. A surrounding forest. Now I take it all in with the kind of focus reserved for what I want to write. It's the only way I know how to enjoy things anymore.

But I'm not here to enjoy anything this weekend.

I'm here to find out what happened to Jess.

Then I remember: Jess and I sat here more than once, just outside the library, one night even watching a sunrise.

Had it been too cold on the roof? Too crowded?

Somehow we fit a lifetime into those six weeks, or maybe just a lifetime's worth of happiness. The late-night drives on 309, playing mixtapes, countering her love songs with *Swing Batta Swing*.

Lake Nockamixon. The Allentown Farmers Market. Musikfest in Bethlehem. Picking apples, carving pumpkins, catching fireflies. Lying in the grass reading Bukowski and Sylvia Plath. Watching thunderstorms roll in.

No six weeks have held quite the same power.

The same magic, the same joy, the same bliss.

The funk that nearly swallowed me earlier at the Marriott hits like a freight train. Darkness falls atop me like a weighted blanket. Helplessness seeps into every thought.

This is how it happens, how you fall through the earth.

Nothing to catch you, nothing to slow you down.

Just darkness.

Weightless, endless.

Until it takes on a physicality. Until it fills your mouth, your nose, your lungs.

And suddenly, I'm back in the dark screen of the TV at the Marriott. Remote in hand. Blank expression. Television flickering like it's on life support.

I dissociated. Again.

"Now that you know what it is," my Hoboken shrink once told me, "you'll be able to manage it better."

Bullshit. The difference is, what I used to call "zoning out" is another on a long list of potential comorbid disorders. Another reason to question what's real. What's memory. What's imagined.

What's past and what's present.

What's sanity.

And what's madness.

I like the smell of gasoline. It makes my head feel floaty, like paint.

I look at Mommy as she stops at the pump. She doesn't seem too mad this afternoon. Not like this morning.

Maybe she had a good day.

Maybe no one messed with her.

Maybe they're learning. The people at her school. The principal and teachers and students and janitors.

I open The Pigman *but can't concentrate. Usually, I focus just fine when I'm in a make-believe world. It's only in this world that I ever zone out.*

When I do, it's weird, like jumping into a magician's portal and disappearing for a while so nothing and no one can find you.

The sound is turned down. A bubble forms around you.

Then, when it's safe, you come out.

But something's tugging at the edges of my brain. So hard it won't allow me to read.

"Ten dollars, regular unleaded," my mother says to the gasman, rolling up her window fast. She hates when they talk to her.

They seem nice to me.

But Mommy says most spickets don't even speak English.

I catch Liv's concerned expression. I hear her voice, distant and muffled, trying to snap me out of it. But I can't snap.

It's like sleep paralysis; I'm conscious yet immobile. Drowning just below the surface. Desperate to break through and breathe again.

Breathe in. Breathe out.

Then it hits me:

Come tonight and die

Come tonight and die

Come tonight and die

I *see* the words, not just hear them. Like the ones from earlier.

Go home

Fock off

Only now they're written in viscera.

Jess's.

From that November morning. Her body on the lawn.

Then I resurface.

Like a drowning man breaking through to air, I gasp and blink. Try to speak, to recover, to mask it as always.

"Sorry," I manage. "I was just thinking of something that . . ."

I trail off.

Liv fills the silence. "Oh my God, my kids have to snap me out of the dead zone ten or twelve times a day."

"The dead zone?"

"That's just what we call it when Mom goes off to la-la land." She smiles but it doesn't reach her eyes.

"So where's the rest of the family this weekend?" I ask. "Is your husband not a big Hootie fan?"

"Les is at a conference in Tokyo," she says, too quickly, like it's rehearsed. "The kids are with my parents. But even if he was here, he'd never come near this."

"A homecoming?"

She grins. "A *Center Valley* homecoming."

"You mean, *your* homecoming."

She stares at the ground. "No, if I'd gone to Penn or Yale or Stanford, or even Brown or Smith, he'd be there, schmoozing with the blue bloods."

"I'm sensing you're not . . ."

"Happy?" She laughs louder than expected. So hard she snorts and makes no apology for it. "Whatever gave you *that* impression? My dating profile? Telling you I cringe when my husband touches me? Inviting myself back to your hotel room?"

It's tragic but I smile. I don't want to discourage that laugh. That chortling snort. That unselfconsciousness I've never seen from her before.

"I'm not a good wife," she says proudly. "Let's just say my parents had more say in who I married than I did."

"So, this *Les* wasn't the type of guy you wanted?"

She shrugs. "I didn't even *know* what type I wanted. I was never allowed to date seriously. Not anyone *I* chose."

I shake my head. "You've been an adult since I've known you. What, is your dad blackmailing you or something?"

She chuckles, bitter. "My father's . . . very much like Kip's. High pressure, high expectations, low tolerance for bullshit. 'My way or the highway.' Didn't you ever wonder why I spent most of my nights in *there*?"

She points to the library.

"I assumed you liked it. It was warm, cozy. I was there once. During the campus tour."

"Yeah, the library was *awesome*." She rolls her eyes. "But I had a scholarship. I *had* to get straight A's or I would've been disowned."

I'd assumed she was naturally brilliant. Maybe Kip was under pressure too. Was that why he never drank? Why I shut him out?

"So why not be disowned?" I blurt.

She's confused. Then something in her softens. "You never had much of a family, did you?"

"I had one," I say, stopping there.

I don't tell her how my mother shrieked about hand towels. How she dragged me on countless errands and kept me isolated from other kids. How she spit venom through gritted teeth.

("If I had it to do all over again, I'd flush you before the first heartbeat.")

"But you weren't close," Liv says.

"No. When I left for Pennsylvania, I never looked back."

"She's still alive?"

"She's alive," I say, the bitterness thick in my throat.

Eighty, alone. Just how she wanted me.

"You're estranged?"

"Thirty years."

She studies me. "You're strong."

I laugh. *Strong?*

No, I'm a coward. A recovering drunk, a prolific pillhead. A fraud who works from his dining table to avoid conflict and responsibility.

Strong? No.

Not strong.

Not the guy Jess saw.

Not the man she believed I could become.

Liv's eyes glisten in the lamplight. "You just walked away."

I'm not following.

She says, "How did you survive without support? Without even the illusion of love? Without guidance? How do you *live through* that?"

I think back and immediately hit a wall.

A massive redbrick wall preventing me from seeing my younger self after Center Valley.

Then, like the blood in *The Shining*'s elevators, the bricks liquefy.

For a moment, they hang in the air, suspended in time.

Then come crashing down on me like a tsunami.

31
The Summer of 1994 and Beyond

Hungry Like a Wolf

By the summer of 1994, I thought of myself as an outlaw. An antihero. Val Kilmer as Doc Holliday in *Tombstone*. Al Pacino in *Carlito's Way*.

I was eighteen and back in New Jersey because it was the only place where I knew a few people who didn't know I'd been kicked out of college.

I took a job in the video department of a massive chain pharmacy called the Rx Spot. I made $5.05 an hour, the minimum wage at the time.

How do you survive on that?

You don't. You *can't.*

So I robbed them blind.

I pocketed rental fees, late fees, even a few hundred bucks a shot for overpriced video game consoles. The only complication was store policy. There always had to be two employees in the department. One to handle returns, the other for rentals and sales.

Anyone could've done the job solo.

The second body was a deterrent.

So, one by one, I cut each of them in.

All it took was a brief speech about the injustice of crass capitalism and the exploitation of teen labor. How it crippled our ability to fill our thirsty gas tanks and expand our anemic CD collections.

In no time, every kid in video was profiting from my system. All but Rebecca, the department manager, a true company woman.

But even she was easily charmed.

Then one day, Carl burst into the store and found Rebecca crying at the feet of her corporate overlords. He zipped to the nearest pay phone and beeped me.

I called him back from a semi-decent hotel room I was renting by the week.

"They did *inventory*," he whispered, as if someone might be listening.

"Inventory? That's not until the end of summer."

"They did it early. I think they suspected something."

"All right, then," I said. "I'm gone. You gotta disappear."

"*What?* I live with my parents *three miles* from here."

"The money we made? Use it to get a place."

I hung up, knowing Carl didn't have the means to vanish.

But I did.

I'd used a fake identity, fake address, stolen Social Security number and birth certificate. No one there even knew my real name.

I felt sorry for Carl but didn't take the next call. I yanked the battery from my pager and unplugged the hotel phone so it wouldn't disturb my conscience, which was growing quieter by the day.

I packed fast, swapped the plates on my Eclipse, and drove four hours north to Rhode Island, a few weeks earlier than planned. For the next few months, I lived on my savings. The money I stole from Rx Spot.

From somewhere far off in space and time, I hear Liv ask me what I did once I reached New England. How did I survive the next three years in college? How did I get through law school?

As I think it, I realize I'm saying it aloud. I feel detached, like I'm narrating someone else's life. Someone I barely know and wouldn't befriend.

Not Gregg Dryer.

Certainly not Del Danzinger.

After shelling out a few hundred dollars for a two-week mixology course, I landed a bartending gig at a Dead Lobster outside Newport. I wanted to go legit. My plan: drink my fill behind the bar and live on tips.

Only there *were* no tips.

Not nearly enough to eat, anyway.

So, I did what I did best.

I robbed them too.

It was even easier than Rx Spot. Bar customers were killing time, waiting for tables. Most transferred their tabs to their servers, unwittingly screwing the bartenders out of any gratuity. For our troubles, each server handed us a couple bucks at last call. The bartenders smiled and thanked them, then grumbled as soon as they were out the door.

I declined my share outright, which not only made me feel like the bigger person but made me popular with the waitresses.

In 1994, cash was king. Credit cards were a hassle. So customers who paid cash got heavy pours and the most charming bartender in New England.

Then I pocketed every dollar of it.

Because screw Dead Lobster and their two-dollars-an-hour plus tips scam.

I earned enough to skip their rubbery popcorn shrimp and cross the street to Chili's for overpriced fajitas and triple-shot margaritas, tipping the bartenders well because I was a friend to the working man. A regular Jimmy Hoffa. Or so I told myself.

Later I cleaned out a tobacconist at a mall in Providence. Then an electronics store in Middletown, followed by the fine men's clothing department at a fancy-schmancy Lord & Taylor in Cranston, where I started pocketing carbon copies of credit card receipts and selling them to a guy I met at a concert near UMass.

In law school, I sold coke to my classmates.

On the days I bothered to show up at all.

Looking back, I was never the self-made survivor I claimed to be.

I was a criminal who took legit jobs under fake names so I could steal as much cash as I could carry. Then I sold drugs.

Why?

Because I had no choice.

That's what I convinced myself.

But the truth?

It all started well *before* I left home.

Well before I stopped calling my mother.

It started when I was six or seven.

It started in Paterson, New Jersey.

It started at the goddamn flea markets.

32
Homecoming 2023

On the bench near the Francis Magee Memorial Library, Liv holds me the way Jess did on this bench thirty years ago. Somehow, it feels like a betrayal.

To be held by someone else.

To open up to her in a way I never did with Jess.

Or Fenton.

Or even Toni.

I finally told Liv about my mother. The ugly things, the cruel things, the things that wouldn't be believable in a work of fiction. The things I'd need to edit out, even if I wrote horror.

How she held a blow-dryer to my scalp as a punishment for sweating.

How she withheld food if I dared to defy her.

How she openly, often wished me dead. Screamed that I was just like my father, even though I never knew him.

How she hurled names at me like javelins: the c-word, bastard, SOB, little MFer, *spicket.*

How she dragged me to sweltering outdoor flea markets, chased me with a hammer if I objected.

How she blamed me for everything: ruining her life, her future, any chance she had at finding and keeping a man.

I told Liv about the flea markets. How I started stealing at seven, first taking a few bills from my mother's cashbox. Then, after she caught on and pummeled me for it, from other vendors. Some who trusted me to watch their tables while they used the restroom.

I swore to Liv I took only what I needed to eat (because I was famished) and drink (because I was overheated). But the truth is, what I needed increased. An extra Dr Pepper. A side of fries. A pack of baseball cards. A ray gun that made noise when you fired it.

Later, I learned to take a little extra to keep in reserve, because cashboxes weren't always within reach.

At my first holy confession I told Father Nolan I was a thief. He sentenced me to ten Hail Marys and ten Our Fathers and reminded me to honor thy mother and father.

What he didn't mention was the eighth commandment.

Thou shall not steal.

That omission clued me in, told me everything I needed to know. That there was a real-life human being with compassion behind that white collar.

Afterward, when I looked him in his hunter-green eyes—no easy feat since he was six four—I knew he hated her too. Until then, I didn't even know priests *could* hate.

I left church that day reasonably certain that, if I regularly hit the confessional, I never needed to miss another meal, no matter how I had to go about getting it.

Liv tightens her grip on me and for those few seconds, a stolen moment, it feels like a hole in me has been filled.

"It's fine," I murmur.

But even I'm starting to realize how stupid I sound.

It's so *not* fine.

It never was.

It never will be.

I'll carry the traumas of my childhood for as long as I breathe.

Living through something is one thing.

Getting past it is another.

Even if the mind cooperates, the body keeps score.

Trauma lives on as physical pain.

I pull away. Liv's eyes are glassy, and I wonder if mine are too. I blink but feel nothing fall. Maybe I've become comfortably numb. Or maybe someone crying *for* me was all I ever needed.

Maybe I just needed to be believed.

Because when an admitted thief and liar says anything, their words carry little meaning.

And that hurts. Because some sins *are* committed from a dark, desperate place that exists through no fault of our own.

It's why, despite the long hours and miserable pay, I initially planned to practice criminal defense after law school graduation.

It's why I shadowed JaMarcus Cooke around Providence.

And it's the reason JaMarcus got me clean.

"I'm going to run inside the library," Liv says, lifting her empty Solo cup and tossing it in the trash. "Restroom."

"They're open this late?"

"Twenty-four seven," she chirps, walking away. "Except on holidays."

"No kidding?"

She glances back at me, walking briskly, smiling. "All those nights I spent there, I was hoping maybe you'd drop by."

Her words stop me cold.

Did she just say what I think she said?

Was Fenton right all this time?

Did Liv have a crush on me all those years ago?

And if so . . . is it a motive? Stronger even than her jealousy over Jess and Toni's friendship?

Or was it both?

No. This is crazy.

The woman I sat here with—the wife, the mother—she's not a killer.

She doesn't have it in her, does she?

Or was I right when I was seventeen?

When I insisted to Detective Harbaugh, it's in all of us.

Minutes later, I see a light in the rear of the library wink off.

Closing time.

In the distance, campus security walks by. A portly man I remember from thirty years ago. *Nash*, I think. An Allentown PD reject, with a fascist's love for authority.

If they find me, I'm toast.

I consider walking away and calling Liv later.

Instead, I wait. I *need* to ask Liv the question I never asked Jess. I need to know what she saw in me freshman year.

I glance at my phone. Almost midnight. Five minutes till.

Now four.

Do they close at midnight on weekends? Today, if not thirty years ago?

These days, most students do their research on laptops and tablets, right from their beds.

Another light goes dark, this one closer to the front.

But my attention shifts to my texts. Toni, Fenton, even one from Alissa.

I push myself off the bench.

That's when I hear it. The scraping of rubber on concrete behind me.

I don't register it as a threat. Not yet.

Then I see a missed call from Creighton.

My stomach lurches as I feel the clock winding down on submitting my blurb.

Another scrape of rubber.

Then, before I can wheel around:

Crack.

A bottle smashes across the back of my skull. Pain explodes, sharp and blaring, spiderwebbing out in every direction. Chilled beer and warm blood pour down my neck, a sickly hot-cold mix that stuns the senses.

My face heads way too fast toward the pavement.

I don't get my arms up in time.

My face hits first and the bridge of my nose shatters. Blood floods the back of my throat.

I hear the crickets and think it's over.

Then:

A kick to my right kidney.

Another to the gut.

I curl up in the fetal position to protect my head and groin.

Another kick to the lower back. *I deserve this.*

A boot to the face.

Spit from multiple directions.

Cursing. *Amateur shit.*

A final warning which I don't catch because my ears are blaring like sirens.

On the brink of blacking out, I somehow manage to roll onto my back.

My vision pulses with static. My ears shriek like banshees.

Painfully, I twist my neck. Scan for them.

They're gone, I think.

And I'm alone.

The stars dazzling against a black felt sky are the last things I see before losing consciousness.

33
Homecoming 2023

When I open my eyes, Toni, Fenton, and Liv are standing over me, right where I was attacked outside the library. Kip paces in the background, on his cell phone.

"Kip's calling 9-1-1," Toni says.

My head is throbbing, my face *burning*, my balls still crawling inside my stomach, searching for shelter.

But my mind is clear. Sober.

"Fenton," I groan. "Tell him to get off the call. Now."

Fenton spins toward Kip and yanks the phone from his hand, unnecessarily flinging it into the darkness behind the library.

"I don't need help," I say as I use Toni's shoulder to hoist myself upright.

"We need to call campus police," she says.

Behind her, Fenton and Kip are arguing over who should run off and find the phone.

Fenton wins.

"No police," I say. "I'm not even allowed on campus. Lindsay will arrest me for trespassing. Dean Anson will press charges. The chief told me herself."

"Then a hospital," Liv says. "We can Uber."

"Hospitals report stuff," I tell her. "I can't risk it."

“There’s a shady urgent care over in Bethlehem,” Fenton says. “They take cash, no questions asked.”

“That’s the place,” I mutter, wincing as Toni presses a brand-new Hootie T-shirt to the gash on my head. “Please. Just you and me, Toni. Get me there.”

She nods. “Okay.” Then to Fenton: “Text me the address.”

From the corner of my eye, I catch Liv’s face fall. She’s disappointed, maybe even devastated. I hate that I can’t afford to care right now. But how can I trust her? For all I know, she had someone waiting for us. She “ran to the library” right before the attack. Apparently, it *does* close at midnight, after all.

The timing’s too clean, too spot-on.

Too much like a setup.

At least Toni, Kip, and Fenton were all within sight of each other at the stadium.

Right now, I want to dissociate. To escape from my body and float above the pain. Instead, I just sit on the bench, clutching the bloody Blowfish shirt to my skull, doing my best not to black out again.

At urgent care, I’ll get X-rays, splints, stitches. Hopefully, painkillers. Though these days, opiates might be off the table.

Who cares?

Just get me off this goddamn campus.

Ladies and gentlemen, Hootie has left the building.

Back at the Allentown Marriott, I lie on the bed while Toni heads out to fill my prescriptions and grab water. When she leaves, I fumble around for the remote but come up empty and have no intention of moving an inch.

The assailants—plural, I assume, unless it was an octopus—broke a bone in my left hand. I’m wearing a temporary splint. They split the back of my head, which is sutured with twenty-three stitches. Pain resides in every part of me. Face, back, nose. Balls.

Apparently, Liv was the first to find me. She screamed, then called Toni, who happened to be aiming her phone at Hootie onstage. She, Fenton, and Kip sprinted from the stadium.

At the moment, I can't think through all the pain. Can't connect the dots. Though it's now *beyond clear* that someone is trying to chase me away. Which means I'm close.

Maybe *too* close.

The key card beeps and the door swings open, with Toni filling the frame, holding up a white bag from a CVS or Walgreens, possibly Pop's Pharmacy. She shakes it like a bag of treats in front of a dog so I can hear the promise inside. My ass-kicking was bad enough to earn me a week's worth of Percocet after all.

Some guys have all the luck, Danzinger whispers.

She places the bag next to me on the nightstand. I tear into it like a kid on Christmas morning. I pop two Percocet. Chase them with a bottle of Fiji.

I wish my life was different.

I wish I hadn't mucked it all up.

I turn on the TV and wait for the pills to get down to business.

Toni climbs onto the bed beside me, fully clothed and silent.

I had *changed, though, hadn't I?*

True, since arriving on campus, I've reverted to my old way of thinking. But there was a *before*. An *in between*.

Between Freshman Orientation and now, I became someone else.

For some reason, I dismissed all the other Greggs, stranding these seventeen and forty-seven-year-old Greggs in my head.

But there were others. Greggs who helped JaMarcus's more admirable clients through the worst point in their lives. Greggs who assisted younger writers in gaining access and recognition. Who sat down and called complete strangers who seemed to be on the brink of suicide in their social media posts.

Greggs who tried.

Greggs who *wanted* to do everything right, everything aboveboard.

Greggs who failed.

But what about the Greggs of Christmas yet to come?

Just as there are multiple Livs, multiple Kips, maybe even multiple Tonis and Fentons, there must be more Greggs waiting.

As the Percocet seduces me into sleep, leaving me in that glorious semi-oblivion between the real world and dreams, Toni lies beside me. I reach for her and she neither pulls away nor moves closer, which seems to me like the perfect response.

High from the oxycodone, I search the entirety of the multiverse to see whether she and I were ever capable of being together. In my journeys, I see one hellscape, a flickering Las Vegas Strip that's burning end to end from the ground up. I hear her fierce laughter and turn to see her in the driver's seat of a neon-pink Mercedes-Benz hovering several stories above the ground.

"I was gettin' sick of Sin City anyway," she says, before stepping on the accelerator, sending us into hyperspace.

Even in another universe, I think she'd make me laugh.

Laugh and have all the wrong kinds of fun.

In the darkness, I feel around for her face. When I find it, my fingers trace it gently and find tiny pockmarks concealed by makeup, miniature scars from a teenage battle with acne. At the time, those flaws somehow made her even more beautiful. More approachable.

More real.

Tonight, the remnants of those blemishes, those alluring imperfections, are familiar enough to soothe me into the first perfect sleep I've had in weeks.

PART IV

Day Three | Cold November Rain

34

Homecoming 2023

On the final morning of Homecoming, I pop up in my bed at the Allentown Marriott and decide last night's violence won't deter me. I'm ready to thaw the coldest of cold cases, whether it's a lost cause or not.

I scan the room. Toni's things are gone.

So is she.

I swing my legs over the side of the bed, wearing nothing but boxers, and try to recall undressing in a Percocet fog. In the mirror, I study the bruises, the swelling, the lacerations, the white tape across the bridge of my nose.

I wonder if any of it will leave scars. Maybe a scar across my face would help the world see what's really underneath.

From the outside, I look like your average middle-aged alpha male. But on the inside, I relate more to the afflicted. To those brutalized by parents or partners. Those men and women who carry pain like rusted steel in their chest, too heavy to extract, too sharp to ignore.

I gather my notes. Crumpled pages torn from several yellow legal pads are scattered around the wastebasket. A reminder of all those missed free throws. Not only here at the Marriott but over the past few decades.

In hot homicides, the procedure is straightforward. A body is discovered, officers respond, witnesses are rounded up and interviewed.

Forensic tests are performed, a manner of death determined. From there, investigators are tasked with solving a real-life whodunit.

Next, police gather a list of suspects. Who had motive, means, and opportunity? Motive is often simple: People generally kill for love or money, power or revenge. Essentially, the same things used to turn upstanding citizens into treasonous spies.

Forensics helps them determine whether the murder was planned beforehand or committed in a fit of rage in a crime of passion.

Detective Harbaugh had almost nothing to work with. No eyewitnesses, no murder weapon, no trail of blood leading back to the killer.

After four years, the case went cold. The main players graduated, married, and moved on. Memories faded. Evidence decayed. People lost interest, some no longer able to invest the hours required of witnesses in a helpless cold case.

With time, most people let go.

But time moves differently for some of us.

Accidents and suicides are some of the most common cases to remain unsolved. Jess's could be either or neither.

I sit down at the table by the window. The sun's already warming the glass, but the forecast calls for cold and rain.

I flip through what remains—notes from campus security, details from Evelyn's private investigator, even some of Harbaugh's old follow-ups. I've pored over everything.

Which leaves me only one thing left to do: Review what I learned this weekend.

One by one, I start crossing names off my mental list of suspects.

Kip. I believe him. He said he and Jess talked about me at the dance. How else would he know about the Night of a Thousand Plushies? I never even told Fenton.

Fenton. Maybe he slept with Jess, maybe not. But even if he did, protecting that secret wouldn't have driven him to kill her. He had no motive.

Toni. She left the Marriott just before dawn. Could've easily slit my throat in my sleep but didn't. With her alibi, that courtesy's sufficient for me to rule her out as a suspect.

Mike Macmillan. I never truly believed he killed Jess. I wanted to believe it. At times, maybe even *needed* to believe it. But he had neither motive nor opportunity. He'd moved on.

As had *Frank Handly.* He didn't even know Jess was gone until the police showed up at his door asking questions. He'd moved on too.

I, on the other hand, hadn't and haven't.

I've always had an alibi. Stacy Rennick. I was in bed with her the night Jess died.

Unless . . .

Unless Jess saw us.

Unless that's what sent her to the roof.

Head in hands, with eyes wet, feet bare and bruised, I consider it.

After everything—the Night of a Thousand Plushies, telling me she missed me, climbing into bed with me, waking up and seeing I sneaked off—was that disappointment, mixed with drugs and alcohol and the hopelessness of a tar-black sky, just enough to send her over the side of the roof?

If so, I'm as culpable as if I pushed her myself.

Even if I hadn't slept with Stacy, I could've done things differently. If I just held her all night when she invited me to her bed. If I told her she mattered. If I told her what happened with Macmillan didn't matter. If I told her I'd be content with being her friend if that's what she wanted. That I'd be there for her no matter what . . .

Maybe she'd be here. Married, a mother.

Laughing. Aging.

Alive.

It's down to two people, then.

Me.

Or Liv.

The same Liv I thought I could be falling for last night.

I slip another Percocet between my lips, but it sticks in my throat like a lie I'm telling myself.

To ease the pain, I say, trying to dry swallow it. *To numb me against what's to come.*

For strength. For focus. But that's bullshit.

I already know it dulls more than pain.

And I can't afford to dull my senses today.

Today I get answers.

What I do with those answers—I'll figure that out when I get there.

I cough up the Percocet, toss it in the sink, then dig into my duffel for a bottle of over-the-counter painkillers.

I grab my most recent legal pad and settle onto the bed. Brunch at McCartney Hall isn't until eleven.

I replay Liv's story about the whiteboard message in her dorm.

Was it real—or just an invention to cover her tracks?

Was it jealousy?

Over Jess and Toni?

Over Jess and me?

Did Liv snap that night? Caught in some silent spiral none of us ever noticed?

Is it possible even *she* doesn't remember?

If she did it, I'll lose another someone I never had. If she didn't and I accuse her anyway—I'll be dropping something precious on purpose again.

There's only one way to find out.

Today, I need to get her alone.

Then I need to break her. As gently as possible.

35

Minutes later, a rare Sunday email from my agent, Creighton the Great, reminds me I need to hand in my quote by tomorrow morning. With my luck, not doing so will ensure *You Oughta Know* becomes the next *Gone Girl* and that author Gregg Dryer is never heard from again.

I swipe open the Kindle app on my phone—then hunger hits me like panic in disguise. When hunger strikes, it doesn't strike alone. With it comes shame, grief, fear, disgust at myself for needing to eat when I have more important things to do.

("If you're hungry again, it's a tapeworm. We'll have Dr. Greene cut it out.")

Three minutes ago, I hadn't even thought of food; suddenly, I'm famished. I close my eyes and swallow hard. Tell myself to grow the hell up. But I didn't eat last night at the concert, or afterward at urgent care or even back here in the room.

Sometimes I can't stand eating in front of people. I don't chew—I inhale. Scarfing down meals like I'm in a contest. It doesn't matter what it is, whether it's cold or congealed or even something I don't like. I guard it like a junkyard dog, as if someone might take it away. Even when I'm eating alone.

At restaurants, when parents tell their child, "Slow down, your food isn't going anywhere," I want to jump up and shout, "Don't believe it, kid. *Finish* it before they say you don't deserve it."

It's wiring that can't be undone. A hunger too old to name. So I rush to the minifridge and pull out a KitKat and small pack of gummy bears. I devour the chocolate first, then tear into the gummies. All the while, the tiny liquor bottles cry out like baby birds.

As I eat, I wonder what will happen to me if I can't sell my next book. If Del Danzinger is DOA, what happens to Gregg Dryer? With my nervous system, practicing law is out of the question. Most days, even leaving the house is a nonstarter. I managed three years with JaMarcus Cooke but only because he saved me. Became my friend, my mentor, my sponsor. Acted like the father I never had.

But I can't work *for* anyone else. I tried.

I can't have a boss.

Every boss is *her*.

Every job is a flea market.

Every instruction carries the unspoken threat of a hammer.

At forty-seven, hunger might be coming for me again—in a way I never expected.

Under the table at the flea market, sitting silent, crisscross applesauce, I watch the heat shimmer off the asphalt. My skin burns. My head pounds. My arms and back ache like an old man's from lifting boxes, loading and unloading the car—twice more today before we're done.

I'm hungry. So hungry.

So hungry my tummy's angry at me again.

But when we get home, Mommy will yell she's too tired to cook, to pop something into the oven or microwave. She'll say I didn't sell enough stuff to order a pizza.

I'll lie in bed hungry.

And when I do, my tummy gets so mad, it doesn't let me sleep.

I leave again.

Not just the room—my body, the world.

If someone asked me what my Marriott room looks like, I couldn't tell them. Not even with my eyes wide open.

But I *could* sketch the parking lot of St. Francis Elementary on command. Every crack in the blacktop, every scorch mark on the sidewalk. Every table at the flea market.

"What you're describing," my Hoboken shrink once told me, "is *derealization*."

"It's just a memory," I told him.

"It's *related* to memory. It's related to *trauma*."

"Why would I intentionally go back there, then?"

"I didn't say it was intentional."

"You said it's a defense. That I use it to escape."

"I said your *brain* uses it. You don't necessarily get a say." He paused, crossing one leg over the other. "Tell me, where *specifically* are you at the flea market?"

"Under the table."

"Why under the table, Gregg?"

"To hide. From the sun, from her."

"Could you see her from there?"

"Only her legs."

"Could she reach you?"

"If she came at me from one side, I could escape out the other."

"In other words . . ."

I stared at him. I was back there at St. Francis again.

I knew where I *really* was. I could *sense* the doc's presence. But I was under that table, protecting myself from the searing sun, hiding from her and her wrath.

Finally, I said, with someone else's tongue, "I was safe. Under the table, I was safe from it all."

Not just from my mother.

From the whole horrifying world.

36

My head splits when someone suddenly pounds on the door.

Fleetingly, I imagine Chief Lindsay on the other side, twirling handcuffs around her index finger, a told-ya-so smile stretched across her face.

Maybe campus security saw me last night after all. Maybe Nash reported it.

I slide out of bed, moving slowly. Each step reveals a new and fascinating injury, gifts from gravity and dwindling opiate levels.

Before I open the door, I already hear Fenton's voice. "Rise and *shine*, my man! Time to gets us some brunchy brunch!"

"What the hell, dude. Quiet down."

"Oh, how's your head?"

"Exactly how you'd expect after last night's bloodbath outside the library."

"Yeah, Toni filled me in on your urgent care odyssey. Still no idea who did it?"

"Logic dictates it was Jess's killer."

"Really?" He laughs. "What the hell kind of logic is that?"

"Who else would want to hurt me?" I ask.

"I don't know, man. You're from Jersey. Pretty much everybody, I'd expect." He chuckles. "Hell, maybe it's some reader who shelled out thirty bucks for your last book."

"Be serious."

"All right, maybe Alissa?"

Her name hits like a cold slap. I stop mid-step yet still feel movement-level pain.

How does he know Alissa? I never mentioned her on Facebook.

I never mentioned our troubles.

Did I?

"You broke up, right?" he says.

I stare at him, stunned. Did I say something this weekend? At the stadium, maybe? I vaguely recall a conversation about Fenton's wife Amy, Queen of the Gig Economy, and her super-huge farm fam. But after that . . .

I must have turned the channel. Zoned out. My memory's as reliable as a best man with a pint of Jack and a microphone.

Then I hear something. Subtle, metallic. The sound of bracelets jangling.

The *Mother of All Triggers.*

"Shh," I hush him. "I hear something."

Fenton tilts his head, listening. Or pretending to.

The sound tightens my shoulder muscles and sends a fresh wave of pain up my spine.

That *chime*. That sound.

Every time I hear it—whether in real life or a dream—it shoves me straight into panic mode. I fall back into muscle memory. I see her face, feel her fists, hear her screams.

("If I go to hell for killing you, it'll be because I didn't do it sooner.")

As impossible as her presence is here in this room, I still flinch.

I *always* flinch.

"Your cell," I say, pointing to the bulge in Fenton's front pocket.

"What about it?"

"It's going off."

"No, it's *not,*" he says.

"Listen!"

"I'm listening!"

"Take it out!"

He pulls the phone from his pocket. But before showing me the screen, he swipes it three or four times.

"You just deleted it," I say.

"Deleted what?"

"The call."

"What call?"

"Or the text."

"There *was* no text."

Rage bubbles up from somewhere dark and deep. Rage as powerful as the pain registering, as every muscle in my body tenses at once.

"Why did you mention Alissa?" I say.

"What?"

"Did you bang her?"

"Your *ex*?"

"Jess!"

"Whoa, man—I can't keep up. What are you even talk—"

"Did you sleep with her, *yes* or *no*?" I step into his space. Feel his breath but can't back away. I'm not in control, not of my feet and not of my mouth.

"It's a *simple* question, Fenton." I say it like I'm not shaking. "The answer doesn't matter. I *won't* be mad."

"Yeah," he says flatly. "Clearly you've got your emotions completely in check." He takes a step back. "Maybe we should run you to the ER after all. Get you a CT scan or some shit."

He slips the phone back into his pocket. If that's the way he wants to play it . . .

"I'm fine," I say, waving him off, my brain buzzing with paranoid static. "Let's just go, huh? Let's get to this alumni brunch. I'm starving. You starving?"

"You know me," he says. "I can eat."

I *do* know him. I've known him for thirty years. I know he chose to hang out with that seventeen-year-old Gregg I like less every day. That he stood by my side as I played Bookstore Bingo with my grandmother's blank check. That he was there at that fateful Saint Patrick's Day party when I assaulted Macmillan. That he wasn't there to console me after Jess's death. Instead, he kept his distance.

I know Fenton as well as he knows me.

Which is why I can't trust him now.

Not anymore.

Not after the game he played with his phone.

37

The Sunday brunch is held at McCartney Hall, same as Friday night's dinner. By the time Fenton and I arrive, most people are seated. We carry our place cards toward the rear of the cafeteria, where Toni, Liv, and Kip are already waiting, with mimosas in hand.

"How are you feeling?" Toni asks, patting the chair beside her.

Truth is, my vision's blurry. I feel dizzy, disoriented. Like I'm floating on some separate plane of existence. The pain's so intense in places, I want to rip my hair from my head just to feel something different.

"Right as rain," I say.

Aside from the KitKat and gummies, I haven't eaten. I took the painkillers on an empty stomach. And now it's been, what, days maybe, since I've taken any other meds.

No antidepressants, no Adderall, no Klonopin.

I should've asked the nurse at urgent care for refills. But not with Toni there. I just wanted out.

I nearly toss back the mimosa in front of me. But no. I've made it this far. No stumbling now. As I set the glass aside and scan the room, I spot a familiar face—Dean Anson, sitting at the main faculty table beside Professor Garland, who I presumed was dead. But there he is, the one-time FBI agent, still stone-faced and grim.

One table over, I spot Chief Lindsay and Campus Security Officer Nash, who was among the first to arrive on the scene the morning Jess's body was discovered. Was he the security officer I saw on campus last night? Right before the attack?

Sitting beside them is Troy, the former RA who vouched for Kip's whereabouts the night she died. And told police to look closer at me.

Something's . . . wrong.

The room's too curated. Too complete.

Across the dining hall, Mike Macmillan sits with his son, Zack. And next to them, someone I haven't seen all weekend.

Stacy Rennick.

Has she spotted me? Would she recognize me? Would she even remember I exist?

Somehow, I doubt it.

Meanwhile, Kip leans into Fenton, whispering something before getting up to head toward the restroom. Liv is chatting quietly with Toni, who has her back to me, keeping me out of earshot.

Stacy and the rest of Macmillan's table are laughing at something he said, probably about his kid, judging by the hair tousle that follows.

At the faculty table, Anson and Garland are deep in conversation. I scan again. Chief Lindsay and Officer Nash are gone. In their place, I find retired detective James Harbaugh.

Staring straight at me.

And then . . . he's not.

His chair's empty.

A chill goes through me. Is this a trap?

Suddenly, my mind spins through possibilities.

Is this brunch going to end with Chief Lindsay slapping cuffs on me after all? Reciting my Miranda rights? Hauling me down to the station?

Could this weekend be a setup?

Could Liv and Toni be in on it? Had they lured me here?

Could Stacy have flipped? Recanted her statement?

Or was her statement in the CVPD file fake? Planted to throw me off?

Was that why the file was stolen? Why it was returned in pieces, with key items missing?

It's possible.

Just when I think I'm free of this onslaught of paranoia, my thoughts pick up speed, swirling, spiraling downward, circling the drain.

Have they notified the press?

Will this arrest turn into a media circus?

Could they have even more on me I'm not aware of?

Danzinger whispers, *They would have to.*

My phone trills. I pull it from my pocket. Creighton's number pops up on the screen.

I swipe and say, "I'm working on the blurb!"

"*Easy*, Gregg-o," he says. "Just checking. The publisher truly appreciates it. They've even agreed to give your next manuscript a good, hard look."

Damn. That's actually . . . good. Pressure, but good.

"You'll have it in the morning," I tell him before disconnecting.

I should leave now, go back to my hotel room. Speed-read *You Oughta Know* and draft a quote. But if I try to leave—will I even make it out?

Minutes later, sitting silently, I open the Kindle app on my phone and shut out the room like closing tabs on a browser. I steal a glance at Toni's unattended mimosa. Then just as quickly tear my eyes from it and lift a glass of water.

I click on *You Oughta Know* and wait for it to download.

Then I close it.

I can't concentrate. Not without my meds. The pain's too terrible, the anxiety too wiring. And my gut feels downright raw.

The over-the-counter stuff wreaks havoc on my stomach.

Especially when I haven't eaten.

"Hey, it's been a minute."

I look over my shoulder to find Stacy Rennick standing over me like I'm some invalid puppy in need of rescue.

"Hey, Stace," I say. "I wasn't sure you'd remember me."

When I try to rise to my feet, I nearly tip over.

"Whoa," she cries as she prevents my fall.

Did someone dose my water?

"I'm fine," I say, waving toward Liv and Toni, who both stare up at me aghast. "Just painkillers on an empty stomach."

And no antidepressants. No Adderall. No Klonopin.

Not a shot at being human.

I turn back to Stacy, whose eyes soften.

"You should sit," she says, concerned.

But I'm already shaking my head. "I've been sitting long enough. Let's go somewhere quieter. These people here—and some kicks to the skull—are giving me a splitting headache."

38

As Stacy and I leave McCartney Hall, it's drizzling. The sky's gone gray again. And it's cold.

"So, you made it down from . . . Toronto? Ontario? Quebec?"

Stacy's presence is unexpected. But now that she's here, I might finally clear the primary suspect in Jess's death—*Gregg Dryer*.

"Narberth," she says. "It's a suburb of Philly."

Way off.

I glance at the diamond she's wearing.

"Married?" I ask.

"Yeah. You?"

"Nah. Your husband here?"

"At a 'work thing,'" she says, adding air quotes.

"Not a work thing?"

She chuckles. "It's officially a global tech conference. Unofficially, it's an excuse. To slip away. From me, our boys, my mom. An excuse to get shit-faced and flirt with tech groupies. Take them back to his room. Ply them, grope them, screw them . . . until they discover what an odious ass he is."

Wow, that's just . . . wow. "That's a lot."

And I thought Liv's marriage was a dumpster fire.

But then, dumpster fires come in all sizes.

"Still together for the kids?"

"I'm stuck," she says. "After he caught me cheating, he forced me to sign a postnuptial agreement."

"A what?"

"A postnup. Before then, I didn't even know the goddamn things existed."

Neither did I. "Can you challenge it?"

"From what I understand, if I leave, I lose everything. The kids. The house. Even the place my mother stays."

"So, your kids," I say. "What, uh . . . *size and type*?"

The small talk's killing me. I need to pivot toward our night together.

The night the music died.

The night Jess fell to her death.

This is our first real conversation since. I hardly saw Stacy the second semester, if at all. But then, I was blacked out most of the time—and steered clear of D'Amelio altogether.

She laughs. "Size and type? Two male teens, full-time hell-raisers. And one son who finished college and moved out of state."

"I saw you chatting with Mike Macmillan at brunch. Were you two friends?"

"We worked on a few projects together," she says. "He's around a lot. His son plays—"

"Yeah, I saw him on the bases yesterday. He's good."

She nods. "Mike was too."

"So, you're around campus a lot, then?"

"Enough. My husband donates. He's trying to buy our sons' way in." She covers the sting with a laugh.

"But your oldest finished college, right?"

"He's got his problems, but yeah—he's made of different stuff." She clarifies: "Different dad."

"They have a relationship?"

"In recent years. It's not how I pictured it, but I'm hopeful."

"Sorry," I say.

She shrugs it off. "We were young. He wasn't ready."

I nod. But it's not much of an excuse. From what little I know it was my own father's justification for leaving me behind. With her.

I think I met him once. My father.

Of all places . . .

At a flea market.

Mommy just broke into my safety zone.

"Out *from under the table," she shouts again. "I'm going for a walk."*

A walk means forty-five minutes to an hour, at least. Under the blazing sun that's roasted my flesh all summer.

I'm thirsty, but there's only puddle water. Mommy didn't bring juice boxes. And she won't pay "flea market prices" for a Sprite.

Twenty seconds later, I haven't moved. I'm frozen despite the 93-degree heat.

She kneels on one bony knee. At times like this, when Mad Mommy takes over, her eyes are two black holes.

"If you don't crawl out of there right now, I'm going to wrap my fingers around your throat and squeeze."

I crawl, but she drags me the last few feet because I'm slow. The gravel opens old scrapes. My knees bleed.

Then the sun hits me.

She smacks my arm down when I shield my eyes.

She points across the table.

A man stands there, holding a reproduced autographed baseball from Harvey's warehouse upstate. It was on clearance because the Mets suck this year.

Mommy walks away. She wants me to make the sale.

"This ball really signed by these guys?" he asks me. "Rusty Staub? Tom Seaver? George Foster?"

"One just like it," I say.

The man has a mustache that looks dumb. I don't say so because I'll blow the sale.

"What's your name, kid?"

"Gregg Dryer."

"Well, that's a coinkydink. My name's John—"

Then, like Jason from Friday the 13th, *my mother appears over Mustache Man's shoulder. Wearing her angry eyes. I'm sure she's about to lop his mustachioed head off with a machete or shoot a harpoon through his chest.*

"You're done," she says to him. "Now go."

"I only asked the kid's name."

"You're through. Go. And send me that goddamn check."

"There's something wrong with you, you know," he says to her. "You're ill."

She raises her voice, which makes me tense up like when I hear her bracelets jingle-jangle. Or when the garage door opens, because she's home.

"Walk away or I'll scream for the cops," she says.

Two patrolmen stand a few folding tables away, drinking coffee from Styrofoam cups. They wear cool sunglasses like Ponch and Jon on CHiPs.

Mommy says Jon is fine, but Ponch is a spicket.

Mustache Man sees the cops too. "Bye, kid." He takes a step away, then turns back. "Hey, kid, you doing all right? Everything okay?"

As my mother shoves him away, he calls over his shoulder: "Sorry, kid."

His eyes are glassy. From the sun.

Or something else.

The sun is a torch. My head throbs, my skin's on fire. My stomach wants to empty itself all over our crappy folding table.

I watch Mustache Man go. Keep my eyes on him until he turns the next corner.

I catch one last glimpse of that dumb mustache.

When that mustache disappears, so does he.

"It wasn't *his* decision," Stacy says. "He wasn't ready to be a father."

I pull myself from my head. She made the decision for him. Unlike Mustache Man, this guy never stood a chance.

The drizzle becomes a light rain. Even colder.

I'm about to navigate the awkwardness when I look up—and feel a wave of strange luck. We're approaching D'Amelio Hall.

Stacy catches my expression. "Bring back memories?"

I half laugh. Unsure how she means it. "You remember our night together?"

"Could I forget?" Her words are flat, neutral. Not nostalgic but not angry either.

"No. Not after what happened the next morning."

"Poor Jess," she says, quiet, distant. "I only knew her to say hello, but she seemed sweet."

"The police never solved it."

"It's a shame."

She veers up the walkway toward D'Amelio's front entrance.

"Want to take a peek inside?"

My stomach tightens.

She means it casually, but the roof feels inches away.

Still, I nod. I'd wanted a look inside D'Amelio but didn't think it was wise. But with Stacy at my side, I'll blend right in. Just another parent visiting their daughter for Homecoming.

"Why not," I say, stealing one last look at Cormac. "I could peek."

39

Entering D'Amelio Hall for the first time in thirty years isn't like driving into Pennsylvania or arriving on campus. It's not like stepping into the Black Pepper and seeing Toni after decades. It's not another time or dimension. It's the same space—just filled with different young women, none of them like the freshmen I remember.

Instead of Tonis and Livs and Jesses, I see my friends' daughters everywhere. Small, young, vulnerable. Adolescents with everything still to learn about the world and its infinite dangers.

At the end of the hall, two towering upperclassmen talk to a single freshman girl. It's *all I can do* not to walk over and ask if she's okay.

I'm sure I'm overreacting, but I suddenly imagine danger everywhere. As a boy abused by his mother, there was always one thing I looked forward to: the day I became too big to hit.

The day I could make clear that if she laid a hand on me again, it would be the last thing she ever did.

When that day came, she could see it in my eyes—what others saw. That I could end her if I needed to.

We skip the crowded first-floor hallway and head to the second.

This hall's crowded too, but no one notices us. We're ghosts. It's haunting but, at the moment, convenient. The other day, when I arrived, I was right—my seventeen-year-old self wouldn't have given forty-seven-year-old me a second glance, except maybe to stash his weed or hand off his flask to Fenton.

I think of the kid with the blue Solo cup in the freshman lot. Hard to believe, at some point, I started looking like a narc. If only they knew how much it takes, how much of my life I sacrifice simply to steer clear of temptation.

We pass the door that once belonged to Liv and Toni. I pause at the whiteboard. Try to picture that note: *One last sunrise, Jess?* But this one reads:

Elly and McKenna have gone 9 0 Days without a one-night stand.

"Jesus," I mutter.

"Well, it's not exactly a Fenton & Dryer original, but they're trying, right?"

We reach the opposite end of the hall in front of Jess's old room.

Stacy says, "This is what you wanted to see, isn't it?"

The door's ajar. The way it was the night I found Jess on Macmillan's lap.

Stacy raps lightly and pushes it open.

A girl at her desk spins around, lowering her glasses. "Hi," she says, brightly. "Are you looking for Faith? She went out for lunch with her boyfriend's parents."

She reads our faces. "Crap, you *did* know Faith has a boyfriend, right? She said you were cool with it."

"We're cool with it," I say, sounding like the reasonable dad.

Stacy frowns. "We're not her parents. We went here. Thirty years ago." Her tone gives it the weight of a prison sentence. "Our friend lived in this room. Mind if we step inside? I promise not to steal anything." She motions to me. "And I'll keep a close eye on this one."

The girl stands. "Sure. My name's Gracie. I'll be across the hall. Just holler."

"Will do," Stacy says.

"Faith *and* Grace in one room," I murmur as the door closes. "And here I expected CVC to be more secular."

"Secular was never their style. Strict Catholics."

"For Catholics, they sure weren't heavy into the forgiveness business."

"Who knows what forces were at work," she says, her gaze drifting to a collection of posters on the wall. Old-school. De La Soul, Arrested Development, A Tribe Called Quest.

"Scenario" starts up in my head.

I shut it down.

I'm running out of time.

"I finally read your statement this weekend," I say now that we're alone.

"You waited thirty years?"

That lands harder than it should.

"Not all of us had the means to lawyer up."

"My parents insisted," she says.

"I tried to speak with you, ya know."

"My lawyer forbade me to speak with anyone."

"But your statement—it's true?"

"Which part?" she asks.

"That we were together all night."

"I said you were there when I fell asleep, there when I woke up."

"You didn't . . . draw any inferences from that?"

"I wasn't asked to draw inferences."

"Were you a deep sleeper?"

"When I was drinking? Yeah."

"You told them you were sober."

"Sobriety is subjective at that age, isn't it?"

I look into her eyes. "So, you think it's possible I got up and . . ."

"Went to the roof?" She shakes her head, shrugs, as if it's irrelevant. "To my knowledge, you didn't leave the bed. But I couldn't truthfully say I had eyes on you the entire night."

"In the statement—"

"Which one?"

"Your statement to the police."

"Oh, that one?" She shrugs. "It was lawyer-polished."

"You gave another?"

"To campus security, yeah. Officer Nash."

"The chubby one. I saw him at brunch today."

"He never left."

"CVPD didn't include campus security's witness statements in their file," I say.

Or they did—and stripped them before handing it over to me.

"What did your other statement say?"

She shrugs. "Pretty much the same. Just my language instead of the lawyer's."

"You think they'd still have the file?" I ask, wondering what else it might contain that didn't make it into Harbaugh's.

"For a death? Maybe."

"I can't ask Nash," I say. "He'll have me arrested for trespassing."

She gazes outside. "My husband paid for that golf cart he drives around in. I might be able to talk him into giving me a thirty-year-old file."

A rare rush of hope fills my chest. "I'm coming with."

She stops me and appraises. "Nash's eyesight isn't what it used to be. And you've *definitely* aged. Still, you might want to find a hat and shades, just in case."

40

Before heading to the main campus security station, we stop at the college bookstore, where I buy a fitted Center Valley Centaurs cap and a handful of key chains.

After thirty years, I'm still constantly losing my keys.

And locksmiths charge even more than colleges.

Bending the brim just right, I slide on the navy-and-red cap in front of the bookstore mirror. With the hat on, I can better see the kid I used to be.

The seventeen-year-old who showed up here thirty years ago in a White Sox hat—just because it was black. Who walked these halls with his chin out, his heart open, his future wide and bright, despite all the darkness behind him.

And who watched it all fall apart.

Or tore it apart himself.

Since I wasn't arrested the moment I stepped out of McCartney, there's a decent chance Nash didn't recognize me. Still, there's no reason to risk it.

We take Stacy's Lincoln across campus. Pulling up to the squat, windowless security station, she glances at me. "I'll go in alone."

"No. We go in together," I say as a steady rain hits the roof. "This is too important. We only get one shot."

Inside, I'm hoping we'll find some young rent-a-cop. But no such luck. It's Nash himself, rising slowly from his chair, giving me the kind of look usually reserved for TSA agents spotting a suspicious bulge in someone's waistband.

But then, maybe he's gauging my injuries.

"Hey," Stacy says, like she's running into a neighbor at a salad bar. "It's been a minute."

Same line as at brunch. This time, more casual. Practiced.

"Officer Nash, this is my cousin Kyle," she adds without missing a beat.

Nash steps toward me, hand extended. Stacy intercepts him with a gentle palm to his chest. "My cousin's immunocompromised," she says. "Since COVID . . ."

She doesn't need to finish. Nash recoils like she'd just whispered *contagious flesh-eating virus.*

Behind my sunglasses, I roll my eyes but keep my mouth shut. Let her do her thing.

"Anyway," she says, "my cousin's working with a nonprofit advocating for stronger mental health policies on college campuses. I told him about Jess Karras—he's interested in looking at the file." She flips her hair back and pins him with her icy blue stare. "Any chance you can help?"

Nash looks at me again. Then at her. Then back at me.

"Uh . . . maybe. I mean, I'd have to dig," he says. "Could take a few days. A week?"

Stacy tilts her head. "Didn't they scan the old files?"

"Some of them," he mutters. "But I'd have to log in, use my personal credentials . . ."

I clear my throat. "I won't use anything sensitive. I just want to review any internal findings. I'll stay on this side of the desk."

He nods, clearly not thrilled, but not objecting either.

"All right," he says. "Let me check what's still here."

As he disappears into the back, Stacy turns to me.

I mouth, *Thank you.*

Several long, anxious minutes pass. My body's buzzing, my mind playing out worst-case scenarios. Maybe he recognized me. Maybe he's back there calling Chief Lindsay.

Then, behind the partition, the old ink-jet kicks to life.

The stuttered churn of the feed rollers feels oddly familiar. Like feedback before a guitar solo. Or the moment just before the lights drop at a show.

For a second, I swear it's Stone Temple Pilots onstage.

And I've got a front-row seat to the final act of the night.

41

I part ways with Stacy after agreeing to meet for coffee at the Coop before I leave Center Valley. Without conscious effort, I find myself back at the Francis Magee Memorial Library, where a splotch of my dried blood still stains the pavement in the shape of Hitchcock's portly profile.

Standing beside the bench, *our* bench, is Liv. "Thought it might be safer in the light of day," she says.

I gaze up at the granite sky as large drops splash off my face. I tuck the file into my jacket to protect it from the rain. "How about today we head inside?"

She smiles. In that smile, I can't distinguish between the woman I've spent the last two days with and the eighteen-year-old freshman who declared me "bad news" all those years ago.

We walk up the paved steps and enter Magee Library.

The smell of dry paper, disinfectant, and dust ferries me like an old song straight to the past. To when I had a twenty-eight-inch waist and walked around with a hard-on for no discernable reason. I'm suddenly sure I spent time here. Maybe not for reference books or the computer lab. Maybe not for anything academic. Maybe this is where I discovered Bret Easton Ellis's *American Psycho* and Clive Barker's *Imajica*.

"There's more privacy upstairs," Liv says.

"I take it this isn't your first visit with a male companion," I joke.

She laughs. "The only things I ever got down with in this building were cognitive, behavioral, and abnormal psych."

"That's right, you were a psych major, like Fenton. Did you ever work in the field?"

"Not exactly," she says. "It wasn't for me."

"Wasn't for you?" I ask, following her up the carpeted steps. "Or it wasn't your choice?"

We settle into a quiet corner on the second floor behind the stacks, sitting crisscross applesauce, like kindergartners. Suddenly, I crave a Capri Sun, a Mott's juice box—anything with one of those tiny straws you jab through the foil.

"There's a certain freedom in not making your own decisions," Liv says.

"Freedom from responsibility for making bad choices?"

"That's part of it, I guess. But it also frees up your mind to live how you want during the times when you're *not* under someone's thumb. When your thinking changes, your behavior changes. Stuff you normally would've eschewed becomes fair game."

"Like dating apps," I say.

"Like dating, period."

"Affairs."

She grins, mischievously innocent. The kind of grin that makes me briefly wonder whether a specific someone was meant to discover her dating profile this weekend.

"How about the rest of the time?" I ask. "When you're back under the thumb."

"You get used to it. In between the doldrums there are escapes. Brunch, wine, Valium, naps. Margaritas. Sitting poolside in summer. In the winter, cuddling up with your cats and crime novels." Her eyes flash on mine. "Catching up with Del Danzinger."

I want to ask what she gets out of them, but the question feels too intimate. Too naked. Even for a writer.

"How about you?" she says. "What does Gregg Dryer do for fun these days?"

Investigate thirty-year-old cold cases.

Corner old friends and interrogate them.

Try to absolve myself of the guilt over Jess's death.

Until recently, the answer would've jumped from my tongue.

But Danzinger's gone quiet.

Once you've made a living writing for decades, you mistake your name for job security. But the market shifts. Trends change. A once exciting series becomes lame. Your champions move houses or lose faith.

Once you're old news, the doors don't just shut, they slam in your face.

Before long, you're doubled over, with your head hovering over the toilet, worrying about the future.

There are no appeals—only long, lonely sentences, with only yourself to blame for the conviction. You lie in your bed night after night, thinking your mother was right after all. You *are* worthless. You *are* lazy. You're *not* good enough.

("No one cares what you have to say, only what you can do *for them. You need a real job. One that pays.")*

You anticipate the pain. In your neck, in your spine, in your gut.

Thing is, my nervous system never resets.

The trauma in my body is trapped.

Pain radiates in all directions.

Muscles inflame.

My spine locks down on itself.

Slipped discs, herniations, facet joint syndrome.

The injuries are ancient, but the trauma is always present.

Since I was a kid.

Since the flea markets.

Since the beatings.

Since I was a boy hauling folding tables under summer's big, hard sun, too scared to ask for lunch.

And they're getting worse.

Some days I feel so broken, I don't want to exist.

Last year I took too much Advil on an empty stomach. Blood pooled in my gut while I was unconscious from muscle relaxers and tranqs.

I vomited in my sleep.

Aspirated on the blood.

Woke up sick the next morning with flu-like symptoms: sore throat, a cough, stomach troubles, aches and pains. I was as nauseated as I'd ever been with a hangover.

Two days later, I collapsed in the driveway shoveling snow.

At the hospital, they discovered pneumonia in my lungs, sepsis in my blood.

My kidneys and lungs were failing.

A priest gave me last rites. Not that I cared one way or the other.

According to my chart, I stopped breathing for a little over a minute until I was intubated.

I was almost gone. Then I wasn't.

But I'm not sure I ever really came back either.

Or maybe Del just never came back. My writing hasn't been the same since.

Danzinger's been angrier, edgier. Darker.

He can't get his father's voice out of his head.

He thinks of ending things on his own terms.

He wants a farewell novel—*Danzinger Is Dead.*

Meanwhile, Liv's question—what Gregg Dryer does for fun—lingers between the stacks.

"I like to travel," I say, neglecting to add that I don't remember the last time I left the Northeast.

"Me too," she says.

I know. I've seen the photos. Paris, Lisbon, Seoul, Tokyo.

Disney at Christmas, at Easter, even on Arbor Day.

"The message on the whiteboard," I say. "The one you think I wrote. Did it really exist that morning?"

"Why would I lie to you now?"

"Why did you lie back then?"

"You *know* why."

"For me, right?"

"No one else would've written those words, Gregg."

"You think I killed her?"

"No. I worried the *police* would think so. They had the voicemails—you *begging* to meet her on the roof 'one last time.'"

"So you think I wrote the message—then never went to the roof?"

"I didn't say that."

"You think I was *there*?" A silence stretches between us. Heavy, unbearable. "That I watched her jump?"

"You're twisting my words. I don't know what happened. But her not being alone opens up . . . other possibilities."

"You're saying someone could've caused an accident."

"Maybe. Or a stupid fight. A push. Or she slipped making a point. I don't know. She was drunk. There are dozens of scenarios. None more likely than another."

The thought comes out before I can stop it. "What if it was you?"

Her eyes narrow. "It wasn't."

"You were drunk, weren't you? You said so in your statement."

"I didn't black out, Gregg. I remember the walk back to D'Amelio, alone, because Toni stayed behind at the Heights to hook up with Rocco."

"How was your relationship with Toni?"

"Fine. Maybe strained."

"Because of Jess?"

"Jess wasn't always helpful. She wedged herself between us. Like she was jealous."

I grab a pen from my pocket and a heavy World War II hardcover from the shelf. I flip to the title page and hand her both. "Show me," I say.

"What?"

"How the whiteboard looked. The message."

"That was *thirty years* ago."

"As best as you remember."

She sighs but she writes:

One last

sunrise

Jess

The question mark she adds is warped, stretched over all three lines, the dot beneath it a sideways slash.

That's when it hits me. "What if Jess wrote this?"

"She wouldn't have addressed it to herself."

I point. "There's no comma before 'Jess.'"

She blinks.

I hold out my hands as if it's obvious. "Do you really think *I* would've left out a comma? Me?"

"You were wasted."

"Half the papers I wrote for the baseball team were done doing kamikaze shots with Fenton. I still used commas."

I trace the letters with my finger. "This 'Jess' looks more like a sign-off. Like she was inviting you and Toni to the roof for one last sunrise."

She studies the words.

The thought crosses my mind: Maybe Liv *knew* this.

Maybe she erased the whiteboard not for my sake.

But for hers.

Or Toni's.

Or both.

"Do you really not remember how devastated you were?" she asks. "How humiliated?"

The Condom Incident. The one even Harbaugh heard about.

"I was seventeen," I say. "I was resilient then. I'd have gotten over it."

"You *say* that. But crimes of passion don't wait for logic. They happen in the moment. When you feel like your whole world's collapsing. So let me ask you, Gregg . . ."

I feel something rise in my throat.

She leans in. "How were you feeling that night? Really."

42
November 1993
The Condom Incident

Of all the nights to forgo a blackout, this shouldn't have been one of them.

But there I was in my room at Cormac, stone-cold sober, sitting on beanbag chairs with Fenton, playing *NHL Hockey* on my roommate's Sega Genesis, when a knock came on the open door.

No one in Cormac knocked on an open door.

Except RAs. Or campus police.

I shifted my eyes from the screen for a split second.

Spotted the silhouette in my periphery.

Recognized it immediately.

I lost focus.

Fenton snuck one in glove-side.

"Gooooooaaaaalllll!" Fenton yodeled, like a frog-throated Whitney Houston.

He raised his Pabst in triumph while tiny pixelated men celebrated on-screen.

I stayed seated, attempting to cool the heat rising into my ears.

I'd already earned a reputation as someone quick to lose his cool. I'd clobbered some poor bastard down the hall for reasons still hotly debated. The fight, not the provocation, was caught on videotape.

I looked like the better fighter.

I also looked like the aggressor.

No doubt I was.

Fifty miles from Philly, all of Cormac Hall started calling me Rocky.

And not in a good way.

The RAs warned me: one more jab, hook, or uppercut and I was out.

Same went for Fenton if he got caught with another girl in his room.

We'd only been on campus two months and were both on disciplinary probation.

People started betting which of us would be kicked off first.

Odds favored me.

"Hey, Mike," I said. My gut turned sour. I kept my face painfully neutral. "What can I do for you?"

I figured he was there to beg me for a paper. By then, the baseball team comprised 70 percent of my client base. And they'd pay practically *anything* to get out of a writing assignment.

Whether they *could* read or write was none of my business. All that mattered was they didn't want to, affording me the means to take my Panamanian suitemate on a daily liquor run.

For a moment, it felt like I had Macmillan over a barrel.

Then I stared at the screen.

No chance I'd write a word for him. Not while he was with Jess.

The wound was fresh. The Lap Glance still stinging like a rubber bullet to the chest.

But I was sure it'd heal.

I was wrong.

"Talk to ya for a sec?" he said.

"Talk," I told him, not budging from my beanbag. I wanted Fenton to hear him grovel. I wanted to laugh at Macmillan's back when he left.

I wanted a drink.

A week earlier, when I caught Jess on his lap in D'Amelio, I'd nearly broken his perfectly aligned jaw.

The only thing that stopped me was the promise I made to myself—not to let her see how much I hurt.

"You got any condoms?" Macmillan said.

I hit "Start." Paused the game.

For a second, I couldn't breathe.

Every instinct screamed: Launch from the beanbag. Smash his smug face in. Watch him crumple like Spinks, ninety-one seconds into the ring with Tyson.

Logic fought back:

He's bigger. Stronger.

He could beat you in a fair fight without breaking a sweat.

But rage? Rage had rebuttals.

Since when do you fight fair?

Since when does size beat being crazy and pissed the hell off?

Rage made a compelling case.

I stood. No idea what I was going to do.

Fenton watched like it was Game 6 of the '86 World Series.

I turned to Macmillan. Caught the *slightest* flinch. A half-second hesitation.

And that broke me.

Not the way I expected.

It made me *soft*. Just soft enough to do what I did next.

The stupidest, most humiliating thing I've ever done.

I walked to my desk. Opened the top drawer. Withdrew the three-pack of Trojans Fenton and I had picked up at Pop's Pharmacy.

I tore the box open. Peeled one off. Tossed it back in the drawer.

Then handed the other two to Macmillan.

For a fraction of a second, I felt noble. Like I'd taken the high road.

Like I was the bigger man.

Then he pocketed the condoms, said "Cool," and marched out.

I turned to face Fenton, who remained seated, his mouth agape like he was catching popcorn.

That's when it hit me.

Macmillan didn't even live in Cormac.

He was taking them back to Wilkes . . .

Or straight to D'Amelio.

To her room.

To her bed.

The same bed where I'd once felt at home.

He'd come to Cormac for one reason.

So I'd know.

So it would become real.

In case the Lap Glance didn't work.

The chicken parm from dinner rose in my throat. I swallowed hard, determined not to fall to pieces in front of Fenton.

Without a word, I walked past him, through the shared bathroom, and knocked on my Panamanian suitemate's door.

The room smelled like fine cigars and imported leather. Because even more lucrative than writing papers for the baseball team was being the only guy in Cormac over twenty-one.

"Mind going for a ride?" I asked. "I'm parched."

Later that night, I nearly died from alcohol poisoning.

I regained consciousness in the ER in the early hours, a pale light searing my eyes. The smell of bleach shot up my nostrils. I almost gagged.

My mouth was bone-dry. My throat tasted like vomit and charcoal.

Toni and Fenton stood over me.

Toni was crying, Fenton leaning back, his hands on his hips, shaking his head.

I stared up at him.

When I finally spoke, my voice rasped, barely recognizable.

"Told you they'd serve their purpose at some point," I said.

Hours later, still lying in the hospital bed, the nurse handed me my discharge papers.

I scanned them for the formal diagnosis, sure it would read: *"Alcohol poisoning."*

It did.

But it was only a secondary diagnosis.

The primary reason for my visit?

"Suicide attempt."

43
Homecoming 2023

Sitting among the stacks on the second floor of the library alone with Liv, both of us remain silent for minutes on end until she asks, "Is there a reason you asked Toni to drive you to urgent care instead of me?"

It takes me a moment to realize she's talking about last night.

I lie. "I'd been bashed senseless."

"I thought maybe . . ."

"What?"

"That you suspected I had something to do with what happened to you."

"Did you?" The words were out of my mouth before I thought them. I force a half smile to soften the blow.

Her eyes become slits. "Are you serious?"

"I don't know," I say, unwilling to backpedal all the way. "You can't possibly believe this had nothing to do with my investigation. With Jess's death."

Her silence is damning. Even she knows the coincidences are stacking too high.

"And you have to admit," I add, "in light of what went down, the timing of your bathroom run was a little too convenient."

She sighs. Rolls her eyes. "You think I hired street goons to jump you?"

"I'm not saying that," I mumble. "I just . . ."

I'm just running out of theories, out of suspects, out of time.

"Were you jealous when Jess started seeing me?" I ask.

"Jealous?"

"I'd never really believed it. But after you broke up, Fenton said you liked me. Said Toni lied about you calling me 'bad news' because she was interested in me."

"Me *liking* you and thinking you're 'bad news' can both be true, simultaneously, you know."

"Were they?"

Her cheeks flush faint pink. But her eyes are more adamant.

"First of all," she says, "Toni wasn't 'interested in' you. She thought you'd make a good . . ." She lowers her voice as if we were in the chapel. "She thought you'd make a fun eff-buddy."

That tracks.

And she'd spotted Fenton's herpes.

She says, "Fenton told me early on Saturday of Freshman Orientation that *you* liked *me*. Did that *excite* me? Yeah, a little."

"Why?" I ask. "Why me?"

"Partly your wildness. You were everything my structured life wasn't. Part of me, I guess, craved your chaos." She pauses. "But you were also clever and funny, even ambitious in your own bizarre way. And you seemed vulnerable beneath it all. Emotionally honest. Like you couldn't be anything but."

My eyes drop to the floor.

She frowns. "But I saw the way you looked at Jess that night. From the moment you laid eyes on her. You fell instantly. I didn't have a chance."

"Unless she was gone," I mutter before I can stop myself.

She blinks. Stares like she didn't hear me. Then:

"Are you *listening* to yourself?"

I look away. "There's an answer here, Liv. I just want to reach it. I just need to *know*."

She studies my face like an abstract painting. Something she once recognized but can't quite name anymore. "What if you discover the answer is something you can't live with?"

"I'll cross that bridge when I come to it." I try to sound firm. But it rings hollow. Like someone quoting an old version of himself.

Truth is, I've come to more bridges than I've crossed.

When I did cross, I usually went kicking and screaming.

Then soaked the bridge in gasoline and lit a match from the far bank.

She doesn't smile. Just nods, like she knew the answer I'd give.

"You told Detective Harbaugh you saw Jess flirting with Kip at the dance in the auditorium," she says.

"They weren't flirting," I say quickly.

"But you *believed* they were."

She's right. I only found out yesterday they were discussing me and the Plushie stunt. All these years, I let a false memory overwrite the truth like a Sharpie over a pencil sketch.

"What if that image from the dance stayed with you after you went to bed with Stacy Rennick?" Liv asks. "What if you couldn't sleep? Or if it woke you in the middle of the night, drenched in panic sweat? What would you have done?"

I don't answer. Not aloud. But I know what I'd have done.

I'd have gone to Jess's room.

Knocked on her door.

If she didn't answer, I'd have gone to Liv and Toni's.

If they didn't answer, I'd have left a message on their whiteboard.

Something desperate. Something dumb.

"That anger," Liv says. "That humiliation over Macmillan's audacity to come to you for condoms. It didn't die with Jess, Gregg. It stayed with you. All year."

"I was a teenager," I protest. What's meant as a defense sounds like a confession.

"Exactly."

I exhale hard. "I had a temper."

She raises a brow.

"But I kept it in check."

"Barely," she says. "And only until March you did."

That last line hits me sideways. Because it's true. She's not even talking about Jess now. She's talking about Saint Patrick's Day. About the right hook that got me expelled.

I look down at the floor between us.

I want to tell her I'm sorry. That I've always been sorry.

But I don't. I sit with it. With her disappointment and what I feel toward myself.

There was a time when I believed I'd grown. When I truly thought I'd changed.

But maybe I never changed.

Maybe I just got better at hiding the truth from myself.

44

March 1994

Saint Patrick's Day

By the middle of the spring semester, my transformation from fun-loving college student to full-throttle alcoholic was complete.

The only shock was how functional I remained.

I'd cleared my incompletes, kept my GPA above 3.3 despite skipping classes—and business was booming.

Every dollar I made writing papers for athletes and upperclassmen too lazy or hungover to string five sentences together went to liquor.

But at least I was drinking the good stuff.

Jess had been dead more than four months.

I thought of her every day. Cried most of them.

We opened our Saint Patty's Day celebration with bottles of Rumple Minze and Goldschläger, because of course we did.

Why not chase awful hard-candy shots with OJ, flat Coke, beer, and warm Gatorade?

By nightfall, Fenton and I were blitzed.

So were the guys we hung with: Marc, Johnny, Loggs, and Little Joe.

I don't remember whose idea it was to leave Cormac and head for the Heights, but odds are it was mine. It usually was.

Within the hour, we were doing keg stands behind Heights number 9.

Inside, the music was loud, the place packed. House of Pain implored us all to "*jump around.*"

The walls shook.

Marc, Johnny, and Loggs vanished, leaving me alone with Fenton and Little Joe.

I must've been scanning for girls when I saw him.

Or maybe I was just drunk and hungry for something to punch.

Either way, I spotted him through the crowd.

Macmillan.

He was standing in a corner, talking to a girl whose name I never learned.

Little Joe once called her Nancy Nipples—because of course he did—and somehow that name stuck. Even in my own head.

That night, she wore a tight green sweater which accentuated them.

She looked a bit like Rachel from *Friends.*

When she glanced our way, Fenton and I turned our heads.

But Little Joe just kept staring.

Like the deer in my headlights the previous semester.

Which is probably what put Macmillan on edge.

He squared his shoulders at Little Joe, whose nickname wasn't ironic.

And I, for some reason, felt giddy.

I don't remember making a decision.

I only remember watching myself from outside my body, walking toward them with purpose, beer in my left hand.

Which meant my right hand had something planned.

Some part of me believed I was standing up for Little Joe, though I knew he was tough and could handle himself. He didn't need me.

If I hadn't intervened, the moment would've passed without incident.

This wasn't some Spock-like sacrifice for a friend.

It was a window of opportunity.

Later, people would say there was jawing.

There was shoving.

Someone even claimed Macmillan threw the first punch.

Maybe.

But I don't think I cared.

Nirvana's "Lithium" came on.

I closed my fist.

Swung.

Made contact.

It sounded like an aluminum can crushed underfoot.

Hollow, sharp, irrevocable.

Then silence.

The music stopped.

Everything went still.

"What the hell did you *do*?" Fenton shouted.

I looked down at the pile of Macmillan on the floor, his arms slack, his face wrong.

"Get the hell out of here," Fenton was shouting. He grabbed me by the shoulders and spun me toward the door. "Get out *now*. They called campus police."

From above, I watched myself move through the house. Watched people part like oil from water.

I remember thinking: *I'm calm. I'm composed.*

But when I stepped outside, the wind punched me in the face.

And I was *slammed* back into my body.

Pain exploded in my right hand.

I knew I'd broken bones.

I muffled a scream into my jacket.

Then I ran.

I ran hard and stupid and fast, not stopping until the red and blue lights of campus police bounced off the Heights like some cursed Christmas tree.

Back at Cormac, I hurried upstairs to the second floor.

It might've been my first time there, ever.

In the hall, I found a kind, familiar face. Some bio major.

I asked if I could use his room.

He unlocked the door, let me in, and left for the library.

I locked the door behind me. Sat on the floor with my back against it.

Breathing hard.

I didn't cry.

Not because I didn't want to.

But because I didn't know how to anymore.

Later, I'd tell myself I blacked out. That it wasn't premeditated.

That it could've been any of the baseball players squaring off with Little Joe.

But I remember more than I like to admit.

Maybe every moment.

Probably every choice.

I remember the satisfaction in the split second between my fist hitting bone and his body crumpling.

I remember standing there, deliberately breathing it all in, like some proud ancient warrior who bested a mythological beast hell-bent on devouring the townspeople.

Like an idiot, I remember thinking I was *owed* that punch. Entitled to it.

And I remember the look on Fenton's face when he dragged me toward the door.

Fear.

Not of what happened.

Not of reprisal.

Not even of getting caught.

Fear of *me*.

The one person on campus who should've had his back.

45
Homecoming 2023

I'd thought I paid the bill for what I did to Macmillan. Served my sentence.

I was expelled.

Exiled.

Lost my friends.

Spent the next few years drinking alone in an off-campus apartment across from a Chili's in Rhode Island.

But there was something I left out of the equation.

Someone.

"And Mike?" Liv says.

Mike.

How had I managed not to think of him as a person in all this?

Had I been too busy feeling sorry for myself?

Had I mistaken my punishment for accountability?

"Do you even know what happened after you ran that night?" she asks.

Not really.

I never wanted to know.

Campus police arrived seconds after I fled. I heard that students pointed them in the direction of Cormac, but I wasn't in my room. I was hiding among the science guys on the second floor.

"He wasn't moving," she says. "He was out cold. You struck him right where the eye socket meets the temple. A few centimeters further back, you could've killed him."

But I didn't, I nearly plead.

But the words sound small. Hollow. Pathetic. Even in my head.

If it had happened off campus—at the Pepper or even the Patio—I'd have gone to jail.

Aggravated assault, at a minimum.

Depending on the injury, maybe even attempted murder.

I'd have been convicted. Sentenced. Imprisoned. And deserved every bit of it.

"They called an ambulance," she says. "The ambulance rushed him to the hospital. While they ran tests, they called his parents. They drove an hour in the middle of the night. When they got there, he still wasn't out of the woods."

I think of Kip and his parents. How I hated him for all the wrong reasons.

For things he had that I didn't.

Things neither of us had any say in.

"I never thought about his parents," I confess.

"Forget his parents for a second. What about *him*?"

I don't want to hear it.

But I need to.

"You *ended* his baseball career. He never played another game. Never even put on a uniform again. He lost his baseball scholarship. Had to transfer to a community college back home. His first year there was a complete loss. He couldn't see out of his left eye. He dropped out and had to start over next fall."

It was my fault.

I was the reason he lost his scholarship.

Not because he was dumb. Because I was.

As she speaks, I drift from my body.

Watching us from above, sitting crisscross applesauce on the floor.

Still, my stomach churns as I imagine the events she's describing.

"After a year," Liv says, "he came back to Center Valley. But he was a grade behind his friends. He wasn't on the team. He'd gained more than a hundred pounds. He was depressed all the time. Almost flunked out."

I wipe away the first tears I ever shed for him.

But they'll never make up for all the ones I shed for myself.

"He changed his major," she says, "from phys ed to history. When he finally graduated, the only job he could get was as a substitute teacher. Meantime, after losing his scholarship, he had massive student loans to pay."

"How about now?" I ask, trembling.

Whether there's a chill or something inside me going cold, I don't know.

"Eventually, he married. Had Zack. But his vision never completely came back. His coordination's off. He never had a chance to throw a ball around with his kid."

I swallow hard.

I was too wrapped up in my own pain to consider the pain I caused.

Too angry about my expulsion to consider the punishment *I* handed out.

Difference is, I deserved it.

Macmillan didn't.

Her next words are unnecessary.

But I need to hear them.

From someone I care about.

Because all this time, I've been hiding under the folding table.

No longer a child but a coward.

"It wasn't *your* life that got ruined that night, Gregg." She pauses. "It was *Mike's*."

46

I don't know how long we sit in the library in silence, only that it's the longest I've sat in silence with another person since my mind-numbing first-year Property lectures in law school.

During that time, I'm away but close. I still see Liv in my periphery, her head down as if in acknowledgment that I need her to be here with me right now, even if I'm not.

Not fully anyway.

In the quiet that follows, the library takes on the feel of a confessional. Every creak of the floor, every breath between us, feels loaded with memory. I think of all the things I can never take back—what I did to Mike, what I never said to Jess, what I buried so deep it never got the chance to age and grow or decay.

And then there's Liv. Still here. Still herself. And still married to a man who, from everything she's said without saying, doesn't deserve her. My eyes trace the slope of her neck, the sadness in her posture, the strength in her restraint. I want to reach for her. But I don't. I can't. Not yet.

"This *Les*," I finally say, the name dripping off my tongue like sour milk. "Have you considered leaving him?"

I'm sure she's about to launch into a ten-minute sermon on familial duty and the sanctity of a marriage bound by an all-knowing, all-seeing God. But that's not what she offers.

"Every. Effing. Day. Since . . ."

"The wedding?" I say. Then: "The engagement?"

"Our first date."

Inside my chest, something melts for her. Everything melts for her, immediately and without exception. Because she means every word. She's being funny, sure, but she means it. Truth in jest and all that.

When her eyes moisten . . .

I see the ivory of Jess's exposed bone.

Hear the crack of Macmillan's eye socket.

Viscerally, I'm liquid.

"Why don't you?" I ask. "Why don't you leave him?"

She chuckles without mirth. "Why do I stay, you mean?"

"No," I tell her. "Why don't you *leave*?"

"It's the same question."

"It isn't, though."

She fixes her eyes on me. "Were you happy growing up without a father?"

I consider my conversation with Stacy. How I nearly judged her for not telling the father of her oldest son without even knowing the situation. But everyone's circumstances are unique.

"I was devastated growing up alone with *my* mother. *It matters who*. It matters who that person is, not just whether they're around or not."

"He's good to the kids."

"Is he good to *you*?"

She hesitates. That and her expression convey everything her tongue won't.

"Then he's doing your children no good," I say. "Every time he treats you poorly in front of them, he's coloring how they see the world. You have two beautiful young daughters. Do you want them to grow up and be with men like him?"

She shakes her head as more tears drip down the sides of her cheeks. "I'm afraid."

"Afraid of what?"

Her sideways glance is enough, but she says it anyway. "Of being alone." When she sees the confusion on my face, she adds, "The girls are about to go off to high school. In a few years, they'll leave for college."

A lump forms in my throat and, with all the emotions coursing through me, it takes me a moment to realize why. Deep down, I've been *waiting* for my friends' kids to go off to college—so I can have *them* back. So I can convince myself that part of life I'd chosen to forgo is over.

She puts it into words as well as I ever could. "I can just imagine myself, sitting around the house, waiting for calls or texts or emails just to hear some version of their voices." She pauses, then moves from the future to the past. "When I was in college, I needed to stay close to my parents. Like Kip. But these days, if you're always available at the touch of a button . . ."

"You're never missed," I finish.

With a tear welling in one eye, I suddenly feel as if I'm split in two. Almost physically. Not just on the issue of Liv and her family but . . . *everything.*

As much as I detest social media, it's the reason I'm here with her now.

As much as I dislike being around people, I miss out on moments like this by self-isolating.

As much as I desire a strong, steady relationship, I'm terrified of being in one and back out whenever I get too close. All these contradictions, these abstractions are . . .

I don't know.

Maybe we had it right in the nineties.

Maybe reality bites and nothing matters.

Or maybe we *make* things matter. We make them matter to *us.* We each decide what's important and what's not. And that's *all* that matters. What we as human beings are programmed from birth to care about: our parents, our children, our siblings, our peers.

Every other human on the goddamn planet.

Every animal. Every plant, every tree.

Every lake, river, and sea.

Every landscape, every skyscape, every last bit of the earth itself from her upper atmosphere to her plasmic inner core.

Liv matters.

Tears roll down her cheeks.

I kiss them away.

Before realizing it, I'm holding her in my arms as she held me last night.

"It's going to be all right," I tell her, then immediately retract it. "That's a lie. I don't know that. Everything could go to shit for either or both of us at any time. For me, everything almost definitely will."

She cry-laughs and it's a beautiful sound. She throws in one of her precious snorts for good measure.

I lift her chin with my finger until she's gazing into my eyes. My lips approach hers slowly, allowing her ample time to decline.

But she doesn't.

Our lips finally touch, then part.

Our tongues find one another.

She tastes like Life.

Not like the end I came here searching for but a beginning I didn't.

47

Several unforgettable minutes later, Liv excuses herself to the restroom.

Alone now, tucked between the stacks, I bask in the quiet glow of after. Our kiss feels like it happened in another time, in a different place, on another plane altogether.

But it didn't.

It happened right here, minutes ago.

Yet the way my brain keeps pumping dopamine, it might as well be happening still.

Each time I think of her taste, her skin, her lips on mine, the pleasure centers in my brain light up like it's brand new.

This time, she left her handbag behind.

"As collateral," she said with a wink.

The older you get, the more you realize there are far fewer movie moments in life than you expected. And the ones that do tend to register seem to resemble a film's "all is lost" moment.

Then there are those that aren't only made for the screen but made for the heart of the picture. That point when your eyes moisten and your mind floods with chemicals you thought ran dry years ago.

This is one of those precious few.

And it happened minutes ago, in a dusty college library, when Liv Latham let me kiss her.

Liv Latham *Todeski*, I remind myself.

Married.

To Les Todeski.

Wealthy Les Todeski.

Outside, the sky has opened as it threatened to all day.

Cold rain drums on the windows in thick, soothing waves.

It means wherever Liv and I go next will be indoors.

Close. Warm.

Closed off from the rest of the world and all its poisons.

The campus security file teeters in my lap. I open it.

Pages familiar and unfamiliar greet me. Much of it duplicates the CVPD file—the official story. Nash warned us he couldn't turn over everything. There were sensitive items he'd need to review and redact and make a determination on.

Still, there's more here than in the police file.

Witness statements from Toni S. Cullen, Liv H. Latham, Josh M. Fenton, and Stacy C. Rennick.

I go to Stacy's statement first.

As expected . . . it's careful. Clean.

Not a contradiction, not quite.

She confirms I was there when she fell asleep. And when she woke up.

Nothing more. No claim of unbroken contact. Nothing that couldn't technically be true and still allow for a very different interpretation to live in the spaces between.

As an alibi, it's airtight in its ambiguity.

I move on.

Toni's statement. Liv's, Fenton's.

All scrubbed by memory and time.

Then I discover another sheet of paper. One I've never seen before.

An *inventory*.

Items removed from Jess's room following her death.

Having just left her old dorm, I see the items clearly—exactly as they were then.

The posters: R.E.M., *Point Break*, *Pretty Woman*.

The school supplies: textbooks, spiral notebooks, folders, highlighters in canary yellow and neon pink.

The plushies: dolphins, sea turtles, bears of all colors. Giraffes, elephants, monkeys.

A whole soft jungle of comfort and innocence.

And this: "Teddy bear with loose head."

One teddy bear even kept her secrets.

It stops me cold.

My mind conjures the mantel in Jess's childhood home, the one lined with framed photographs.

Jess with her parents on a boardwalk.

Jess with ponytails and braces.

Jess at her eighth-grade graduation.

At senior prom with Frank Handly.

And in the center:

A single, worn teddy bear.

Its head lolling to the side, barely hanging on.

Stuffing breaking free from the neck.

Maybe from age.

Maybe from use.

Maybe from something else.

One teddy bear even kept her secrets.

Maybe something no one ever thought to check.

I stare at the page again.

The inventory doesn't say *brown teddy bear* or *small teddy bear* or *worn teddy bear*, like the others.

It says: *Teddy bear with loose head.*

And suddenly I know:

Detective Harbaugh never really *saw* this.

Not in the way I'm seeing it now.

Not with the proper context.

Because if he had—he'd have already done what I'm about to do next.

PART V

You Oughta Know

48

Twenty minutes later, I'm back in Nazareth, pulling Liv's Audi to the cracked curb outside Jess's childhood home. This time, I'm not armed with falsehoods but wielding a white flag of truth.

As I wait for Evelyn Karras to answer the bell, I glance back at the car, thankful Liv allowed me to borrow it without any questions or conditions. I need to do this alone. Have my first and final heart-to-heart with Jess's mom after all these years.

Together, perhaps we can finally get to the bottom of what happened to Jess, possibly without having to look very far.

It's taking her longer to answer than last time and, fleetingly, I worry she's out of the house. But no, her slate-gray Dodge Aries remains in the driveway. This moment feels familiar—an eagerness and exhilaration laced with terror and dread.

Like flying to Paris alone after Chloé dumped me.

Evelyn opens the door and, standing in its frame, she looks different. Tired, sour, perturbed. As she stands back to allow me in without question, I step forward as if my legs are being lifted by strings. My feet feel heavy, the carpet like quicksand.

Immediately, I sit on the sofa, my eyes returning to the mantel with its framed photos and lone teddy bear.

She follows me into the room and takes the same comfy seat directly across from me.

Her eyes have changed. Earlier they'd been curious, cautious, concerned.

Now her look feels darker: desperate, dour, almost disturbed.

"Mrs. Karras," I say, as my eyes fall from hers to the right arm of her chair, where she holds a—

Oh, fu—

No, it can't be.

But yup, that's . . .

That's definitely a gun.

"How dare you set foot in this house again, Mr. Dryer."

My gut fills with a degree of fear I've never felt.

She said my name; so much for hoping this is just a senior moment.

"I was about to tell you who I am, Mrs. Karras. And, more importantly, why I'm here."

"Bullshit." She levels the gun at my midsection.

I flinch, throwing my hands out at my sides. "Oh, you don't get upstairs *that* way, Mrs. K. That's a *no-no.* That's one of the big ones."

"An eye for a *goddamn eye.*"

I shake my head like a dog with a rope between its teeth. "That's Old Testament stuff. It really doesn't fly under the new regime. At least from what I hear—"

"Shut up."

I shut up. I shut up *good,* as my mind drifts back to all the times I thought I'd welcome death to the door like an old friend.

But no. *Death can kiss my ass.* I don't want to die.

I really, super-duper *don't* want to die.

"Please, listen, before you use that thing," I say, trying to stay calm. "I'm not going anywhere as long as you're holding the gun. I'm forty-seven and frankly *never* ran fast. I dislocated a kneecap playing an angel in the second-grade Christmas play, and every time it rains—"

"Shut up."

Okay, that's twice. There's no way I can talk myself out of this if I'm not allowed to speak. Not allowed to humanize myself, tell her my side of the story. Or what I hope to find here in this house, in this room—exoneration.

I'm drawing a blank.

She cocks the hammer.

Now would be an excellent *time to dissociate.*

Except dissociation isn't a superpower.

I have zero control over it.

"I didn't kill your daughter," I suddenly say.

Hearing the words emerge from my mouth, they sound truthful, *convincing*, even to me. For the first time, I fully believe them.

I didn't kill her daughter.

"You think you can *lie* to me? I've known men like you my entire life. I *married* one."

Jess's father.

"I knew everything I needed to the week you two got together," she says. "Jess told me. First, you were moody. Then you were a drunk. I told her to get the *hell* away from you right then. But you were so *funny* and *handsome* and *charming.*"

Somewhere, deep down but crying out, I'm crazy flattered.

Evelyn says, "I told her it means nothing. 'He's your *father.* Cut from the same cloth!' She said, 'It's not his fault. He's *damaged.*' I told her, 'You found him that way, *leave* him that way. That's what men do—they turn their pain into anger and lash out at the world. Men like that can't be fixed. They *don't* change.' Know what she did?"

I shake my head.

"She hung up on me. For days, she didn't call back. When she finally did, she was crying."

"Crying?"

"You'd *yelled* at her."

No, never.

"You were *drinking.* You'd punched a wall. She had to drive you to a doctor. Said you were lucky you hadn't broken your hand."

My sprained wrist.

It hadn't happened going out a first-floor window at D'Amelio after all. It must've happened in the dorm itself. In front of Jess. Probably in her room. The single place on campus she should've felt safest.

"You were jealous," Evelyn says. "Of a *high school* kid. She'd *told* you she was done with him. But you didn't believe her. As if she had any control over who called her phone."

Frank Handly? Had I really been jealous of him back then? Had I been frightened of losing her to him? To anyone? Was I so terrified of . . . *abandonment*?

Of course I was.

"To put it mildly," my Hoboken shrink said when I first asked. "Abandonment issues are extremely common in people with childhood trauma as severe as yours. You were betrayed by the single person who should've loved you most in this world. The one who brought you into it. Instead, she tried to wish you out of existence."

The slightest perceived provocation, the tiniest threat, even a minor frustration triggers fight-or-flight in some trauma survivors, he told me. They become frightened and, in turn, *frightening*.

I didn't want to believe him.

But I did.

"What happened to you," he said, "caused intolerable loneliness and despair—and yes, *rage*. When rage has nowhere to go, it gets redirected against the self. It's why you drove like you did, why you nearly drank yourself to death, why you fought giants with a slingshot for side-eyeing you."

He paused to let me process it, then added, "You only feel *alive* in the face of actual danger. It's not your fault. Neither are those feelings: that pervasive guilt, that fear of being abandoned, that *anger*. Those are feelings you came by honestly. You didn't *choose* them. They were produced by your experience."

Is that why Jess left me?

During my blackouts did Jekyll become Hyde?

If so, she never tried to one-up me.

She needed to escape me.

"I've been talking to Jess's friends all weekend about what happened," I tell Evelyn. "They would've told me if I'd behaved like my moth—"

"She never told *them*. She told *me*. I was her *mother*. Her *best friend*. And until you came along, she'd always listened to me. But she *loved* you. She loved you like a drunk loves his bottle."

Jess never told Toni because they were never alone.

Liv was always around.

"She *did* listen to you," I say. "She broke up with me. For good."

"Only *after* you left her that nasty message on her door."

I blink. "What message?"

Her own rage starts to simmer, her gun hand trembling, but steady enough to remain aimed at me.

She says, "The note telling Jess to go the *hell* back to her high school boyfriend."

"There *was* no note," I cry.

She practically leaps to her feet, swings around, and snatches the teddy bear off the mantel. She rips off its head and tosses the body at my feet.

"Pick it up," she yells.

As I suspected when I perused the inventory, this was the plushie.

One teddy bear even kept her secrets.

The bear she confided in, the one she could trust with anything. A stuffie with a detachable head and hollowed-out insides.

I drop to my knees, grab the bear, and reach in with my fingers to shovel out crumpled yellow Post-it notes, dozens of them, each containing a sentence or fragment.

Still on my knees, I flatten them against the living room floor, trying to put them in sequential order, but some aren't dated. Those that are all fall between August and October 1993, her two months as a freshman at Center Valley.

Finally a Centaur, yay!

Met someone and saw the sunrise!

I think we're pretty much dating?

GD + JK. I am sooo thinking impure thoughts. ☺

Going to a Phillies game!

Gregg drives like he's in F-1. Thought we'd die on the PA Turnpike. ☹

Definitely prefer him in the backseat. ☺

Another sunrise!

Frank came by. Luckily, I was at Gregg's.

He gets so angry when my phone rings. ☹

OK, so Mike's kinda HOT! Shouldn't have said so to Liv.

I think Liv likes Gregg. I think I Luv him. Hehe.

Yup. Liv told Fenton who told Gregg, who's pissed about Mike.

He threw a shit fit.

Liv told me she thinks Gregg did sleep with someone that first night.

I think Gregg's lying about not remembering.

Oh, damn Liv! Can I get 2 minutes alone w/ Toni???

Someone told him Frank was here.

He went nuts, almost broke his hand. We spent the night in urgent care. ☹

He scares me sometimes. But it's out of fear. I see the pain in his eyes.

Maybe Mom's right.

I miss her so much. I'm homesick. Yuk.

Gregg and I just had the biggest fight! ☹

It's over. He's falling apart. I don't have the strength to keep picking up the pieces.

Don't know what to say to him. Do know his feelings on exes.

Anyway, he's an all-or-nothing kinda guy.

Hung out with Mike tonight. We . . . kissed.

Things are heating up with Mike. He moves fast. Maybe too fast?

Jerk left the door open! Gregg saw us.

So pissed. Mike went too far. I feel rotten.

Gregg couldn't even look at me in class today.

Saw him talk to the girl in the black leather jacket again.

Well, Mike's a cheating piece of shit.

Swearing off men.

Liv's a bitch. Then you die. Haha.

Went to bed w/ Gregg, woke up with . . . my Stuffies?

He hasn't called. Should I call him? What would I even say?

Can't believe the note he left on my door.

This one's attached to a peculiar, crumpled purple Post-it, alone among all the yellows.

I reread the first—*Can't believe the note he left on my door*—and set them both aside.

By *he* she must mean *me*, and I can't bear to read it just yet.

I can't face my own words.

So I continue with hers, all dated the night of the dance.

The night the music died.

Dance sucked.

Don't know what to do. Kip says lay it all out.

But if he was jealous before . . .

One of the conditions: counseling for his anger.

And we'll continue to move at a glacier pace. I'm not ready to have sex with him.

Liv just saw him go into D'Hall with Stacy.

Hate my life. Miss Gregg. Feel like I lost a best friend.

Should I go down there? Or am I way too messed up?

All told, there are roughly three dozen yellow and one crumpled purple Post-it I assume is the message she discovered on her door. I stare at it like it's lethal.

Finally, I pick it up, my hand trembling.

Keep screwing

Frank

I'm done

My breath catches.

It's not just the rage in these words. It's the heartbreak. The finality. It's the presumptiveness. Over a decision Jess thought she'd already made on her own.

Then I notice the punctuation.

An oversize exclamation mark—stretched across the lines, with a slash beneath it instead of a dot.

A twin to the warped question mark Liv drew on the whiteboard sketch.

She didn't remember it at all, she said.

She humored me, hadn't she?

Which means, this might be her actual handwriting.

"Mrs. Karras, I think you're confused."

"The *hell* I am."

"I was with someone that night, *all* night," I tell her. "I have her original statement to campus security in the car parked just outside."

"The *whore*, you mean?"

"What?"

"The French Canadian? You know *damn well* who I'm talking about."

Her old-lady fingers are twitchy and, at any moment, she could pull the trigger, intentionally or not.

"Stacy?" I say. "Jess told you about Stacy?" I think of the *visits* Evelyn receives from Jess, who's *upstairs* getting their place ready. "Like . . . *recently*?"

"Not *recently*, you jackass." She points with her foot to one of the Post-Its. "She told me thirty years ago. Right before you made her *kill herself*!"

I look down at one of the earlier notes, which reads: *Saw him talk to the girl in the black leather jacket again.*

As I stare into the blackness of the barrel, I don't piss myself as I'd have expected.

Instead a dubious feeling of warmth flows through me like morphine.

It's almost like there's a heated washcloth lying gently atop my gray matter.

Blissfully hot water seeps into its crevices, clearing new pathways. Then:

She squeezes the trigger.

The sound of the gun firing deafens me. Like a slammed door. Finally:

An all-too-familiar blinding white light spreads like an industrial chemical spill across my vision.

49

My Hoboken shrink said everyone experiences it at some point.

Driving a dull stretch of highway. Weather fair. Traffic mild. Favorite song on the radio.

One minute the road's in front of you. The next—it's gone.

Your hands stay on the wheel. Your eyes don't close.

But your mind?

You miss your exit. You don't notice for ten miles.

Call it highway hypnosis. Muscle memory. Autopilot.

Physically there. Mentally elsewhere.

That's *dissociation.*

The last thing I remember is the gunshot.

I stare down at the dead center of my chest, waiting for a scarlet circle to appear, then slowly, suspensefully, expand outward, the way it does in the movies.

That's when I'll finally feel it inside me.

Something burning, hot and fast.

I smell the chemical tang of gunfire.

The body of the teddy bear at my feet becomes fuzzy.

My eyes tear.

In a moment they'll fall still, gazing up at the heavens.

When the pain doesn't come and the blood doesn't appear, I look up.

Evelyn's laughter bursts out wild and high-pitched, like a child caught doing something wrong. But it falters. Cracks mid-breath. Turns to sobbing.

The kind I heard at Jess's funeral.

She collapses into herself, tears blotting her blouse.

Somewhere between gasps I hear it—*blanks*. She's muttering about blanks. Whether this was a mercy or a mistake, I don't know.

For a split second, I think: *Maybe there* is *a god.*

But that lasts only a moment.

I need to find Liv.

I need to know whether she killed Jess.

Or whether Jess jumped after Liv told her I slept with Stacy.

No more autopilot. No more blaming my brain, my past, or the weather.

I'm behind the wheel now. *I'm* driving. Eyes open. Straight into the fire.

One way or the other, we're both responsible.

But then . . . this isn't about justice.

At least not anymore.

It's about knowing once and for all what happened that night.

Then what?

I'll cross that bridge when I come to it.

Liv, maybe, can be forgiven. Depending on her role.

But me? I deserve no forgiveness.

And maybe that's the next truth I need to face.

50

"Hey, *Dryer*," someone calls from behind me as I hurry toward the Francis Magee Memorial Library.

I freeze. Slowly turn around with my arms low but out at my sides to show I'm not carrying a weapon. My eyes are glued to the concrete.

When I'm fully facing the figure who spoke, I lift my head, expecting to see Detective Harbaugh, probably with his weapon drawn on me.

Or Professor Garland with Harbaugh beside him, gun in hand. Dean Anson and Officer Nash, even former RA Troy watching, severe-looking yet inwardly enraptured.

But it's not Harbaugh. Not Garland. Not any of the ghosts I expected.

It's someone worse.

Someone I haven't spoken to in thirty years.

It's Mike Macmillan.

"Hey," I say.

Macmillan stands before me near the bench Liv and I occupied last night. Presumably where he and his pals kicked the hell out of me, leaving the Hitchcock-shaped bloodstain that wasn't washed away by today's rain.

The sky, which emptied earlier, promises something much heavier is coming.

Macmillan starts toward me. I stand my ground, no longer because I'm a tough guy—but because I'm frozen like that deer in my Eclipse's headlights.

He moves faster than anyone his size should, no doubt gaining momentum to run me over. To throw real force into the fist headed for my face.

I have this coming.

I deserve this.

I deserve worse.

And from the looks of things, maybe I'll get it.

At least the bullet would've made things fast, Danzinger whispers.

"I owe you an apology."

The world stops.

Once Liv told me what happened to Macmillan after my expulsion, I'd asked myself, *Should I apologize?*

The answer was, *Of course I should.* But then:

Is that something he'd even want? Or would it be embarrassing for him? Would he relive trauma he never should've lived through in the first place?

I owed him an apology. Still do. But I haven't said the words yet.

Because he beat me to them.

But what's he apologizing for?

Suddenly, it occurs to me. *He* was the one responsible.

For the beating last night.

For vandalizing my Prius during the game.

For ransacking my room at the Allentown Marriott.

For stealing my pills.

After what Liv told me became of his life after that punch, whatever it is, I had it coming.

Instead, he says, "Your buddy Kip just told me you were struggling with something, and he figured it was what happened between us. I'm not gonna say I had it coming. But the shit I pulled—that wasn't right either."

I try not to be shocked. Try to handle it all with panache. "You liked her, she liked you. I don't hold any grudges . . ."

"That's not exactly what I . . ." He studies my expression. "I'm sorry, I thought you knew. I thought she told you."

"Told me what?"

He kicks lightly at the ground. His cheeks become peach, almost orange.

"The condom thing," he says, "and the night you caught Jess in my lap . . ."

The Lap Glance.

"They weren't my ideas. But I went along with them. That's on me."

It takes me a moment to process.

While I'm elsewhere—partly on the bench with Liv, partly at Evelyn's getting shot at—Macmillan waves a hand in front of me. In a different time, a different world, maybe an alternate simulation, I might've bitten off his fingers.

But this is here, this is now, and I'm wondering if the bad guy who walked this campus thirty years ago stayed behind in Rhode Island after all.

Because that's where I eventually got clean. Sober. Finally—after shadowing JaMarcus Cooke beyond the courtroom to a lawyer's recovery group.

After making him a promise I was determined to keep.

"Who?" I say. "*Whose* idea was it?"

I'm expecting to hear him say "Liv," which would allow me to confront her. To end this once and finally, thirty years late, but at least not never.

"Cecilia's," he says.

The name lands with a thud. Not familiar, not even faintly.

"Who the hell is Cecilia?" I ask.

Immediately, the Simon & Garfunkel song gets stuck in my head.

My phone vibrates in my pocket.

I automatically excuse myself, reach in, and pull it out.

It's a text message.

From Creighton.

About *You Oughta Know.* By C. C. Candiotti.

Except this time, he doesn't use her initials but her nickname, which sounds the same.

Ceecee.

A lump forms in my throat.

I swallow hard and wonder:

Could the answers have been in my pocket the entire weekend?

51

Minutes later, on the bench in front of the Francis Magee Memorial Library, in a thickening rain, I unlock my phone and tap on the Kindle app. I touch the icon for *You Oughta Know* and only now see that it's just a couple thousand words, barely a short story.

What the hell, Creighton?

I almost close it before reading the first line of prose and realizing I should've read this much sooner. Because:

The story opens on a roof.

That night on the roof, the wind was still. The only sounds: music and mindless shouting from the Hills. That's when Kerry spotted him crossing the square, from the auditorium toward the freshman dorms.

She didn't hesitate. She ran downstairs and made it outside in time to catch him.

"Hey," she said, "are you okay?"

He looked angry, frustrated, but softened once he started talking. "Yeah, I'm cool. I'm just . . ." He motioned toward his building.

She gestured back toward hers. "Wanna come in for a drink?"

The last time she asked, he stood her up. Left a clipped voicemail saying he was meeting up with people. He promised to call her later to tell her where.

He never called.

Now he stared off toward the auditorium for what felt like eternity.

Finally, he said, "Sure, let's drink."

She felt an immediate twinge of excitement that she hadn't felt since her first night on campus.

Her first night with him.

The phone slips from my wet hands, takes a bad bounce off the bench, and lands face down on Hitchcock's bloody silhouette. When I bend to pick it up, a bolt of pain shoots through my lower back and I can't straighten up.

When I finally do, I almost faint from the agony.

Inside her room, he removed his boots and dropped to the floor.

Kerry grabbed two icy bottles of Michelob and handed him one. She snatched the bottle opener off the fridge door, but he twisted the cap, said, "It's all right. All domestics are screw-tops. Only imports need an opener." He lobbed the cap in the direction of the wastebasket but missed by a mile.

They drank. Well, he *drank. She turned on music, caving to his demand to hear Phish.*

Her roommate Hannah was away this weekend, leaving them two full nights together, alone. Enough time to seduce him, maybe even break it to him gently that this wasn't their first time together. Maybe she'd tell him about their first night at the Hills.

Maybe she'd even tell him about—

This time the rumbling thunder interrupts me. It's distant, but the valley creates an echo, carrying it closer. Across the campus, darker, heavier clouds are headed this way. They won't reach me for ten minutes at least, long enough to complete this short story.

And, one way or another, maybe put Jess's death to rest once and for all.

Kerry brought the Michelob to her lips for show, never actually sipping. She thought maybe he'd catch it, ask questions, leaving her an opening to tell him everything.

But he didn't.

He suggested drinking games.

Kerry humored him, watched him get plastered playing Six Degrees of Kevin Bacon against himself.

Her presence felt unnecessary. Until they ran out of beer and he turned and kissed her, deeply, passionately.

When she pulled back and looked into his eyes, she could tell he didn't see her. He was staring at someone else. Not gazing into her eyes but into his ex's. Into Jazz's.

The sex was great, even better than the first night.

After the second time, Kerry longed to tell him everything.

Well, almost everything.

What she privately called "The Sexy Adventures of Mighty Mouse" needed to stay between her and Hannah. Or else he'd never speak to her again.

"Do you remember our first weekend on campus?" she asked.

He struggled to keep his eyes open. His head lolled and he muttered something about needing to get back to his friend.

She smoothed her hand over his chest, returning him to a state of calm. Within sixty seconds, he was asleep next to her in bed.

She laid her head on his chest and let his heartbeat lull her into a light, dreamless sleep that promised forever.

Until a knock on the door at 3 a.m.

52

Kerry shot up in bed after the first knock. She glanced at the clock and tried to make sense of who'd be at her door at this time of night.

She wiped the sleep from her eyes. Slipped into her panties and Hannah's robe. After checking on her passed-out guest, she trudged to the door, expecting to find his best friend slumped against the wall, unable to keep his chin up, muttering gibberish.

She didn't even bother with the peephole. She was beyond cool with the RAs and other upperclassmen because her sister graduated the year before.

Kerry had been visiting the college since she was fifteen. Membership came with privileges. Like having an RA look the other way when you sneak a boy into your room. Like using an upstairs bedroom when you meet someone at a party at the Hills.

When Kerry opened the door, her jaw locked. Her heart pounded, loud and hard, in her chest. The room was dark, the hallway dim. She didn't know if the girl could see him asleep in her bed.

Kerry was afraid of what she might do, the scene she could cause. As the far less popular girl, Kerry would be left standing alone when it came time to choose sides.

Kerry held a finger to her lips. "Let's speak somewhere else."

The girl frowned but nodded okay. "We'll go to my room," she said.

But no. The thought of being in her room made Kerry sick. All the while, she'd picture him in her bed doing things he should've only done with Kerry.

"Is there anywhere else?" Kerry asked.

"I guess we can go to the roof."

Just minutes earlier, Macmillan admitted to staging two of the worst moments of my life. The worst two moments on campus before Jess's death.

The Condom Incident. The night Macmillan came to my room at Cormac, asking for a condom to sleep with the only girl I ever loved.

The Lap Glance. The night I peeked into Jess's room and found her on Macmillan's lap, their lips millimeters apart, as if they were about to kiss or just finished. Or both.

After he said it, I'd stood there, gobsmacked, drops of rain pelting my face. Macmillan looked up, saw it was falling harder. "I got to get a move on," he said. "Just wanted to let you know, if you're harboring any guilt, we're good, you and me. Or as good as we can be, anyway."

"Same," I said. "And for what it's worth, I'm sorry too. About what I did—and that the apology is three decades past due."

He nodded. "I know you paid your dues with the disciplinary committee. And that was my dad's doing. He threatened the dean. Expel you or face a lawsuit. He was an asshole." He paused. "He's dead now, so . . ."

I bowed my head.

The rain started coming down harder.

So we left it at that.

Hours after Kerry stood there on the roof, the wind made it difficult to hear. Music played in the distance, but the shouting was over. The campus was as silent as she'd ever heard it.

"I know you brought him to your room," the girl started.

Even as Kerry denied it, the girl assured her it was all right. She and Craig weren't together. She'd dumped him for a jackass juicehead who was cheating on his girlfriend back home.

Kerry pretended this was new information.

It wasn't.

Kerry and her roomie Hannah had dubbed the juicer Mighty Mouse so they could speak freely once Kerry shared her plan.

Initially, Hannah begged her to let it go. She considered Jazlyn ("Jazz") a friend—"a close *friend." But following a couple bottles of Mad Dog 20/20, Hannah was as excited about Kerry's plan as she was.*

It didn't require much thought. It was brilliant in its simplicity.

One night, Kerry told Mighty Mouse that Jazz was hot for him. That was all the encouragement he needed. It didn't matter that he had a girlfriend back home. He'd ride the wave as long as it lasted.

"What a pig," Hannah said that night.

Kerry wasn't sure if she meant her or Mighty Mouse.

Meanwhile, Kerry continued working on Craig. Sitting next to him in class. Approaching him in the caf. Following him to parties.

The problem was, he was in denial. Craig thought he and Jazz would reunite once she saw Mighty Mouse for what he was, an idiot only there because he could hit a baseball four hundred feet.

Kerry needed something Craig couldn't come back from.

"Let him see you together," she told Mighty Mouse the next day. "He's always with his buddy roaming the girls' dorm. One night, when she's showing affection, just leave her door open a crack."

Craig saw everything before Jazz jumped up and slammed the door, realizing she might've hurt him. She'd been careful until then and became indignant when Mighty Mouse laughed at Craig's expense.

She nearly dumped Mighty Mouse there and then.

Kerry's plan had backfired.

Regrettably, Craig was no less obsessed with Jazz after seeing her on his lap.

So she returned to Mighty Mouse for another favor. Hannah was sure he wouldn't go through with it. But when Kerry told him Craig was talking smack about him, the Good Mouse Almighty was ready to disgrace him in the cruelest way possible.

And Craig would have no one to blame but Jazz.

Mighty LOVED the idea. Especially since he hadn't even slept with her yet.

Kerry briefly worried about Craig's temper. What if the plan ended in disaster? It was a gamble she was willing to take.

The next day, as he passed Kerry's room, Mighty Mouse flashed a pair of Trojans and winked at her.

Kerry nearly fainted. Not metaphorically with joy. She literally had a dizzy spell and needed to lie down for a while.

She lit a vanilla- and lavender-scented candle, put on some Tom Waits, and rested her eyes, pondering how well her plan was working.

Kerry had continued chatting up Craig in their creative writing class. He confessed he'd been writing papers for money. She pinned the notation in her head but didn't think she'd need it. Not after the condom quest.

But even after that humiliation, Craig hadn't been swayed. And once Jazz dumped Mighty Mouse, it looked as if she and Craig might actually get together again. They spoke, they flirted. Once Kerry even saw Craig enter her room and stay.

Catholics and all their forgiveness bullshit!

She was about to give up, really she was. Kerry wasn't some desperate stalker who couldn't find someone else.

She'd arrived at college brimming with hope but shackled to the same crippling insecurities that made her invisible in high school.

But another four years like the last four just wouldn't do.

The first Friday night on campus she was emotionally charged yet tried to pace herself with the alcohol. But as the Hills filled up and groups gathered in circles, her pole position on the main sofa became a liability.

There, she was not only alone but on display. The comfiest spot in the entire town house was open right next to her, yet no one took it. It reminded her of her first day of first grade, when Audrey Briggs branded her with cooties. A severe case that lasted twelve years.

When Craig walked into the party, she thought nothing of him at first. He was cocky, bordering on arrogant, a shame because she thought she'd seen the real him eyeing her across the cafeteria earlier that day.

He had seemed quiet like her, shrinking into himself so he wouldn't be seen. Now he was with a friend, jabbering with upperclassmen he'd never met. She looked away in disgust. She was about to get up when the strangest thing happened.

Craig sat next to her.

Something fluttered in her chest. Fear and expectations swirled together in her stomach, and she almost scrambled upstairs to beg her sister's old friend for a spot to lie down. Then he said something to her.

"What's your name?"

To Kerry, he might as well have offered to fly her to Milan for breakfast. The intimacy she felt in that moment—and over the next forty minutes—was like none she'd ever experienced.

Here she had what she came for. Male validation and proof that her reinvention was successful.

That night she used sex in order to feel something new and exciting.

Craig used it like he used liquor and weed—to avoid feeling anything at all.

When he acted like he didn't know her the next day, she felt sick, wounded, cursed. Did he really not remember? Or was this just his way of saying they'd been a mistake?

Commiserating with Hannah, she became convinced he was a dog, a player like the ones she knew in high school. A child in grown-ups' clothing.

Then she saw him with Jazz.

Night after night, she watched from her window as they crossed the freshman parking lot, heading to the cafeteria for dinner.

One night, visiting a friend on the second floor, she heard his voice and Jazz's laughter, and it felt like an ice pick to the heart.

He seemed to love her.

Week after week, she watched in awe and horror. Thinking constantly: That could be me with him and the four others. Had Kerry's fate really hinged on the dorm lottery? She felt so close, yet so, so far.

It was like her father's definition of hell: "God's light is visible but forever out of reach."

Using Mighty Mouse as a pawn, hope had returned. But by then, she'd seen the true Craig. The jealous, needy, territorial alcoholic who now reeked of desperation himself.

Then, one morning after breakfast, Kerry rushed back to her dorm and stuck her head in the toilet.

With all the drinking she'd done the past few weeks, it seemed normal. Except she hadn't drunk the night before. Not a drop.

Could it be withdrawal?

Did she catch the flu?

When Hannah returned from class she found Kerry on the floor in the bathroom.

She told Hannah she'd been sick.

Hannah took her temperature. No fever.

"When was your last period?" Hannah asked.

Kerry thought she meant her course schedule that morning.

Then it hit her. Her period.

She didn't know!

Kerry ran to her closet to check the tampons her mother stuffed in with her other supplies. The box hadn't been opened.

"Not since I've been on campus," Kerry said, suddenly short of breath.

"Were you with someone this summer?" Hannah asked.

But Hannah knew that she hadn't been. And she hadn't told Hannah—or anyone else—about her first Friday night on campus.

A night Craig didn't even remember.

Only now am I certain what I hold in my hand. The killer's confession.

It's been in my possession the entire weekend.

Whoever sent this to Creighton, pretending to be from Trigger Finger Press, *wanted* me to read it. Presumably, before now.

I only waited two days because I'd been so consumed with the investigation—and someone stole my meds.

And beat me senseless.

Which likely means someone also *didn't* want me to read it.

But who?

Not Macmillan. He'd told me everything. How Stacy was going by her middle name these days—Cecilia, a.k.a. Ceecee, a.k.a. *C. C.*—and, of course, her husband's surname. *Candiotti.*

All of which could've been discovered through a simple Google search. If only I'd ever considered my concrete alibi a serious suspect.

If only I'd ever taken Stacy C. Rennick Candiotti seriously.

Like a woman.

Like a human being.

53

On the roof, Kerry sympathized with Jazz about the juicehead, really. She'd dated assholes like him, which was why she had been attracted to Craig in the first place. For his mind, for his wit. For the way he looked at her that first night.

The way he chose *her.*

Headlights appeared in the freshman parking lot. Both girls ducked, crawling to the ledge to peek over the side.

Just some drunks coming back from the Black Pepper Pub or Coopersburg Diner.

Once the drunks were inside, the girls rose and retreated to the rear of the roof, where they wouldn't be spotted from the parking lot.

"I know this is sooo inappropriate," Jazz said. "But I absolutely need *to speak to Craig tonight. Can I bring him up here to talk for a few minutes?"*

"About what?" Kerry said, surprised by her own boldness, her defiance.

Jazz, too, was surprised by Kerry's reaction. She folded her arms across her chest and said, "Sorry, but that's really none of your business, Kerr."

"It isn't? He's in my *bed. I'm pretty sure that makes it my business, at least for tonight."*

Jazz uncrossed her arms and dropped them at her sides in resignation. "I made a huge mistake," she confessed. "The way I left things with him. I just want to tell him that. I need him to know that I'm sorry and . . . that I care about him."

As the wind picked up, howling like it was hungry, Kerry's mirthless laugh startled even her.

"Listen, Jazz," she said, "as much as I'd like to oblige, Craig is with me *now."*

Jazz laughed.

She laughed in Kerry's face.

"With you?" Jazz said with incredulity. "You think he's going to stay with some girl who dug him up wasted from the square the night of the homecoming dance? Are you crazy?"

"We've been together before," Kerry said.

"What? When?"

"Our first Friday night on campus."

"So, you're the one I saw him with at the Hills?!" Jazz said, covering her face with her hands. "Well, if you really were, I wouldn't brag about it, because he doesn't even remember!"

"Shut the hell up," Kerry warned in a tone more menacing than she thought herself capable of.

"You're nothing and no one to him, Kerry! You're just some freak dressed in black annoying him in his favorite class." When she saw Kerry's shock, Jazz went for the jugular. "That's right, Kerr, he spoke about you. How you follow him around and try to get a seat next to him in creative writing. He called you a goddamn stalker!"

Kerry didn't know who she was angrier with at that moment, Jazz or Craig. She saw them both standing there in front of her, the tiny dotted lights from Wilkes Hall just past them over their shoulders. Then:

Something came over Kerry, a fury she'd never felt before.

Her arms were already extending outward when she realized they were in motion. They were moving so fast, with so much strength. Strength Kerry never knew she possessed. She tried to pull back but couldn't.

Her palms connected with Jazz's upper chest.

Jazz sprang backward, with a confused look on her face that swiftly turned to pleading as she lost her balance.

But it was too late.

Jazz's momentum was carrying her over the side.

With futility, Kerry reached out, grabbed air. Then held her hands to her ears so she wouldn't hear the accompanying scream.

She heard it anyway.

It was loud but brief.

Immediately followed by a hard, stomach-tossing thump that would forever haunt her sleep.

54

The morning after the homecoming dance, Craig stirred next to Kerry as she pretended to sleep. He shifted, probably guessing where he was again. Waking in strange places had become a habit for him in the three short months since they first met. The three short months since they slept together.

Kerry worried he'd notice she was breathing too hard, sweating. But lying on her stomach, she didn't know whether he even glanced at her, let alone recognized her or took stock of her physical condition.

He certainly never touched her; he went to great efforts not *to. After several anxious seconds she felt his weight lift from the bed.*

Then, for an extended moment, she did *feel his eyes on her. He was studying her bare back from a few feet away. She'd thrown off her robe, slipped out of her panties, and managed to pull the sheet halfway up. He was likely staring at the curve of her ass, determining whether to wake her or flee.*

He chose the latter. Again.

Kerry heard him gathering his clothes. Heard him slip into his jeans and flannel shirt. Heard him gather his Timberlands and shove his feet into them.

Then a chill as he opened the window—sharp enough to make her shiver. She froze for a moment, unsure if he'd noticed. If he did, he didn't act on it. Instead, he climbed onto her desk and, the moment voices came from the hall, flung himself out the window.

She heard him hit the ground. Hard. He landed with a groan. Briefly, there were footfalls on grass, then no sound at all except for the baying wind, its chill clinging to her bones.

She jumped out of bed naked, crossing her arms over her breasts. She watched Craig round the corner just as a professor passed him on the pavement. She resisted the urge to slam the window shut and instead eased it down so as not to make any noise.

Then she climbed back into bed and curled up tight, chasing whatever warmth she could find beneath her comforter.

Curled up there she waited and waited for . . .

What. Felt. Like. Forever.

Until, like a nail through her eardrums, she finally registered a girl's scream emanating from the lawn behind the freshman girls' dormitory.

Someone had found Jazz.

It wasn't until the scream—*"Oh God! Jess!"*—echoed in my memory that I fell out of the fictive dream and realized where I was.

Back on the bench.

Rain soaking my Centaurs cap, my jeans, the stitches on my eyebrow.

The Kindle app still open.

The bloody silhouette of Hitchcock still visible a few feet away.

I'd just read it all.

Stacy's story. Cecilia's confession. Kerry's revelation.

Whatever name she gave the killer on the roof, she wasn't the girl I remember.

This was someone lonelier.

Smarter.

Sicker.

And me?

I was the object.

The accidental catalyst.

The boy passed out in bed while two girls circled each other in the dark.

Over me. *But no . . .*

Over the me they thought they saw beneath the surface.

The me that didn't even exist, at least not then.

There's no version of this story where I'm the hero.

No version where I can say: *I saw her. I understood her. I stopped it.*

All I did was sleep.

Sleep through the most devastating moment of two women's lives.

I always thought learning the truth would feel more . . . satisfying.

Especially if it cleared me. But this . . .

This just feels like more grief. More guilt.

Not the kind of guilt that collapses you.

The kind that burns clean through.

55

Minutes later, Center Valley University is no longer waiting for rain.

The rain isn't just falling—it's coming down in sheets, thick as a tarp.

Atop the roof of D'Amelio Hall, I stand alone—bruised, broken, and soaked to the bone.

Gazing out over the three hundred acres of campus, I witness Center Valley University release its alumni back into the wild for another year.

But I'm not going anywhere.

Because after all that, I'm confident I finally have the answers to the questions I've been asking myself for the past thirty years.

The answers are in the Kindle app. On my phone. Still damp in my pocket. And this roof is exactly where I expect to find its author—C. C. Candiotti, a.k.a. Stacy Cecilia Rennick.

This wasn't just some game to her. She wasn't simply a jealous girl crushing hard. She was a saboteur, a savage, a sociopath. And Jess—Jess had no idea.

"It's been a minute, hasn't it?"

I turn at the sound of her voice and find Stacy Rennick standing several yards away under the overhang from the door that exits onto the roof.

"What happened that Friday night of Freshman Orientation?" I call out to her.

She pretends she doesn't know what I'm talking about.

I pull my phone from my pocket.

The Kindle app is still open, the words now blurred by the downpour. I hold it up so Stacy can see it.

Rage rises in my chest.

I attempt to slow it down by managing my breaths.

Gradually, I regain focus.

"Did you just pass this on to my agent to have a good chuckle this weekend?"

I step under the overhang, soaking wet, but standing eye to eye with her.

Stacy continues her silence, her eyes speaking volumes of the contempt she holds for me, which I don't yet fully understand.

How do I get her to talk to me?

"Your protagonist's a creep," I say. "Despicable even. *Irredeemable.* Your prose? Pedestrian. Juvenile. And your title? It just plain sucks."

I can't tell whether she's squinting from the rain in her eyes or still trying to deny that she knows what I'm referring to. Or maybe after thirty years and a homicide between us, she can't believe I'm standing here on the roof skewering her story.

"At least tell me what really happened," I say.

"You *read* it, didn't you?" she cries in a voice that sounds identical to Jess's.

I look past Stacy on the stairwell but see no one coming up behind her. *Did Stacy's lips move?* Did her voice echo as if she was standing *inside* the stairwell instead of outside under the overhang with me? I'm almost certain it did. I've experienced auditory hallucinations before but never anything so intense.

I glance down at the phone again. There's a call coming in.

It's Creighton.

As I'm about to hit the red ignore button, Stacy says, "I'd answer that if I were you."

I pause with my lips parted. "You *know* him?"

"Yes," she says. "I know him."

I stare at the phone, my thumb still hovering over the red button.

I hit the green one instead.

"Creighton?" I say, pressing the phone to my ear.

"How's tricks, Gregg-o?"

56

“Creighton,” I say into the phone as the rain pelts the roof, “I’ll call you back.”

Once I’ve ended the call, I stare at Stacy Rennick, who’s as beautiful as she was back then. But now there’s something in her bright blue eyes that portends the kind of trouble that’s overwhelming, sometimes even final.

“What do you *want*?” I ask her.

“He’s always wanted to meet you.”

I take a step back. Back into the steady, hard rain as the darkening sky threatens to empty the heavens onto us.

“I *told* him what you were like,” she says. “I told him you were striking to look at, especially your eyes. But you were *stricken* too.”

Kerry Maven was pregnant.

Lightning crashes in the distance, soon followed by earth-trembling thunder.

Meaning, Stacy was pregnant too.

I’d assumed from the story that she lost the baby or terminated the pregnancy, neither of which I wanted to dwell on.

But no.

Stacy had the baby.

I stare down at the phone in my hand, and the puzzle pieces fall into place like a game of *Tetris*.

The hunger in his eyes.

A look I once had.

A look that fades with time.

Stacy smiles thinly. "Congratulations." The sentiment is a cold slap in the face. "It's a boy."

Time stands still.

I finally realize why the hole's still there, why it's growing, why it's been so much larger than father-size for so long. Not knowing who your father is—that's a hell of a thing. But not knowing all this time—these twenty-nine years—that you have a child . . .

A son.

Creighton.

"Why?" I cry, though I hardly have any voice.

"You really should've opened the book earlier."

The irony splits me like an axe. Especially having written eighteen papers on Joseph Heller's *Catch-22* thirty years ago. I've been sideswiped—and *why*?

For not doing my goddamn *homework*.

"Why now?" I hold up the phone, her story still on the screen. "Why like *this*? How did you even know I'd *be* here this weekend?"

She pushes some hair out of her face. "I know everything that's in your phone. It took my PI all of six minutes to install an app when she asked to borrow it at ShopRite. Who, besides the Big Lebowski, grocery shops in their bathrobe, by the way?"

I eye my phone like it's betrayed me. "She installed spyware?" My lower lip hangs down as if it's being pulled by a fishhook. "You've been watching me this entire time?"

"We've even been talking, Gregg. Remember Toni and Liv sending you messages begging you to come to Homecoming? I bet when you arrived, they were surprised to see you, weren't they?"

I was catfished.

Spied on and catfished.

Spied on and catfished and *lured* here.

With a sardonic laugh, I ask, "Why not just *kill* me?"

"Because this isn't the nineties, Gregg. Murder is so last century. You'd know that if you spent more time in the real world."

I manage to summon indignation. "Excuse me if I like to get away as *far* as possible, as *fast* as possible."

"You always have."

I instantly catch her meaning.

"I didn't know about him," I tell her. "About Creighton."

I think of all the years I missed with him.

All the milestones.

All the memories never formed.

As if the past three decades were one great blackout.

"What do you *want*?" I ask her again.

"Creighton's compensation."

I bark a laugh. "You think I have *money*?"

She smirks. "I *know* you don't. I have access to your phone, remember? To your bank accounts, credit cards, email. You could've *handwritten* every copy of the last book you sold. Del Danzinger's *done*."

The hell I am, Danzinger whispers.

"Then what's this all about?"

"Books today are all about lies, lies, lies," she says. "The word's in every other title. I wanted to write just *one* story that was all about telling the truth."

I hold the phone up again. "This isn't the *truth*. This story is about *your* choices, Stacy. *Not* mine."

"We *both* made choices."

I blink.

She's right.

Drinking may aid in clearing your conscience, but it doesn't absolve your sins.

Lifting my brows, I suddenly look at Stacy differently. In a serious way, a way I never have before. As much as she deserved to be taken seriously.

Stacy Rennick. The mother of my son.

My son.

My son Creighton.

Creighton the Great.

Creighton, the literary agent.

"What happens now?" she says.

"Do you mean, do you go to prison for killing Jess?"

When she doesn't respond, I work the answer out in my head.

I could call Chief Lindsay right now and end this thirty-year nightmare. Tell her what Stacy confessed on the roof and in her short story. Tell her Jess's death isn't some cold case mystery but the result of a shove, a flash of temper.

Maybe Jess's mother would finally sleep at night.

Maybe I'd feel less like a coward.

But then, I think of Creighton. My son. My second chance to do something right. And the idea of ripping his mother away guts me.

I've spent most of my life angry at the world for what I lost. What does it say about me if I'm willing to make him feel the same?

Yes, Jess deserves justice. But Stacy's been carrying her own prison around for three decades.

And me?

I'm just trying to learn how to live without burning down what's left.

If it were cold-blooded, I tell myself, I'd turn her in. But it wasn't. It was stupid and cruel and impulsive, like everything we were back then.

If Macmillan's story taught me anything, it's that vengeance doesn't heal. It only destroys more. Not just the target but everything and everyone in its path.

Besides, Creighton would never forgive me. And if he's willing to accept me, I'm finally ready to be his dad.

"Are you sure he's mine?" I say.

"Positive. While I was back home pregnant—you never noticed—you were sleeping with Hannah. She snagged a few hair samples."

I reach for my head.

"Not *those* hairs," she says.

I wince, my hand reflexively heading south.

"How do I know that's the tru—"

"We can do another test at the lab. First thing tomorrow if you'd like."

In my head, JaMarcus reminds me that agreeing to a test can be as effective as taking one.

But that's not the case here. Stacy Rennick isn't bluffing.

"Does your husband know?"

"He knows. The first one did too. This one's even a good stepfather. They get along okay, him and Creighton."

"But Creighton's drug problems . . ."

She throws up her hands. "I can't imagine *where* he gets them from," she says.

Is that all I've given that poor kid?

I've given my son nothing in twenty-nine years. *Nothing*. Except for a coke habit and 15 percent of my dwindling book sales.

And the look.

That hunger in his eyes.

That I gave him.

"But his personality . . . ?" I say.

This time she laughs. "Mostly fake. Just for you. He knows it bugs the hell out of you, and he loves it. You've never met the *real* Creighton. Just the mask he made for you."

I attempt a smile that doesn't quite make it. But I think I *did* meet the real Creighton. Just once—over the phone at the Allentown Marriott—a couple nights ago. When he called drunk and snorting lines on the Upper East Side. When he all but cried out for help.

I shrug, immediately regretting it, as an intense pain surfs down my spine. "But after all this time, why now?"

"There have been advances in DNA technology," she says. "Recently, Ancestry told us something else you might want to know."

"About Creighton?"

"About *you*." She pauses. "About Mustache Man."

Mustache Man? "I *told* you about him?"

"You told me about a *lot* of things, Gregg. When you were drunk—which was pretty much all the time—you held nothing back."

While she speaks I can't help but scroll through my memories of the past thirty years. If Creighton had been in my life, would *I* have turned out differently? Would I have married Stacy? Would I have taken them both up to Rhode Island with me?

Or would I have never gotten expelled and left Center Valley in the first place? Would I have realized I didn't want to be an attorney? Would I have skipped law school and hundreds of thousands in debt?

Would all those dark years at Bristol have gone differently?

Without booze, without drugs?

"Things would've been different had I known," I tell her with a certainty I feel in my gut.

"I know," she says. "That's why you never knew."

My eyes well. "You kept my son from me."

"You weren't ready."

"How can you *know* that?"

"Because I knew how you grew up," she says. "You told me everything. I was terrified you'd become your mother. *Or* your father. Because, at the time, you were sure it was Mustache Man. You even called him Mustache *Dad*. You thought he left you there at the flea market, knowing you were suffering, knowing your mother wasn't well. You thought he *abandoned* you, so I thought so too. I didn't want that for my son. And your behavior those first few months of college . . . It didn't seem like a phase anymore. I believed that's *exactly* who you'd become."

"So, why now?"

"Because now I know your father didn't abandon you."

"What?"

"He never even knew about you."

"He *did*," I say. "He left my mother because he didn't want me. Never wanted anything to do with me."

"She lied to you, Gregg. Mustache Man left *her*, yes. But he *wasn't* your father. He was a man your mother married for the sake of appearances because she was pregnant. She convinced him you were his. Then, right after you were born, he ordered a paternity test." She hesitates before adding, "You aren't even the same ethnicity as him."

That last bit hits me like a brick to the face. Suddenly, so many of my mother's racist rants that oddly seemed to be directed at me hit me right where they were meant to.

"My private detective," she says, though I can barely hear her for the blood rushing through my ears. "I had her track down people who knew your mother at the time."

"You had your investigator dig into my past?"

"I'm sorry for everything you went through as a child."

I nod, lost somewhere I've never been.

"I just . . . I thought you oughta know."

It's 1983. Mommy's car idles at the gas station. Once I asked her why she keeps the engine running even though all those big red explosive signs say to shut it off. She says they're just trying to scare us.

She never says who, but I assume the spickets because they're the ones who usually work these crappy jobs. Because they're lazy, she says. Like me. They have no education and don't belong in our country. She calls them animals.

I wish I could begin reading again, but all my thoughts are getting in the way. I don't like to think. At least not about things in the real world. Like school, where I need to get all A's. Because what would the other kids' parents think of her, a teacher, with a failure for a son? She'd be a failure too.

I don't want to make Mommy a failure.

I've already ruined her life so much.

57

Minutes later, following alternating rounds of awkward shouting and deafening silence, I hold up my phone and say, "This story is a full confession, you realize. It's . . ."

Stacy shakes her head. "This is a work of fiction, Gregg. Names, characters, places, and incidents are either a product of the author's imagination or used fictitiously. All that matters is that the intended audience gets the message."

"The intended audience being me?"

"I thought it was about time you finally paid me some attention."

I stay silent.

Her phone dings. It's a chime, like bracelets jingling-jangling together, and it causes my neck muscles to instantly harden like a rock.

The sound is almost like a signal. Not like the Bat-Signal but an alert, like Spidey Sense.

As soon as I hear it, my back gets *really* stiff *really* fast, and I shift my face in the opposite direction of the sound so it won't get hit.

Even though the bracelets, even then, didn't necessarily mean a hit was coming.

Sometimes Mommy just moves around like a normal person.

Stacy looks at her screen and says she has to go.

"Stay here," she tells me. "Don't let Liv see us together. She might get the wrong idea. I think she really likes you."

"What about Jess?"

She shrugs. "What about her?"

"Who wrote that message on Liv's whiteboard?"

She takes a step back toward the stairwell but lifts a single finger in a gesture that's an admission. She's the author. Not just of *You Oughta Know* but *One last sunrise, Jess?*

Which means she also wrote the message Jess awoke to following the Night of a Thousand Plushies. The one telling her, *Keep screwing Frank. I'm done.*

Had Jess not read it, we might've spoken in class the next day.

We might've gotten back together.

Or not.

True, I wasn't ready to be a father back then.

Maybe I wasn't even fit to be a boyfriend.

What I needed most from Jess was her friendship.

And I lost it.

"So, you killed her," I say quietly.

My stomach turns as I think of Jess, pushed from the roof. Falling, falling, falling—until she broke into pieces.

All because of my recklessness, my insensitivity, my obliviousness.

"You killed her and you're getting away scot-free."

"You can always turn me in if you think you have the evidence," she says.

As a lawyer, I *know* there's insufficient evidence to convict her and, therefore, insufficient evidence to charge her. No prosecutor wants to take on a case they know they're going to lose. Especially one thirty years old.

I think of the jacket copy and how she refers to her ex as the person actually responsible for Jess's death. "You blame me, don't you."

"I think you do too. No less now than before this weekend."

She lets that settle on me.

I *am* to blame. I need to own the choices I made. To recognize the harm they've caused. Some that can't be undone.

I thought I survived my past and outgrew my worst impulses.

But I didn't survive it.

I *escaped* it.

And, in doing so, left behind a trail of damage I've never acknowledged.

"So what happens next," I say, "assuming the story continues. *Tell* me. Why not just spare me the suspense."

She nods, compassion and understanding finally warming her face.

But not her bright blue eyes.

They remain ice cold.

"She kills him," she says as her hands move toward both pockets.

For a moment, time slows.

As I watch her hands slide into her pockets, I fear I'm going to piss myself because I absolutely *know*, as sure as I do in any movie, that she's about to pull out a gun.

About to aim it at me from point-blank range and squeeze the trigger, putting an end to the life of one Gregg Dryer.

Because what are the odds, even in the worst fan fiction, of two guns, both loaded with blanks, being fired at me on the same day?

The last face I see will be Stacy's.

A woman I should've cared more for.

A mother who only wanted to protect her child from his boogeyman.

His Mr. Hyde.

But no . . .

This time I'm wrong.

Her hands are clearly stuffed into her pockets for warmth.

"So, this weekend," I say, trying to steady my trembling. "This is my punishment for a pair of one-night stands thirty years ago?"

There's a hint of a smile on her lips when she asks, "Do you think you deserve more?"

Do I deserve more? Of course I do. But there's no reason to tell Stacy Rennick that. Not here, not now, certainly not on the roof.

"So it's over?"

"Not entirely."

"What more can we possibly take from each other?"

She tilts her head, surprised to hear the words spring from my lips. "Jess's death haunted me. From your books, I knew it haunted you too. In *Another Man's Hell,* Danzinger loses his young wife on their honeymoon. It destroys him. But . . . he had nothing to do with her death. Not a shred of guilt. So he's spent nineteen books pitying himself. Blaming others. Being bitter. Feeling entitled to his anger. It made me wonder if *you* felt that way. If you did, I wanted you to feel how I felt."

She's got us there, Danzinger whispers.

"Part of me always felt like I robbed myself and Creighton of a life with you," she says. "When you first got published and seemed so happy on social media, I *missed* you, I even *wanted* you for a while. But at some point, I realized it was all an illusion."

Frigging Faceland.

"Besides," she says, "regardless of who your father was, I don't think you would've wanted us, Gregg. Maybe you would've tried. Maybe you'd have even made it thirty years, I don't know. But I'm pretty certain that if you did, you'd resent us for it today."

I say nothing.

How can I argue with that?

But I also need to know what's coming. So, I ask her. "What's . . . ?"

"Next?" she says. "Remember the first thing we learned in creative writing? For a character to truly learn a lesson, there needs to be real-world consequences."

"What . . ." Frozen and fogged, I stumble on my words. "What . . . do you mean?"

She shrugs as the last trace of a smile falls from her face. "Hell hath no fury . . ."

Like a woman scorned, Danzinger whispers.

As Stacy slips slowly backward into the shadows of the stairwell, four much larger forms come forward. Not just large but *ginormous.*

"Running out on me isn't all you did here freshman year," she calls out.

I think of the trashed hotel room, my vandalized Prius, my ass-kicking outside the Francis Magee Memorial Library. Stacy wasn't behind any of that. Those weren't the actions of a middle-aged woman. That was the work of . . .

College freshmen.

One of them, Zack Macmillan.

I take a step in reverse, tilt my head backward to eye how far I am from the ledge and thus, death.

Zack and his friends continue approaching as I backpedal. "I apologized, Zack—your dad and I *both* did. We worked things out. You can *ask* him."

The giants keep coming. I'm running out of room.

Mike Macmillan may have forgiven me.

But his kid Zack sure as hell hasn't.

"Oh, shit," I mutter, holding up my hands. "All right, *listen*, Zack and Zack's friends. What happened between me and your dad . . ."

Then the beating commences.

As I throw my arms up in front of my face and pull my legs in tight to protect the family jewels, I remind myself that, if nothing else, I've demonstrated—ever since I was a little kid—that I can take a beating. I can take a beating and get back up.

Every. Goddamn. Time, Danzinger whispers.

As I register new levels of pain in parts of my body I didn't know existed, Stacy Rennick, the cute French Canadian from my freshman year creative writing class, cries out one final thing.

"For what it's worth, Gregg, it was nice seeing you again!"

Strangely enough, it was nice seeing her too.

But I have no intention in hell of ever saying so.

At the gas station, I finally give up and close The Pigman *in my lap. I trace my finger over the design on the book jacket, which is protected by plastic because I borrowed it from the library.*

I imagine my name being where Paul Zindel's is.

That's it! That's what's been nibbling around my brain this whole time.

I'm so excited (like Pointer Sisters excited) to tell her because she always asks me what I want to be when I grow up and I never give a good answer.

She hates everything I come up with.

"I decided what I wanna be when I grow up, Mommy!"

She's not interested, which maybe is for the best. Maybe I shouldn't say anything. Maybe if I don't tell her, she won't remind me how stupid and selfish I am.

But I can't help myself. This one could make her happy because it's hard work and you use your brain, unlike the animals who pick up garbage and pump gas and clean classrooms and toilets for a living, like the spickets.

"I want to be a writer!" I say.

When she turns to look at me, I expect her to smile. But she doesn't. Instead, she scrunches up her face like she just sucked on a lemon. She wants to know, "What kind of writer?"

I didn't realize there was more than one kind.

What if I pick the wrong one?

I hold up The Pigman. *"Like this writer. I want to tell stories about fake people in fake worlds."*

"Writing isn't a career," she hisses. "No one gives a damn about what you have to say. They only want to know what you can do *for them. Like a doctor. Or even better, a lawyer, so you can sue the shit out of anyone who takes advantage of your mother."*

That doesn't sound fun. "I don't think I'd like suing shit out of people," I tell her. "I think I'd rather tell stories." I think about it, hard. "Maybe I can tell stories about lawyers suing shit out of people!"

Angry Mommy appears. "Only if you want to do it on the streets with the other bums, because writers die starving and drunk and penniless. They're scum! Books aren't a career. They're barely a hobby."

I don't like starving. Sometimes, when Mommy's mad at me, I'm not allowed to eat. Like when I try to hide under the table at flea markets so I won't get sunburned too badly.

"But writing's a job, right?" I ask her.

"It's not a job, not a real job. You need a real *job. One that pays a salary."*

"But some people do it for money," I say, holding up the book.

Her face darkens, her anger rising with each word. "Writing is a pipe dream. You're a bastard. You don't get to dream. You get to work*."*

Something inside me dies when I hear those words. Something in my tummy, something in my chest. The whole idea of being a writer dies in my mind. And I want to cry. But when I cry, she says I sound like a pig being slaughtered. Loud and stupid. And helpless. Because no one's coming to save me. Not now, not ever.

I look down at the book, wondering why people don't get paid to tell stories.

The Pigman *is so important to me—even when I'm not reading it, even when I'm just thinking about it, trying to fall asleep.*

Sometimes even just holding it makes me feel better, like if Mad Mommy comes, I can open the cover and dive in and hide in the pages with the Pigman, where no one will find me.

That night I stare at the author photo on the back of the book and cry like a big crybaby for Mr. Zindel, who must be lying somewhere, starving and drunk and dead and penniless.

He must not have a smart mommy always looking out for him like I do.

58

Awakening is painful. Even as a metaphor.

I regain consciousness at the edge of the roof so that I'm looking down onto the freshman parking lot. I have no clue how much time has passed, but it's all but stopped raining, and any additional cars that arrived for Homecoming weekend are gone.

Except one.

Is it Toni's?

Fenton's?

Kip's?

"Hi," she says, hovering above me.

Painfully, I roll over. *"Liv."*

"Let's just get this out of the way," she deadpans. "I didn't do this."

"How'd you know where to find me, then?"

Ow, it hurts to laugh.

But I'm still alive.

"That bitch Stacy Rennick said you were up here. You didn't . . . ?"

I spit blood.

Oh, damn, and a tooth.

I roll my tongue over the survivors.

And, yup, it's a front one.

"No," I assure her, "I only kissed the rooftop gravel and a bunch of knuckles."

That sounds weird. I think I'm somewhat concussed.

Hell, maybe that'll fix things upstairs. Like in those Bugs Bunny cartoons.

That rabbit cracks me up.

Ow, that's right—it hurts to laugh.

Seeing me grimace in pain, Liv comes to my aid. Slowly, she helps me sit up, then sits down next to me, at first crisscross applesauce, then (realizing that's just not happening with my gimpy legs) with both our feet dangling over the side of the building like two middle-aged parents at the deep end of the swimming pool. A couple who only wants to get their feet wet and nothing more.

Sucking up the pain raging through my body, I tell Liv everything. Starting with why I came to Homecoming and my suspicions about my friends. About what transpired all three days: at the Black Pepper Pub, during the alumni dinner, the baseball game, the trip to Nazareth, the Hootie concert, today's brunch, Evelyn's blanks, and everything in between.

I also tell her everything I remember going through my head, which I may regret when I'm less concussed. I tell her, too, about Alissa, about Chloé and my other relationships. Given the kicks my head has taken this weekend, maybe I even repeat a few things.

Only now, sitting here battered and concussed, do I finally see it—that the violence I inherited didn't just haunt me. It spilled out. Onto people like Mike Macmillan.

Now that I see it, I can't *unsee* it.

Now that I know everything, I'm overwhelmed with remorse.

Just as my mother tried to steal mine, I *succeeded* in robbing Macmillan of his chance of pursuing his dream.

Of course, his actions need to be considered too.

Not by me, though. Only by him.

And, unlike me, he seems to have done his homework.

Because we're all responsible for our own choices. And the problems they cause.

All our decisions ripple far into the future in ways even the finest storytellers can't imagine.

"Gregg," Liv is saying as she waves a hand in front of my face.

I snap out of it. "Sorry," I tell her. "Dead zone."

"Where were you?"

She looks at me like I just stepped off an alien spaceship.

That's right, I haven't gotten there yet.

"Turns out, I have a twenty-nine-year-old kid," I say. "His name's Creighton. Creighton the Great. He's a literary agent."

"You have a son with *Stacy*?" She shakes her head in disbelief. "What does she want after all this time? Money?"

"Nah, she's got plenty of that."

I tell her about Mustache Man, who *isn't* my Mustache Dad after all. And the unknown Hispanic man who *is*. Who likely doesn't even know I exist.

If he's still alive, that is.

Every day I don't find him makes it a little less likely I ever will.

"Gregg?" Liv's saying, waving a hand in my face. "You left again." She waits for me to say something. When I don't, she says, "Let's get you back to urgent care. You're going to need more stitches. Hate to break it to you, but you're going to look like Frankenstein for a while."

"Frankenstein's *monster*," I say with something akin to a wink. "I don't want to boast, but I know how much women love to be corrected by men."

She laughs, so over-the-top she lets fly a double snort, and I think: *What a beautiful geek.*

"After urgent care," she says, "we can stop off at the Coop for a hot open-faced roast beef sandwich with brown gravy."

My heart stops for a moment. I stare at her the way we all stared at Kevin Spacey at the end of *The Usual Suspects* back in the nineties.

"How do you . . . ?" I start as dizziness begins sweeping over me. "How do you know that's what I order?"

My mind races back through the lines of C. C. Candiotti's *You Oughta Know* for some second conspirator hidden between the pages, one only revealed at the very, very end when you think the writer's just tying up loose ends, dotting their t's and crossing their i's.

"Because," she says, "you ordered it when we met at the Coop Friday night."

"Oh yeah." I collect my thoughts. "So where did I leave off in the story?"

"You were alone here on the roof of D'Amelio—'bruised, broken, and soaked to the bone.'"

I'm pretty sure she's having fun at my expense, but she's right. I spend too much time in the dead zone these days.

I end the tale with Stacy's exit and Zack Macmillan's entrance here on the roof.

"So, Zack—" she starts.

The beating will last longer than the bruises or the broken rib I feel shifting when I breathe too deep. It not only cracked open bones and flesh but something I didn't know was still locked down. The dumb kid who showed up here in '93 thinking he was bulletproof is finally gone. What's left is a man who knows pain, knows how it lingers, and how sometimes it's the only thing that proves you're alive.

Whenever I catch my reflection, I'll see Jess's ghost in the swelling around my eye, in the jagged scars that'll form across my forehead and lips. It's like the universe finally listened and forced me to wear my grief on the outside instead of in.

This beating wasn't about today. It was about everything I never faced, everything buried under decades of silence. Maybe it needed to happen. Maybe I needed to get knocked down more than once this weekend, to finally feel the weight of it all, to remember why I returned here in the first place.

"So, what's next?" Liv says, rising to her feet. "What are you going to do about Creighton?"

It's a good question and, like most good questions, I don't have an answer to it.

"I'll call him when I'm back home," I say, using every last scintilla of strength to push myself off the gravel and rise to my feet. "Play it by ear. If he wants me in his life, I'll be there."

She nods her approval and places a palm on my chest, near my heart.

"How about you?" I say.

Liv lifts her slender shoulders. "I guess I go back," she says with a sadness that makes me ache for her. "Back to my life. Back to my home. Back to my marriage."

I look at her, my broken and bloodied face in pain, my vision blurred, but my head never clearer. "What if you don't?" I ask her.

Her gaze falls on me, though I can't tell what she's thinking.

I never could.

But only now that I've shared with her the entire story do I realize that this narrative, if I write it—*when* I write it—must be nonlinear. Because every part of our lives affects every other part, no matter what lies we tell ourselves.

No matter where we hide.

Or how far we run.

It all matters, Danzinger whispers.

Liv rests her head on my shoulder. "It's not the worst idea you've ever had," she says.

"It's not," I say, leaning into her for warmth and finding it. "Not by a long shot."

Epilogue
Fall 2025

August & Everything After

I never wrote *Freshmen.*

A day after I returned to Jersey, I called Creighton to invite him out to dinner in the city.

"Before I accept your invite," he said, "I need to tell you: *Freshmen*'s a no-go. The short story I sent you was really an excerpt from my mom's novel, which Trigger Finger bought six months ago. It hits the shelves next summer."

Instinctive heat rose in my cheeks but instantly cooled. Truth is, I was relieved. Mainly because Del Danzinger had started talking to me again. On the drive back from Pennsylvania, he laid it all out for me. Stacy had given him the idea.

Danzinger said, *My wife's case from twenty years ago is being reopened after new evidence exonerated her convicted killer, who's been released from prison and wants revenge against everyone who testified against him—including me.*

The spotlight's back on Danzinger, he told me. *A new, ambitious Honolulu prosecutor has me in her crosshairs. The progress I made over the past nineteen books is swiftly unraveling. I'm drinking again. Using. Back east, my law license is on the line again.*

Remember what we did back in Danzinger on Trial*? Yeah, that's about to come back and haunt us.*

He even had a title picked out:

Danzinger Defends Danzinger.

I told him we'd work on that.

I couldn't get started on it right away, of course. I had things to do.

My first priority was Creighton. Getting him clean. Sober. I could hear it in his voice; he wanted the monkey off his back. The coke, the alcohol too.

But the blow was the big *problemo.* The one that dwarfed all the others.

For Creighton. For JaMarcus. For me too.

Except I smoked it after one too many bloody noses.

I hid it well. From law professors, fellow students, friends, even JaMarcus for a couple years. Then, late one afternoon, I showed up at an arraignment high and reeking of gin.

JaMarcus didn't blow up at me. He didn't yell.

He drove me to his home in Mount Hope and sat me down.

He told me the full story about his son.

Not what happened to him. Not how he died.

But who he was, the potential he'd shown, what he loved, the future he wanted.

"I've already buried a kid, Gregg," he said in the silence of his kitchen. "Don't make me do it again."

The next day we went to a meeting. That night I got drunk and high.

The following day we went to another. That night I got drunk and high.

By then, there was no lying to him. I expected him to fire me, maybe even inform the school. Do something radical like call the police when he knew I was carrying.

He did none of that. Instead, he gave me more hours. He talked to me. He took me to meetings. He became more than my professor, my mentor, my boss. He became my friend.

Then he gave me a future I could actually look forward to. Not the one I expected. Not as his associate. Not clerking for some appellate court judge he was friendly with.

We were in an interview room at the maximum security prison in Cranston, waiting for a client charged with a gangland double homicide. He turned to me.

"Ya know, Gregg. Some people are just made for this shit."

I nodded. His tone was serious enough I thought he was going to offer me a job after graduation.

"*I'm* made for this shit," he said, looking me in the eye. "Not you, though."

I felt the room spin. He was finally going to drop the hammer. Fire me, write me off as a lawyer *and* a friend. He'd given me too many chances already, and I disappointed him every time.

"Nah," he said. "You do this with me—as much as I want you to—you're never going to get clean. Because you're never going to be happy. The adversarial system is a death trap for someone with your trauma. At twenty-five, you're already experiencing neck pain when you're stressed. By forty-five, your life will be just one great stretch of agony. So I'm going to make you an offer."

I waited in silence.

"You're going to continue coming to meetings with me. You're going to put in some actual *effort* in trying to get clean and sober. You're going to take and pass the Rhode Island bar exam on my buck and get sworn in as an attorney. Then you're going to do what *you* were made to do. You're going to write."

("Writers are scum.")

JaMarcus *was* cutting me loose. After the bar exam, I'd be on my own. Hustling for clients at the courthouse or holed up in some studio apartment in Warwick, sending out query letters to *P.I. Magazine*, *Diabetes Self-Management*, *Pizza Weekly*.

("They die starving and drunk and penniless.")

"JaMarcus, I can't—"

He held up his hand. "You can't do it alone, I know. You can't do it without support. You can't do it without love." He paused as if posturing for a jury. "But I've read your stuff. You *can* do it with all that. And that's what I'm prepared to offer you, *if* you'll do your damnedest to get clean."

After I passed the bar, JaMarcus offered me his son's old room at his home in Mount Hope. I could stay for as long as I'd like. Leave whenever I wanted to. I'd have food, a support system, a family who cared about me.

I took the offer.

I took the bar.

I got sworn in as an attorney with JaMarcus at my side.

When I told him I wanted to move back to Jersey with Chloé, who'd just passed the bar there, he didn't bat an eye. He wrote me a check for $25,000 and made me promise not to spend it on drugs.

"Keep track of your finances," he said. "When you run low, I'll reup you. For however long it takes you to earn a living."

"JaMarcus, I can't accept a—"

"A loan? Of course you can. You just borrowed a couple hundred grand to get a degree only Del Danzinger will ever use."

He took the check and wrote something on the memo line, then handed it back to me.

I expected it to say *loan*. I worried it would say *gift*.

But it said neither.

It said only: *A bet.*

Fast-forward twenty-five years.

I didn't push Creighton into rehab. I knew better than to come at it like a rescue.

Instead, I showed up, again and again, in small, stubborn ways.

Lunch at Delmonico's. Tickets to *Hamilton*. A season pass to Citi Field.

I told Creighton stories I never told anyone. How I nearly drank myself to death freshman year. About JaMarcus and the deal he made me. About the fight it took just to *want* a better life. To believe I even deserved one.

Somewhere amid all that, Creighton cracked. Not all at once. Like I was with JaMarcus, he was obstinate with me. Blow had him by the throat.

When he was arrested, I was there to bail him out. When he was too hammered to drive, I went and picked him up.

And when he finally said "Yes," I checked him into a program and visited him three times a week. It took time. It took multiple tries. But when he came out the other side, he was a different human being. He was tired of reading manuscripts, so I bankrolled him for a year and told him to write one.

"All this time I wanted to be a writer," he said, "I never considered what kind of novel I wanted to write."

I handed him a spine-creased paperback of *Another Man's Hell*. "Start here. I made a career pretending to be the man I wanted to be. Might work for you too."

Creighton's recovery happened to coincide with Liv's divorce. She rented an apartment near me, and we've been seeing each other since Homecoming.

Tonight we're celebrating the finalization with dinner at River Palm Terrace in Edgewater.

"So did you read it?" she asks me over her wineglass.

"I read enough of it that day on the roof."

Stacy's fictional account of our freshman year, retitled *August & Everything After*, was a moderate critical and commercial success.

"She changed *everything*," Liv says.

"Everything?"

"Everything that matters."

So, everything, Danzinger whispers.

She reaches across the table for my hand. When she holds it, I feel like there's nothing in the world I can't take on. She squeezes it, and I can tell it's time.

"Move in with me?" I say with a question mark on my face.

Her smile is all the confirmation I need.

After dinner, she wants to dance. Not here in front of the linen-draped tables and tuxedoed waiters, but out there, past the river's edge, where the city twinkles like all the stars we can't see.

We settle the check, step into the brisk fall night, and wander down the Hudson toward my Prius. There's a band playing somewhere down the waterfront. Maybe a wedding. The music carries like a promise on the breeze.

As we pass it, Liv pulls me in without asking. I follow without resistance. We step onto the dance floor, unnoticed, and sway beneath the soft lights, a little off rhythm, a little older than the last time I let myself believe in this kind of bliss.

How about Danzinger's Last Dance*?* Danzinger whispers.

Works for me.

Liv leans her head against my chest, and I realize I'm no longer haunted. Not by what I didn't know, or what I couldn't face, or who I used to be.

There are things I'll never fix. Things I'll always carry.

But for the first time in thirty years, I don't feel as if I'm running in place.

I'm alive.

I'm in love.

And for tonight, that's enough.

Author's Note

Ever since I read Bret Easton Ellis's *The Rules of Attraction*, I knew I wanted to set one of my books at a rural northeastern college. I also knew my novel would focus on the first few months of freshman year. The trick was combining four years of experiences into one cohesive story that would resonate with readers. But once I turned a metaphorical death into a literal one, the rest came naturally.

Center Valley University is a composite of the five campuses on which I spent the most time in the early to mid-nineties. Likewise, each character is a composite of several people I met during my college years (and a few I met in law school and beyond, sometimes just in my head). Although I've no doubt old friends will wonder, *Was that the night we . . . ?*, none of these events happened in real life the way they're told in this book. Yes, beer was drunk, fights were had, loves were lost, hearts broken, speeding tickets received, and disciplinary actions handed down. But if you try to fit the pieces together with actual occurrences, you're going to end up with one very strange, disjointed puzzle.

Likewise, to the chagrin of my proofreaders, certain liberties were taken with respect to musical release dates. Guns N' Roses' *The Spaghetti Incident?*, for instance, came out two months after Fenton comments that "Axl Rose should cover every song ever." Additionally, K7's studio album *Swing Batta Swing* arrived that November—but in the novel, Gregg's actually referring to the single "Come Baby Come," which was released in July. The real title didn't have the same juvenile punch I was looking for to counter Jess's love songs. In my defense, the lyrics *"Swing batta batta batta batta batta swing"* are the song's most memorable.

Which is simply to say, the mistakes—both intentional and unintentional—are mine and only mine.

Douglas Corleone

Kapolei, Hawaii

November 30, 2025

Acknowledgments

Contrary to popular belief, novel writing isn't a solo pursuit but a collaborative effort with your literary agent, acquiring editor, developmental editor, proofreaders, jacket designers, and countless others behind the scenes. Roll the end credits.

Special thanks goes out to my editor, Liz Pearsons; my developmental editor, Charlotte Herscher; the editor who originally acquired the novel, Chantelle Aimée Osman; and everyone at Thomas & Mercer and Amazon Publishing who supported their efforts.

Thanks to literary agent James Mustelier of the Bent Agency, who sold this novel, and to my current agent, Danielle Egan-Miller of Brown & Miller, who is working with me—with saintly patience—during the most pivotal period in my writing career.

Thanks also to everyone who's supported me from the early days of attorney Kevin Corvelli through the evolution of crime novelist Gregg Dryer. To name just a few who've actively encouraged me since my last novel: Jennifer Badgley, Dotty Morefield, Stuart Goldstein, Sarah Baglin, Nicole Raffa, Vincent Antoniello, Katrina Jagher, Brad Coles, Jason Quintero, Tricia Schmidt, Tara Staup, musician Beth Rudetsky, and illustrator L.M. Labat.

Thanks, too, to fellow writers David L. Tamarin, Robert W. Walker, Timothy Miller, Joseph Mark Glazner, Lori Wray White, Michael Miller, Gary Turner, Bonnie Traymore, and the multitalented crime novelist Robert Gregory Browne, whose sober wisdom helped me live through a turbulent 2025.

To absent friends I'll never forget: Norman J. Civensky, Aida Corvelli, John Krusas, Michael Kennedy, Pete Ryan, and Kimberly Kopp—thank you for enriching my life by sharing yours.

A more personal thanks to *New York Times* bestselling novelist Allison Brennan and her husband, Dan Brennan, who took my silly 2024 Father's Day Facebook post with the seriousness of its underlying sentiment and carried me across a personal finish line I'd dreamed of reaching for decades while running in place. Without their intercession, my own lifelong search for identity would've continued until my last breath.

Finally, a superspecial shout-out from Honolulu to Quakertown, Pennsylvania, home of friend and frequent collaborator Ray McManamon, to whom this book is dedicated and whose fellowship has been the bedrock of my faith in humanity since fall 1993.

About the Author

Photo © 2024 Jill Corleone

Douglas Corleone is the international bestselling author of *Falls to Pieces*, *The Rough Cut*, and *Robert Ludlum's The Janson Equation*, as well as the acclaimed Kevin Corvelli legal mysteries and Simon Fisk international thrillers. Corleone's debut novel, *One Man's Paradise*, won the Minotaur Books / Mystery Writers of America First Crime Novel Award and was a finalist for the Shamus Award for Best First PI Novel. A former New York City criminal defense attorney, Corleone now resides in Honolulu, where he is currently at work on his next novel. For more information, visit www.douglascorleone.com.